MW01602796

clare,^{loving}

Also by Emily Meier

Suite Harmonic: A Civil War Novel of Rediscovery
Time Stamp: A Novel
In the Land of the Dinosaur: Ten Stories and a Novella
The Second Magician's Tale
Watching Oksana and Other Stories

A Novel in Three Novellas

clare, loving

EMILY MEIER

SKY SPINNER PRESS
SAINT PAUL, MINNESOTA

© 2011 by Sky Spinner Press
117 Mackubin Street
St. Paul, MN 55102
skyspinnerpress.com

All rights reserved. No part of this
publication may be reproduced, stored
in a retrieval system, or transmitted in
any form or by any means—electronic,
mechanical, photocopying, scanning, or
otherwise—without the express written permission of the publisher.

Published in the United States of
America
Sky Spinner Press Books Distribution
through Itasca Books
itascabooks.com

ISBN 978-0-9838983-1-3

First Sky Spinner Press Printing, 2011

Library of Congress Catalog Control
Number: 2011913832

9 8 7 6 5 4 3 2 1

Cover and book design:
Jeenee Lee Design
Cover painting:
Painted Mirror © Eric Rimmington

For Whitney

CONTENTS

SYLVIE

"A boy? And Sylvie's all right? A boy, how wonderful," Clare McHenry says, gripping the phone when the call comes at eight on Saturday night. *A boy. How strange. Really, a boy?* she thinks as she lifts the phone cord and moves sideways to a kitchen stool.

Her son-in-law gives her the particulars: eight pounds two ounces. Twenty inches. Damien. Not a name she would have thought of, though of course she's not thought of boys' names. She was sure Sylvie would have a girl. "Damien Gabriel," Jack says, and Clare immediately stops herself from asking if Gabriel is for the angel and Damien for the leper. She keeps on listening.

"Oh, a caesarean," she repeats when he tells her. Tears flash in her eyes at the sudden image of her daughter cut open. "If she needs me to come—if either one of you wants me to be there, I'll catch a plane right now. I'll go straight to O'Hare," she says, hoping Jack will actually say yes, picturing a scar on Sylvie that matches her own.

Not a happy bond, such a scar. Though a baby. That was happy. What was she thinking?

"She's asleep. With everything. With both surgeries . . ."

Clare feels her eyes tighten. Both? *Two* surgeries?

Jack waits. Then he continues when Clare doesn't ask anything. "She had her tubes tied."

Clare nods at the phone, realizing just what he has said. No more pregnancies. No other baby.

"Kiss them for me. Damien too. Tell Sylvie—" Clare starts, but Jack has already said good-bye. The line is dead, and Clare puts the phone in its cradle, cradling the word in her mind. *Sylvie's cradle.* The sweet wooden curve. The just bumpy hitch in its swing. How she wishes she'd kept it.

Clare's forehead is damp. She is keyed up, excited. She feels agitated, and she wants to tell someone her news. Well mostly she wants to talk to Sylvie, though she knows she'll just have to wait. She scribbles *Damien!* on the grocery pad on the fridge and adds *1-20-06* below it. Then she scratches the *6* out and writes a *7* in its place. She stares at it, stares at the floor.

Somebody's missing. It really does feel that way. Is this maybe what husbands are for—to be part of this sort of thing? Is this maybe the place where it helps if your child isn't fatherless, or a time when you wish you still had your own mother? At the least, is it a time when your friends are your bailout position?

Yes! Again. Friends for backup.

Clare dials three numbers and gets three voicemails—three friends who are out on a Saturday night. She considers calling Elizabeth a second time and leaving a message but she decides against it. It's the kind of news to tell an actual person, though of course an actual person would ask when she's flying to Dallas. Soon, she could say. When they need me. Soon.

The dog is sniffing at the stove where Clare's dinner is still in the skillet. "You wouldn't like what I'm eating," she tells him. She turns the burner back on and stirs the tofu and broccoli she bought as part of a New Year's resolution. "Harold, we're grandparents. Not you exactly, although maybe you're an uncle. Uncle Hal."

Clare pulls her apron over her head. "This is nuts," she says, turning off the burner again. "Get your leash. I really do need to tell someone."

When she and Harold go out in the Chicago night, the air is nippy, but the sidewalks are clear with the snow banked up beside them. Harold is ready to run and Clare is, too, though she isn't dressed for it. She compromises. She lets Harold set the pace, and then runs if she needs to to catch up. She's remembered to forward calls to her cell phone, and she keeps checking her pocket. Still, she's surprised when she hears her ring tone: the announcing chords of Beethoven's First. Without her reading glasses, she can't make out who's calling.

She's hoping for Sylvie, but the voice is male. "Finn," she says. She's not certain her brother is drunk, though chances are good that he is. He's talking about her Christmas card, which she sent out late. "Yes, it's an amazing Christmas tree when you realize it was painted with a foot," she says, agreeing with him, and then she wonders if this will be it, if her brother—she can hear the ice clinking in his glass— will be the very first person she tells.

He has moved on to talking about Sylvie. Clare listens and tries to keep up with the dog. Finn is glad about Sylvie, pleased she's finally going to have a baby. He's sorry about the miscarriages (why, Clare wonders, did she ever tell him?). Did Sylvie have an abortion or something when she was a kid that she's had all this trouble? He hopes she'll be all right; he hopes the baby will be OK, though it will probably be lazy after so much bed rest with its mother. He's kidding, of course. She knows that he's kidding?

"I have to go. I'm at the store. I'll call you." Clare clicks the phone shut and tries to bring her anger down to a simmer. She loops the dog leash around the bike rack and points at the window. "I'll be right there. Just beyond the vegetables. Don't bark. I'll be back in one minute. Two minutes tops." She pats Harold, looks in his mutt eyes, and then leaves him whimpering.

She intends to head straight to her favorite checker, but in the store—the fluorescent lights buzzing and a cart squeaking in front of her—Clare decides she needs something to buy or she'll look like an idiot. She stops at the flowers and then picks up a pineapple and sets it down again, concluding it might spoil while she's gone. She stands looking around her, aware that buying just one thing would be a lot easier if she smoked. Her eyes lock on the cough drops. She picks up the large bag, the kind with zinc, and clears her throat a couple of times, trying to sound sick. She sounds phony instead. Still, they're not a bad idea. She may not have a cold, but she doesn't want to pick one up—on the plane or something—and give it to Sylvie. To Sylvie or the baby.

Waiting behind a man with a baggy coat and a hand in his pocket, Clare wonders if she's arrived just in time for a stickup. She tries visualizing the kickboxing move that would knock a gun away if she got it just right, if she didn't lose her balance instead. She looks at the windows, but they're nighttime reflective. She can't see through the glass to check on Harold, so she turns back to the line and studies the hair on the man's neck. It's both wispy and curled at odd angles, and it looks as if he slept on it when it was still wet—wet and maybe slick like a newborn's. He's buying a rotisserie chicken, and Clare hopes Harold won't lunge for it when he leaves the store. She keeps an ear tuned as she puts down her cough drops.

"I don't really have a cold," she says to the clerk, the girl with the beautiful eyes and lovely dark skin. "But my daughter just had a baby. I don't want to catch anything. I don't want to give it to them. She had a little boy. Damien Gabriel."

"Congratulations. Wow, you're a grandma." The checkout girl gives her a big smile, ringing up the cough drops, and Clare remembers election day and the "I voted" sticker on the register and the girl saying she'd just gone to the polls with her grandmother. "Have you seen him yet?" the girl asks looking back at her.

"They're in Dallas. But I will. I'll see them soon."

"Great." The girl gives Clare change for her ten and starts pulling cans across the scanner for the next order.

"It really is." Clare waits a moment longer and then, clutching her bag of cough drops against her chest, she goes out to the dog.

"There. Somebody knows besides us," she says, undoing Harold's leash and checking to make sure there aren't any chicken bones on the sidewalk. "It's a start. Harold, the secret is out."

———

Closing the front door and rubbing her fingers through Harold's cold fur, Clare stands quietly for a moment and wonders if the news from Dallas means the house feels changed. She's lived here for Sylvie's whole life and she still thinks of it as Sylvie's, too. Except for the addition of a computer, she's even kept the den off the living room as Sylvie's sewing room, though it's not Sylvie who uses it but Clare's occasionally frugal friends who stop by to shorten hems or repair seams. Clare listens to them race the machine and pretends that they're Sylvie.

She puts her coat in the closet and takes the picture book of European cities Sylvie gave her for Christmas out to the kitchen. It's a stunning book of aerial photographs, and Clare has looked at every one of them, though now she's determined to read the text, which has so far eluded her. It's an oddly impersonal gift and Clare really wonders if Sylvie even chose it. By the time she's stretched out on the settee and read and reread the description of Latin cultures without anything registering, she's yawning and checking her phone and no closer to an answer.

She gets up, pushing the book aside, and grinds her tofu and broccoli in the garbage disposal and cleans the pan, cleans the counter. It's Sylvie who's missing, of course. Tonight that feels so achingly true. But like a single pool of misplaced persons, all the people Clare has ever missed seem absent as well. Her mother, of course. Her father. Her grandfather. In a minuscule way, Finn. And, too, Sylvie's missing father, for whenever there are complications for Sylvie and her, he is part of the equation.

Clare calls Harold and listens for his feet padding toward her through the hall. When he nudges up against her, she rubs his neck with a bare foot and catches a tuft of his hair between her toes. "You wouldn't understand, but secrets, Harold. Complications," she says, aware they were out there hovering right from the start. "*Always, Harold*," she says, and she wonders for the zillionth time if she and Sylvie kept them at bay by acts of will or by plain dumb luck.

Yet Sylvie had barely started school when she'd first asked the question Clare had been stymied about answering since before her birth. "I've been thinking," she said, leaning on the counter after school, "shouldn't I have a father? Other kids do."

Clare had put her glasses on and busied herself in the papers she'd brought home from work. "Lots of kids at your school just have moms," she said. "We're good, chickie—you and me."

"Yes. But they've got dads somewhere. In California or Hyde Park. Or at Christmas. It seems I should have a father somewhere."

Clare took a breath and opted for the higher end on vocabulary. "And you do. Everyone does. For procreation—reproduction—there's a need for a biological male and female. It was no different with you. But we've done this pretty much on our own almost ever since—you teaching me to be a mom and me helping you be a kid."

"What's almost mean? You said on our own almost ever since. What was it like when it was almost?"

Clare hesitated, considering various truths, a wave of emotion engulfing her at the sudden memory of Sylvie's father. *Luc.* She steadied herself. "There were doctors and nurses helping when it was almost," she said. "There were lots of people to help. Drink your milk. I've brought tons of work home. I'm not good for much else tonight."

Clare is a blank on when and where she actually told Sylvie more, and on what exactly she said. She doesn't remember if Sylvie's questions came in a sudden barrage—*So was there a donor? Were you raped? Did you know him? Were you in love? Where is he? Was it incest? (My God, Syl-vie!! Sylvie!)*—or if there had been a slower, but still intense drilling by an adolescent Sylvie determined to root out the facts. Clare does remember she felt hunted. Marked and haunted by her inquisitive daughter, but as utterly clueless about what to tell her as she had been since her birth. Her instinct, as always with Sylvie, was to offer the straight truth but it was hardly an option. The weight for Sylvie would be too heavy. The whole thing felt impossibly fraught.

Clare guesses what she must have said: "When you're older. Sylvie—sweetheart, it will be so much simpler for you if you can just wait."

Yet when Sylvie was older, it wasn't easier at all. Sitting across from her at lunch on a college campus just budding into spring, Clare had known that with a sudden dread. Sylvie, impossibly beautiful, her legs tucked up on the bench and a gray scarf tossed carelessly around her neck, was staring at her. "In a few months, I'll be here or at some other school. I'll be gone, Mom. I'll be of legal age and off on my own. You have to tell me. *Now*, Mom. Who is my father?"

Clare had swallowed hard at the frontal assault. Then, to her own surprise, she rolled out the story she'd created for just such a moment, just such a loss of nerve. "I met him in a bar. He asked me to dinner. I asked him back to my apartment. I never saw him again."

Sylvie didn't reply at once. She had a suspicious look on her face. "Did you happen to catch his name?" she said finally, a just acid tone to her voice.

"Fred. He said his name was Fred."

"Any last name? It's not like Fred has a ring to it like Sting or Bono. I'm guessing he had dark hair since I do. What was he? Maybe a stevedore? Did you go for his muscles? Was he some kind of salesman or a businessman passing through town? What? Was he eighty or twenty? For Christ sake, Mom, who exactly was he? I can't believe you waited all this time and came up with this. A guy named Fred. Fred! A totally untraceable name. And a totally not credible story."

Clare was fiddling with her straw. She wanted to tell Sylvie not to swear, but she stopped herself.

Sylvie kept on. "And I should assume with this story that you were quiet all these years because you thought I'd turn into some sort of slut if I knew? Mom, if this was the real deal, you'd have all sorts of add-ons—extenuating circumstances, a grand explanation of why you'd have a baby by just some guy named Fred. Think about it, Mom. You make a bigger production out of a trip to the refrigerator."

Clare still said nothing, her silence, she knew, condemning not only the story but herself as well. She closed her eyes. "I almost miscarried. I almost lost you," she said. "I can't even imagine . . ."

Sylvie didn't skip a beat. "Well you didn't. I'm here. And I'd like a better story, please."

Clare was trying to stay calm. She was determined not to cry. "And you deserve one, of course. It's just that for a lot of reasons, I don't have one now. But I will. Sylvie, I promise you the truth, but I need you to wait a while longer. Be angry if you have to, but please try to trust me."

"Thanks. For the permission. Trust you and Fred?" Sylvie's voice had a hard note of disdain to it as she pulled her jacket on. "I want to go to a church," she said. "Isn't it finally time for that? Isn't it time you stopped protecting me from everything? I mean—even church?"

Clare nodded, clutching at the compromise. Yet when she and Sylvie entered the steepled church they found near the campus and she saw the glowing vigil lights, Clare knew that her uncertainty about what she was keeping from Sylvie was tied inextricably to the awkwardness of going inside. All the old guilt.

And all those years. Once, as a child, she'd felt grace when she prayed—grace that was part of the church way up at the vaulted ceiling. She hunted the old memory: *Herself at nine. She sat next to her mother who, this Sunday, had come with the family to Mass. Clare could not lean against her father's shoulder and ask to use his handkerchief and think that grace was love, that it came down from the ceiling and was part of the handkerchief, part of her father's shoulder, and something her brother would never feel. Her mother was in the way.*

Sylvie touched Clare's sleeve, and the memory, both real and evanescent in the echoing church, disappeared. "It's Roman Catholic?" she whispered, and Clare nodded. "And what are those pictures on the walls with the little roofs on top?"

"Stations. Stations of the Cross. They're about episodes on the road of Jesus to be crucified. They've inspired a lot of art," Clare said. Then she was quiet. For all the gaps in knowledge that a lapse of twenty years had meant for her, she knew it was nothing like the chasm she'd insisted on for her daughter.

She watched Sylvie walk down the aisle, looking at the statues and tabernacle, at the windows and ceiling. Then she came back and slipped into a pew and knelt as the other visitors in the church had done. She looked up at Clare. "I'm going to pray that my mother will stop treating me like a child," she said. "So tell me how to pray, Mom."

When she thinks of this moment, Clare invariably feels a muddled kind of anger. She feels it now, checking the bolt locks and getting ready for bed, giving Harold a dog bone to clean his teeth. She hears her own deep sigh. Always, she's assumed that Sylvie, on the cusp of eighteen, was intent on punishing her, not just for her silence, but for all she'd done wrong. Ever. Sylvie's perceptions of what was wrong. Yet when it came to religion, hadn't Sylvie known that Clare had raised her to think for herself, that she'd expressly shielded her from a lifetime of guilt? Clare had certainly told her that often enough, and Sylvie seemed to agree it made sense.

"Right. Guilt about what, though?" she always asked, and Clare had never found an answer that quite satisfied either one of them. One answer was too large: guilt about everything. The other was too small. Armed with the explicit and ubiquitous knowledge of her generation, Sylvie had merely giggled when Clare first told her her distressed childhood memory of the boy who'd tugged aside the crotch of her underpants. Clare understood that, to Sylvie, the rest of the story would seem even slighter.

But in the church aisle, Clare had stood as if slapped. "You pray however you want to, Sylvie. Some people ask for things. Some give thanks. For some people it's more of a meditation. And some can't pray with their mothers in the way. I'll meet you outside. When you're done."

Later, in the hotel room, Sylvie had crawled across the bed and rested her head on Clare's shoulder while the news was on. "Mom, sorry if I was rude," she said, and Clare, looking down at her, decided she was roughly fourteen. For the moment, the girl who'd walked confidently across campuses, turning all heads, had lost her self-awareness. She'd taken her retainer from the case and clicked it into her mouth. Her face was scrubbed. A wayward curl was stuck to her cheek.

"We're even," Clare said, patting the knee that poked up beside hers and feeling she'd dodged a bullet. But she knew it had been just one bullet from one advance scout. The posse, of course, was still on the way.

⸺

One a.m. Fumbling for the bedroom phone, and scaring herself awake enough to read the luminous numbers on the alarm clock, Clare is hoping for Sylvie, but expecting Jack. Instead, it's her brother's slurred voice. And the ice cubes again. "So when did you say she's having her baby? Sylvie. When is Sylvie? When's her baby due?"

"You woke me up."

"I called her first. I called her house but there's nobody home. She having her baby now? I'm looking at hospitals on the Internet. Dallas? She go there or the suburbs? I could talk to a nurse. Find out. Talk to her right and she'd tell you the whole damned story."

"Go to bed. Finn, you're drunk. I need the line open." Clare drums on the phone.

"You don't have call waiting?"

"No."

"I'll get it for you. You want it for your birthday?"

"I don't. And don't start calling hospitals. She had a boy. OK? Damien Gabriel."

"After the leper? Gabriel? She want her kid to be a dancer?"

"Finn, shut up. Don't call her. Don't call me."

"You going to Dallas?"

"Yes. And I'm hanging up now."

"You told me you'd call when she had it."

"Well you know now, and so I don't have to."

"This Damien's got one hell of a grouchy grandmother."

"He does." Clare slams the phone down so hard that it bounces. She stares at the trace of light that leaks through the blinds from the streetlamp and wonders if it would wake up the neighbors if she screamed really loud. It would, of course, and they'd be ready to call the police. But there's a bigger factor restraining her: her fear she might break. Her head is pulsing, and her stomach is funny. She didn't eat, so she can't blame the tofu, though maybe the broccoli. She managed to scorch it, and she still smells the acrid odor, pictures the black-rimmed florets.

Clare rolls over the rumpled sheets. She pulls her feet away from the bumpiest part. She is *so-o-o* wide awake, her head filled with all sorts of warring impulses: to be headed to Dallas. To be asleep. To have Sylvie in the next room—a younger Sylvie with her pillow pulled over her head and her legs uncovered where the blankets are untucked. No Jack, of course.

And just what about Jack? What? Clare can't escape the recurrent questions: Why did Jack call? Why not Sylvie after all that has happened? *Really!* Isn't this finally the place—*when you've had a baby!*—that you call your mother yourself? Why did Jack fill up the frame—Jack running interference, Jack blocking Clare away from Sylvie? If that's what was happening.

Clare bats at her pillows, realizes it feels like she's punching at something. From the first time Sylvie brought Jack home, Clare had wanted to like him. He was handsome, but not too handsome. He was smart. He could be funny in a remote sort of way. He was reserved with her, but polite and respectful and, though it made her feel old at times, she didn't really mind. How could she not be fine with it? She thought it was one of his ways of treating Sylvie well. And, too, she had it firmly in her mind that if this was an important boyfriend, she needed to let Sylvie have all the space that she could.

But it hadn't been easy. Clare had rapidly collected a long list of advice starting with her own mistakes that she wanted to protect Sylvie from making. Because she'd read the books about letting go, she said nothing. She'd long since adapted her favorite line from *Cheers*, which she and Sylvie—their feet up on the chair in the kitchen—had watched together: *Let your child follow her own path, and that path will always come back to you.* Clare had an impulse to try it in cross-stitch for Sylvie's room. Mentally she started it, mentally she threw it out with the trash.

The fact was that the whole situation was challenging, and Clare had felt left-footed in all sorts of ways. It was different from Sylvie's adolescent years when any friction between them had been the rare exception. But watching her with Jack, Clare had seen the implicit bristle in the line of Sylvie's back and known it was for her.

"It's not that I don't want her to have a serious boyfriend," she'd told her friend Elizabeth when they met for coffee, though she left out her suspicion that Sylvie, in the autumn of her last year of college and never quite good at transitions, was seduced, in part, by the promise of something new that would replace what was coming to a close.

Elizabeth, with her usual casual elegance, was wearing—well what had she been wearing? Clare's memory puts her in her green bulky sweater and skinny jeans, but the sweater was new this fall. It scarcely matters. Whatever Elizabeth had on, she was tugging at a nub on her sleeve. "Are they sleeping together?" she asked.

Clare shook her head. "I don't know. She hasn't told me. But, oh God, of course they are. They must be. Doesn't everyone? Didn't I?"

"Just so she doesn't feel she has to marry him," Elizabeth said, and then she blushed—a first for her, Clare was certain. "I'm sorry. I didn't mean anything. About marriage or something. I meant—you know what I meant."

She did know. Even with easy Elizabeth, the complications were always there.

Clare has made a decision. She's getting up. She is up, her legs hooked over the edge of the bed. She hunts for her slippers with her toes and, when she's found them, she maneuvers them onto her feet. Yawning, she heads to the hall and takes the afghan off the alcove chair Sylvie reupholstered years ago as her birthday gift. Harold is following her, and Clare feels the tug on the afghan when he steps on the fringe. She nudges him off and then pulls the afghan up and around her.

At the living room window, Clare lifts a slat on the blind. Her eyes adjust to the blotchy darkness. She can feel the night. She can imagine the city stretching far, far beyond her. Gangbangers hanging on street corners near Howard Street. Traffic streaming on Sheridan Road where it takes the turn to head downtown. Between tree branches and past the shadows of brownstones, the dim reflection of car lights she thinks she can see, just as she almost hears the rattle of the El in the distance though it's not running. Chicago is out there. Her city for years with its web of neighborhoods. She plots their demographics. It's her job, which she loves, and she loves the town. She has it by heart and, in her own way, so does Sylvie. Clare wonders if Sylvie ever misses it.

The radiator clanks and starts to hiss and Clare feels how alert she is, listening for the phone to ring. It doesn't, it's not ringing, and she drops the slat. She crosses the room to her TV chair and plunks herself down in the dark and turns on the weather channel, which is her latest nighttime addiction. She loves it for the computer-generated, very weird speech patterns. She's actually recommended it to Sylvie and Jack thinking they'd like it as much as she does. She was wrong. Jack doesn't. Sylvie doesn't.

Clare watches the map, and then presses the off button on the remote and holds her legs out in front of her, tightening her quads, wondering if they'll stay strong forever. She pulls her legs under her in the chair. She's so ready to go. She has her suitcase packed. She's had it packed for a month. She put in enough clothes for a week—two weeks if she washes her underwear. And a china cup for the baby. A book of Beatrix Potter. A silver dollar. A black and white toy that's meant to be educational. A lavender dress with eyelet . . .

She'll have to give it away now, that perfect little dress. Clare clasps her hands to her ears, her neck. It is such a stunning thing that this child is a boy. The only child that Sylvie will ever have is a son. It's a crystal-clear fact that dazzles Clare with its strangeness: the line of mothers and daughters, descended from some misty savanna and running to Madelyn Wheatley and Clare McHenry, stops now with Sylvie and a baby named Damien. A boy. A demographic likelihood, as she knows, and far too commonplace and fine to be an occasion for grief. Yet grief, in a small way, is what she feels. For eons, that vessel was whole, balanced carefully on the head of a woman who passed it to a daughter who passed it on. And now, what's this—Humpty Dumpty time?

Clare drapes the afghan around her again and wonders why she has had this thought. Is it something easy like a signal that it's time to brush up on her nursery rhymes? She understands, of course—the doctors' advice. Sylvie's decision. Distressing as it is to think about, she knows how hard it has been for Sylvie to have even this one child. Though Jack said she was all right. Sylvie's all right . . .

Harold is at her feet, ready for a walk. Ready for a meal. "Forget it," Clare says to him. She pulls him onto her lap and lets him lick her face and then raises her head, listening again for the phone, though it's still not ringing. "Harold, you're lucky I tolerate this. You should feel honored you've even got my ear. I could be talking to Sylvie. I could be talking to my daughter."

Clare twists a finger in his fur. If only she weren't lying. This whole baby thing has made her feel odd. It's such a long time since she's even thought of Sylvie's birth, but tonight it's here again, a little room stuck in the back part of her head or lodged above her shoulder. The horrible hours of labor. The hours of pushing that didn't stop until she was finally rolled into an operating room, abruptly cut open, and Sylvie tugged out. Yet what a miraculously easy baby Sylvie had been. Clare had cared for her in a painful fog and Sylvie, clear-eyed, had seemed to understand. "She was born with patience," Clare always tells her friends.

"Wasn't your mother there to help you? After she was born?" It's the regular inquiry, and Clare always shakes her head and says she didn't ask her, that she wanted to prove she could do it alone. That, anyway, she didn't think that she'd need her. "I was wrong, of course," she adds.

"You didn't get along with your mother?" is the usual next question, and Clare always denies it quickly, says it wasn't that, that she was simply out of the habit of asking.

"And . . . the circumstances, the situation? Was that a problem?"

Invariably, Clare shrinks from this question. She's evasive. She says she doesn't know, that she certainly didn't tell her mother everything. Really, did they? She never says a word about Sylvie's father—never—but with her best friends, she does concede that the fact she'd had Sylvie on her own had to seriously bother her mother, though her mother adored Sylvie and thought Clare was raising her well. Not that she saw her often with the distance to travel and then Clare's father being ill. And, of course, she thought of asking her mother to live with them when he died, but her mother had her own life, and both of them thought it was important she stay near her friends. And, too . . . well, her death was really very sudden. Clare always stops at this point when she hears her own rationalizing, knows that it verges on dishonesty.

But everything about Sylvie was just as she claimed. Sometimes Clare imagines Sylvie small again, wrapped in a towel and snuggled against Clare's terry robe. They sit in the rocking chair, Sylvie's dark hair still damp and tightly curled from the bath. In this memory, they are like an ad for cotton. French doors. Sunlight streaming into the whiteness of robe and towel. A hibiscus blooming on the windowsill. As Sylvie sits forward and turns the page Clare has read, her cheek is a spot of pink. Young as Sylvie still is, Clare already knows she will be creative and artistic in a way that she herself is not. Sylvie gathers everything with her eye.

Had she actually had a hibiscus when Sylvie was that small? Clare isn't sure. Memories jigsaw together, the slight misfit always invisible when she tries to see into the past. So maybe no hibiscus until Sylvie, at eight, skidded with her bike, flying over her handlebars and into a rosebush and, for weeks, that perfect face was starred with the tiny scabs from thorn pricks. It was then that Clare had settled permanently on flowers she could keep indoors and ripped out the rosebushes herself.

Clare tries to remember the scent of hibiscus. She settles deeper into the chair, shuts her eyes. In her mind, she taps in Sylvie's home phone number. But even though what she's doing is imaginary, she stops, lifts her hand without pressing the final number in case Jack is home.

———

Groggy from the few hours of sleep she's cobbled together in chair and bed and eating a bagel at the kitchen counter, Clare nudges the crumbs around the plate, her mind snagging again on the one intractable fact of Sylvie's missing father and her old relentless uncertainty about what to tell Sylvie. And when finally she did reveal the truth, Jack hijacking the story and using it against them both.

Clare knows Sylvie would reject the last point, and maybe she does herself, though not now when she's upset with Sylvie, mad at Jack. Lodging her coffee cup between the portable phone and the cell, she tests the coffee with her finger. Then she almost knocks it over at the sound of the phone ringing. For a startled instant, she's frozen between both phones. But ridiculous—the cell doesn't ring. She's almost collected herself as she picks up the portable. She hits the talk button, waiting for Sylvie's voice.

"Did I wake you?" Elizabeth asks. "It's so gorgeous. Blue sky and three inches of new snow. Get your skis out. I'll pick you up. We can hit the trail early."

"I tried to call you last night. Sylvie—"

"She had the *baby*?"

"Yes."

"Is she OK? That's so exciting! What did she call her?"

"Damien. She had a little boy. Damien Gabriel. Jack said she's fine. She was sleeping."

"You haven't talked to her?"

"No."

"So I should get off?"

"Probably. She had a caesarean."

"Oh-hh." Elizabeth is quiet, but just for a second. "I think you should take a boyfriend when you go down there. Make it seem like you've got a life. It might pique her interest."

"And you're offering a boyfriend? You have extras?"

"What about that guy you were seeing at Halloween?"

"What about him?"

"I thought he was nice."

Clare laughs. "Did you ever even see him outside of a Dracula costume?"

"I saw his face. Is that enough? If you needed somebody to suck your blood, I thought he looked fine."

"It seems a little personal, don't you think? Call a man you haven't seen in months and ask him to hop a plane to your personal crisis."

"It's a crisis?"

"Is that what I said?"

"Well what I meant—it just seems like a time when you might want a man in on your feelings. Sylvie's a mom! That's a rush you really shouldn't waste."

"Incorrigible friend."

"My job description."

"I'm leaving your name with the kennel for Harold."

"And you're going when?"

"I'll let you know."

"Give her a kiss for me."

"Of course."

"And call me. Or e-mail me. Stay in touch."

"Right. Sure." Clare presses the "end" button, glad she hasn't said she might be in touch from her own house for the foreseeable future. She puts the phone down. Then she picks it up again, along with the cell, and hikes the afghan up off the floor. She keeps it bundled around her as she makes her way to the shower.

In the bathroom, she sets both phones on the sink and looks at them uncertainly while she starts the shower. She knows she could make a timeline of the essential moments in her life simply by plotting phone calls on a graph. Deaths and births. Eavesdropping. Admissions of fault. Rejections and acceptances. Announcements. Devastations. Accusations. The gossipy bits of diversion and entertainment that keep all the larger parts together. She e-mails for work. She e-mails with strangers and with the network of scattered family her mother's death left her in charge of. But it's the human voice that she's always lived for.

"I should send flowers!" The water is comfortably pounding Clare's back and pasting her hair flat when flowers are all she can think of. She forgot to ask Jack for the hospital name. She didn't ask for the room number. She can find them, of course. If Finn could hunt on the Internet, she can do it too (and Finn's flowers are probably already crowding the space on Sylvie's bedside stand). But didn't it make more sense to arrive in Sylvie's room, flowers in hand? Of course, she can do both. Send a bouquet, and appear with lilies wrapped carefully in paper. She won't get roses. Roses are best coming from a man. Coming from Jack.

Clare is still toweling off as she ducks into the bedroom to get her clothes. With her jeans and a turtleneck on, she stands in front of the dresser rubbing her hair and eyeing her favorite picture of Sylvie (the untamed McHenry curls), and the smaller wedding photo tucked into the mirror frame: Sylvie calm and beautiful; Jack gazing at her adoringly. Though she's tried every time she looks at this picture, Clare has never thought of another word.

For a second, Clare stands still listening, holding the towel away from her ear. Nothing. Still, she retrieves the phones from the bathroom. When she's back at the mirror, she slides the wedding photo out and leans the Jack half behind the picture frame so she has both Sylvies together: Sylvie at seventeen, and Sylvie, the very young bride, at twenty-two. Clare knows she's never really gotten over it.

She sits down on the edge of the bed. Then she lets herself fall backward, feeling the wail that's stuck in her throat. Could she miss Sylvie any more than she does? Really, where's Sylvie? Just *where* is her daughter? How could Sylvie possibly be so far away?

Her hair is getting the pillow wet. Clare feels the dampness spreading behind her head, which bothers her, though she doesn't get up. She pushes her heels hard against the mattress and then lets her feet flop to the sides. Really, the whole thing still surprises her. Sylvie the fiancée, Sylvie the bride. Clare had been caught so entirely off guard. She was totally stunned when Sylvie came home at spring break her senior year sporting a ring and announcing that she and Jack planned to get married at the end of June.

"Really? June?" Clare said, and Sylvie asked if there was anything wrong with that.

Clare had suppressed her real answer (that soon? are you sure? *oh, Sylvie*) and hurried into her reply. "No, I'd just imagined you as— well, say a November bride."

Sylvie was just as fast with her response. "Decorations with squash and crepe paper turkey wattles?"

Clare had laughed. "It's just that you've always had your own style."

Which Sylvie did. Eye-catching is the word. In high school, she'd always preferred doing the theater costumes to being in plays. Clare has been told—and by people who know—that Sylvie has an exceptional eye for cutting fabric. She doesn't need to be told how good Sylvie is at assembling the oddest things into a particular kind of perfection. Clare knows that her prom dress is legendary. Coming home with bags full of remnants—organza and lace, spandex and sequined knits (the common denominator some shade of champagne or pale peach)—Sylvie had set to work cutting and basting. She threaded twisted lace through half the bodice and quilted the other half. For the skirt, she cut layers of ruffles at odd angles, their edges left raw. Then she swirled a bangle of beads across the bodice and around the skirt, and crowned herself with an upside down, V-shaped ice cream cone. Clare might have been amused if the whole effect had not been so gorgeous. Well she did laugh, but with real appreciation. And she was quick with her denial when the other mothers wondered if she'd helped.

"I can barely thread a needle," she told them, which wasn't so different from her answer when the mothers asked if she wasn't going crazy helping Sylvie write her college essays. "Hardly," she said, and then she showed them one of the padded books Sylvie had sewn for an application, its text her cross-stitched haiku. Clare still remembers the most haunting one: *Make swings from green vines. / Let children fly in the trees / When death is certain.* It was Sylvie's answer to this: You have been sent alone to an African village in a region where massacres are occurring daily. What will you do?

Clare had always thought that one day Sylvie would take her costuming skills to New York and work in the theater or at a fashion house. Instead the surprise. She'd been the June bride, just as planned, with a purchased wedding dress and a determination to teach kindergarten. It made sense in its way, and it still does. Sylvie has plenty of patience for five-year-olds and her good voice and ear and her limitless ideas for art projects. And Clare was never one of those mothers so thoroughly invested in her daughter's offbeat ways that a more conventional career path was a disappointment to her. She'd been all right with it.

Still, the change was unexpected. "You never even told me you switched majors. How did you stuff in all those credits?" she said.

Ah, Clare thinks now and, oddly, for the first time. Was it earlier than senior year when Sylvie met Jack?

But even that idea seems murky. And, anyway, why would it matter? After all, it was Jack who fell in love with Sylvie just as she was—Sylvie, the beautiful girl with the funky look. There'd never been any question about that.

———

Always, there is something exposed about the city on an early Sunday morning, drained of traffic, drained of its hordes of people, the debris from Saturday night blowing in the gutters or pecked at by the scavenger pigeons who've become the main pedestrians. Clare isn't going all the way downtown. She's only heading as far as her office and, driving, she sketches in all the landmarks she doesn't normally think of when she's going to work in a rush hour. Somehow, that includes the pigeons as they cluster beneath the clangy blackness of the El, but mostly it's the city's pride of buildings, glassy and facing the lake. As she drives, cell phone on her lap, Clare understands she is letting go of idle daydreams that were never quite plans. No taking a granddaughter to the American Girl doll hospital to have her dolls mended. No holding a young girl's hand as they go past the posters of toy soldiers and sugar plum fairies to join the *Nutcracker* crowd. It was what she did when Sylvie was young, though the tickets then were bought with a check mailed from her mother with the word "Nutcracker" printed neatly on the memo line. Clare thinks of a little girl with Sylvie's curls. A perfect little girl dressed in navy blue velvet.

She shakes her head, trying to clear it, to focus again on the skyscape of buildings, but moments and bits of ancient conversations stay floating in her mind—Sylvie at nine as they drove north for Clare's mother's funeral, soggy Kleenexes piled between them on the seat: *Mom, how come you're crying so much? I didn't know you liked her that well.* Clare herself at eight sprawled next to her mother on a Sunday afternoon and craning to read a newspaper article over her shoulder: *It says she had kids. That's so awful. The woman in the car crash. I couldn't get along without a mother.*

But she has, Clare thinks. She's gotten along without a mother for almost twenty years, and she'll get along without a granddaughter. But she can't get along without Sylvie. Even an argument with the simple premise that she could would be utterly and totally false.

Clare changes lanes. She knows there's a part of her that wants to head out to the freeway. Take the default trip on I-94 that leads to the house outside Milwaukee that Sylvie and Jack bought and remodeled and that Clare liked a lot, though of course she'd hoped they'd eventually settle in Chicago. (But Dallas. How did Sylvie ever wind up in *Dallas*?) Or maybe she could keep on going, take the familiar route across Wisconsin and into Minnesota.

Decades ago, before there even was an I-94 or I-90, she and her parents and Finn had come all the way from Delaware and made that journey for the very first time. Clare has no idea what highways they took. She doesn't remember going around Chicago or through it, but she's sure that they did. What has stayed with her always is the excitement she felt as they drove farther and farther north. It had been so very cold. Her feet wouldn't get warm. The windshield was frosted and her father could only see the road if her mother kept scraping a spot on the glass. Clare knew her mother believed Minnesota was the end of the earth.

But the soggy Kleenexes piled between Sylvie and Clare when her mother died seemed more like the end of the world. Clare remembers passing O'Hare. She remembers coming up on Six Flags, abandoned to the winter and shrouded with snow. Sylvie, seeming to ape the quiet landscape, folded her hands in her lap and sat very still. Her accusing words still hung in the air.

Clare had tried to compose herself, struggling with her answer, putting it together. "Sylvie, of course I liked her. I loved her. When people grow up, they have their own lives. I have work. I have you. Grandma has so many friends."

"But I think she would have liked me to visit her. To stay with her by myself. You never let me stay with her."

"You didn't ask."

"But I should have. Or *you* should have asked."

Insistent child. She was right, of course. Clare knows she was right, and she knows it's one of the reasons she still feels bereft when it comes to her mother. Guilty and bereft. And how unfair is that, all these years later, to still feel the loss of her mother when Sylvie is so far away?

Clare punches her fist against the steering wheel as she pulls into her parking spot. She's changed her mind. She doesn't want to be here and she doesn't need to be here. She backs up sharply and turns into the street to go home. She feels the sting flaring through her knuckles, and isn't this right—shouldn't it soothe rather than worry her when she thinks of her mother? She pictures her, the not-quite-good skin that has always been her main reference point for comfort. She remembers her parents' high bed, and lying next to her mother, both of them talking, heads on pillows, Clare in her flower-sprigged pajamas and her mother in a nightgown with a Peter Pan collar. Sometimes they whispered even if there was nothing to confide. Her mother in this memory doesn't wear glasses. Her bare eyes are surprising, the outer corners with the slightly downward turn that Clare has seen in three generations of family pictures. On her grandfather's side. Her grandfather did not have those eyes himself, but his father and grandfather did. Wheatley eyes.

Clare knows she doesn't have a single early memory that isn't intertwined with her mother and with knowing or gauging exactly where she was. Increments. Places. The few toddling steps it took her to cross a sunlit kitchen to reach her and hold on to her skirt; the five long minutes she waited with Finn in the car until their mother finally emerged from a store. Then primary school in Delaware. When Clare was home sick, she would call with her scratchy throat and listen for ages for her mother to answer and start up the stairs. Then they would bargain. Clare would want her to stay forever, to read forever, and her mother would tell her how many more minutes before she was going back to her housework. If Clare was very sick, her mother would stay longer. She would give her Cheracol for her throat. She would give her sulfa from the doctor. She would sing to her after the stories. She would take her temperature and wait while Clare grew dozy. When she stood up to leave, Clare would lift her eyelids and ask when she was coming back. She wanted her company. She wanted what, in adulthood, she has always described to herself as a sense—not really even physical—of being gathered up, of being sheltered and buoyed.

It was nothing she could explain to Sylvie in the car. "Should I be crying more?" Sylvie had asked, looking at the Kleenex pile and Clare shook her head and laughed through her tears.

"I want you to remember this," she said. "Everything you did made your grandmother happy."

"Is that true for you, too?"

"Well . . . not as much."

Clare knows that if Sylvie could still ask such a thing, she had hardly wanted to attack her innocence on the subject. She didn't want to tell her that, at some point, things could be challenging, that at some point a mother would likely be disappointed and hurt, a daughter hurt and—very possibly—furious.

"Something got in our way at times, Grandma and I. It started when I was stolen by nuns," she'd said.

"You always say that, but I don't think you were."

"Not exactly stolen." Clare had patted Sylvie's knee, at the moment not really willing to follow her own lead. "No, of course not. Not exactly. No, Sylvie. Not really stolen."

⌒

As soon as Clare opens the front door, she knows it's cold in the house. Her next thought is that the furnace is off—really off as in something wrong with it. She tries to remember when she had it checked last. There's a gap in the fall.

"It's so cold in here," she says to Harold when he jumps up to greet her. She leans down and scratches his chilly ears and under his collar and then, first things first, goes out to the kitchen to take the call forwarding off. She's back to two lines when the cell phone beeps. She really can't believe this. Why didn't she plug in the charger when she went to bed—or at least before spending part of the night asleep in a chair?

Clare gets the charger from the bedroom and fiddles with both phones, following the instructions stuck on the fridge until she's sure her cell calls will go to the house line. Then, feeling technologically successful, she's ready to turn her attention to the furnace.

But the phone is actually ringing, a sound so sudden and shrill that, for a second, Clare thinks maybe she's called herself. Then she's absolutely sure it's Sylvie, and she feels something dry and choky cutting off her vocal cords. She can't really swallow, and she wonders if blinking will help. Something eases in her throat. The frog jumps free and she says hello. She peers hard into the middle distance, which feels like acute listening.

It's not Sylvie. It's a woman Clare doesn't know calling to ask if she's still interested in a yoga-for-knitters class.

Clare tries scanning her mind for past phone calls, for notices or applications in the mail. She's pretty sure the image she's conjured—a room filled with women in the full lotus position knitting with their arms extended—is entirely new. "Was I interested?" she asks. "I don't actually knit. Are you sure you have the right number?"

Elizabeth, she thinks then. This is Elizabeth's idea of a grandmother joke—Elizabeth's reminder that there's life after anything.

"You can send the directions to my friend who put you up to this," Clare says, and she gets off the phone without being entirely sure she guessed right, and not even certain that the woman said knitters. She's tempted to hit *69 and call her back, but she doesn't. Instead she feels the moment adding itself to the larger limbo where she feels herself stranded.

"Phone, ring! Be Sylvie," she says, and it makes deplorable sense to her that the house is cold, that even that comfort is gone. She gets her heaviest sweater from the bedroom and reads the 62 on the thermostat in the hall. Back in the kitchen, she tries to remember the furnace man's name. She has no idea what she did with his magnetic card, and she cringes to think what a weekend service call would cost. She wonders how long it takes for pipes to freeze and what her own tolerance is for dipping temperatures. What if she needs to head for Dallas when there's no heat in the house?

Clare lets Harold out and paces the kitchen, waiting for him. Then she leaves a message on her neighbors' voicemail asking them to call when they get back from church. She actually asks them if their furnace is off too, which she realizes is a dumb thing to say as soon as she says it, though it's captured there, waiting for her to ask it again when they listen to their messages.

"Harold, what do you think? Two phones to keep track of me," she says, when she calls him again and he bounds in the door, skidding on the tile. He comes toward her, his head down and tail wagging. Clare checks the cell to make sure it's charging. Then she looks at the answering machine though she knows it says zero. "Puppy, why do I even have a cell phone? How did that happen?" And when, Clare wonders, did answering machines and voicemail become so everywhere? Don't real phone memories need people on both ends of the line?

Clare takes the eggs from the fridge. Then she puts them back and looks for sandwich meat and pours herself some flat diet soda and knows she's about to cry. She pushes her hand against her mouth. It's all such a muddle. Sylvie with a baby. Sylvie in Dallas. Sylvie wounded. Clare wounded. Sylvie angry. Clare angry. Jack so impossibly *what*? How in the world did it ever come to this? And how after all the time that she's been a mother could her old, searing question have stumbled into this new variant: what if all those years ago she'd reached an answering machine instead of a present tense voice? Would things have been different? Would she actually have left a message? If she'd heard a recording saying words besides *hello . . . hello*, and then a puzzled, slightly irked *is somebody there*, would she have made a response instead of just sitting there, uncertain in every pore of her being, but wanting to say it's me. You need to come back. Everything feels different now.

Why didn't she answer?

Clare sees herself eyeing her graduate student woolens that she'd taken out of the closet only the day before. Her hand is on the phone cord, and the light from the nearest window is falling into colors that make a shimmery quilt on the wall.

Her Sylvie quilt. This is how she always thinks of it. She'd stared at the colors, and these were the last words that she heard Luc, Sylvie's father, say: *I'm hanging up now. If nobody's there.*

Clare grips the counter. She inhales a deep, airless breath. It was right here in the kitchen. It was just one month before her wedding when Sylvie learned about Luc. In spite of the scenarios Clare had thought about, there'd been nothing ceremonial about it. No special dinner. Not an offer of anything to drink. Not the preliminary gift of the Wheatley flatware.

But there'd been the ultimatum she couldn't avoid. She still recoils at the ambush from Sylvie that launched it. They'd come home with the boxes of lingerie and nightwear from the shower Elizabeth had given, and Sylvie had confronted her: "Mom, do you really expect Jack to marry me when he doesn't even know who my father is?"

Clare remembers how numb she was the next morning as she drove to the bank and retrieved the envelope she'd kept at the bottom of the safe deposit box. When she finally pushed it across the counter to Sylvie, her body felt as fragile as crystal tossed in the air. How long did the moment last? Forever? A second? She thought Sylvie looked curious, and her heart rose at the possibility until she thought again that Sylvie might hope her father was still living—a living legend, Mick Jagger, anyone alive . . .

Then Sylvie picked up the envelope. She took out the clipping Clare had saved in silent obedience to her own mother—*darling, do keep his name where it won't be lost.* She read it. She read it again, and then she put it down on the counter and got up to leave without saying even a single word.

Clare had quickly grasped at her hand. "Ask me anything you want," she said, trying to keep her composure when all she really felt was terror. "Of course there's a story . . ."

"I'm sure there is." Sylvie had pulled away from her, the whole rest of a book of expressions shifting swiftly across her face. Surprise. Anger. Distress, and a desire not to care. Her voice, though, was icy. "Put it back, Mom. Put it back wherever you've kept it all these years. This ship has pretty much sailed."

"But you can see the complications, the ways I needed to protect you. It was always about that."

"No, Mom. Face it. It was always about you."

"Sylvie . . ."

"And you're all rehearsed, I suppose. Sorry, but I'll skip the drama." Sylvie pushed the clipping at Clare so the headline screamed in her face: *Priest's Death on Near Northside Ruled Suicide.* Then she grabbed her car keys and went out the door. It slammed and Clare felt the sound like a punch in her chest, in her belly.

And Sylvie had been so entirely right. Clare knows she was more than prepared, though her script varied. She'd tried her story out by talking to herself at her desk. When she was walking Harold. Looking in the mirror. Anywhere, anytime. Frying eggs. And because there was no good way to tell it, she'd decided to be blunt and straightforward: *Sylvie, that's him, the man in the article. Luc-Cristof Étienne. Your father. As it says, he was a priest and he shot himself. It happened seven months before you were born.*

What followed that invariant opening was whatever Clare picked from the grab bag of possibilities. Sometimes she stressed the distant background, the fact she'd met Luc when she was a child and he was already ordained, and only then added that she'd met him again much later when she was in graduate school and he was teaching. At other times, she made it all about Luc: *He was a wonderful man, a brilliant man, and I loved him. Sylvie, he was French.*

The most changeable part of Clare's story was her attempt at an explanation. Sometimes she would say it could seem foolish now, that it was foolish, but she'd seduced Luc because of her lasting anger from a childhood when she'd felt terrorized by the church. (Hadn't nuns crippled her with guilt? Hadn't they created a *chasm* between her and her mother since her mother wasn't Catholic?) Occasionally, Clare even considered adding in Cody Dawkins, her college boyfriend whose religious scars were worse than her own. Her point, in these tellings, was that she'd wanted institutional payback and, if that was hardly fair to Luc, it was what had happened.

In these versions, Clare was the instigator, with the caveat she hadn't at all planned to get pregnant, though she generally spared Sylvie the demographic footnote she provided herself—that nobody exists without a whole legion of unintended children in their ancestry. Usually, she concluded with words that were musing—"I knew it was a time of doubt for him. What I didn't realize was just how vulnerable he might be. I didn't know him well enough at the deepest level, the priest level really, but I think he died, in part, because of disappointment in himself." Or she chose words that were far too dramatic: "He thought I wanted an abortion and that his death could prevent me from having one. That it would raise the stakes. So he died to save you. Vicar of Christ, as it were. There you have it."

This was the Luc the Anguished Hero rendition of the story. Another version—a more self-serving one—was that Clare hadn't wanted an abortion, that the idea was Luc's, that the seduction itself was as much his as hers, and driven by passion. Even now, Clare is pulled by both narratives, unsure where to carve out the middle road that is closest to the truth. And, because Luc died—a sorrow that has never really left her—she lacks the voice of a second witness to add to her own, though she does have the idea, born of long perspective, that his suicide was the result of depression, that his spiritual crisis and the questions about Sylvie were merely the proximate causes. Sylvie has never heard any of this.

Not that Clare didn't try again to tell her. She tried the very next day. Sylvie had instantly raised her hands in a stop signal. "I know who he was. I know that he died, I know how he died, and I know when he died. That's what I wanted. If there was an honest way to make this an easier story, you would have told me long ago. So just stop, Mom. I don't need to hear how you made it so I don't have a dad. I mean it. Case closed."

"*Sylvie!* But it's all right if you're angry."

"Angry that I exist?"

"Not that. Just angry."

"Thank you very much. Thanks for the permission."

"If you want to talk to someone—"

"You'll pay for the shrink? I'm not crazy. And it's not like I didn't expect something basically weird. Or like I need to hear this is what made you so anti-religion."

"It doesn't explain that," Clare answered, thinking she should try again about the nuns, maybe even about Cody Dawkins. Sylvie shook her off.

"I don't want to talk about it," she said. "I really don't." And then she'd gone quiet, keeping their conversations to the bare minimum as the month ticked away.

Nervous and edgy as she was, Clare had still been deeply moved that Sylvie dressed so much like a regular bride for her wedding day. There were Sylvie touches. She'd eyed her dress and cut off the sleeves. She'd bought the sheerest tulle and drenched it in fabric softener so that, dried, it fell like air from head to toe, front and back: a veil with the size XXL wedding garter Sylvie had bought and snapped around her head to make a perfect, anchoring band.

"I love it that you look like a bride—and that you look like you," Clare had said kissing her and then waiting quietly while Sylvie did up the cuff buttons on her mother of the bride dress. Watching Sylvie as she stretched a loop over the last button, Clare wondered desperately why she'd given up her secret. Why she had caved. She wanted to erase the entire month.

"They're nice buttons," Sylvie said when she looked up from the sleeve, and Clare thought she seemed, if not unhappy, at least subdued in her wedding dress. Clare wanted to put her arms around her and ask if she was all right, if she was still sure. She even wanted to ask if she'd decided to get married just so she'd find out who her father was, though she knew that was her own crazy projection and that Sylvie was hardly that foolish. But she didn't ask. Instead, she focused every bit of her will power on banishing her feeling about Jack and his appalling need to know—on blocking her recurrent thought: *blew my chance.*

"I wish your grandparents could see you," she said.

Sylvie was stunningly quick with her reply. "I can assume they're all dead?"

Clare knows that she visibly flinched. She waited, trying to compose herself before answering. "Since you ask," she said then, "I know very little about your father's family. But his parents would probably be a hundred by now. Or close. I was thinking of Grandma and Grandpa McHenry."

"I know you were."

"Sylvie, put your sadness and resentment aside. We'll work on this later. You're a bride. It's your wedding day."

"You're right. At least about that, Mom." Sylvie turned away. She went off to join her bridesmaids, leaving Clare with the flickering images of the parents whose names she'd evoked. The father she pictured was already old. She watched him struggle for words that wouldn't come, wondering the whole time just what he understood. Anything? Did he know that Sylvie, the baby wrapped in Aunt Sophie's shawl, was his granddaughter? Did he even know she was a baby? Could he suspect, as Clare did, that the very fact of Sylvie's existence was part of the reason he'd had a stroke?

Clare doesn't know the answer to these questions, though she's always wondered. Her mother's reaction had been so much clearer. She was worried. Though careful in what she said or asked, she was clearly dying of curiosity. She was disappointed in Clare. She was passionate about Sylvie. She held her in the crook of her arm and, very carefully, didn't look up as she spoke the words that became indelible for Clare: "You don't have to tell me who her father is. I know you don't want to—and Clare, I'm not asking. But just make sure—darling, please be certain you keep his name where it won't be lost. Whoever he is, he's her father. She'll need to hear who he is. Someday she'll want to know."

It was the closest Clare had ever come to telling before she gave Sylvie the clipping. She was angry first. Then she had the impulse to straighten her mother's glasses as she held Sylvie, to settle them evenly with the dispassionate gaze of an optometrist. But her strongest urge was to sit on the floor and close her eyes and whisper what had happened. She'd wanted to offer the burden to her mother exactly as she'd handed her Sylvie. Or to give half. To have her mother—just by knowing—carry half.

Yet the burden had stayed hers alone until Sylvie knew, and then it had grown even heavier, which Clare, doing her best to look calm and welcoming in Elizabeth's garden, was entirely aware of as the wedding oboist began the Albinoni and Jack's friend put out his arm to escort her up the aisle. Walking on the white rose petals that were scattered on the ground between the chairs, Clare felt as if there'd been a brief flurry of snow.

Finn had given Sylvie away. Clare and Sylvie had had the idea together.

"It's a morning wedding, and he'll still be sober," Sylvie had said.

"For you, he'll stay sober the whole day, the whole evening if he has to," Clare had added, pleased at the fact she had this bit of family for Sylvie on her wedding day, pleased for that matter she could offer her brother such a moment in the sun. And in some way she didn't particularly care to understand, she knew she was glad for the appearance of things. She had always felt a man in a tuxedo should accompany a bride down the aisle. Certainly, it was more traditional and certainly, if she had married herself, she would have wanted her father beside her on her wedding day. She would have wanted him pre-wheelchair or post, when his right hand was the one extremity he could still move.

Clare was happy with Elizabeth's perfect garden, with the flowers and food, with Sylvie's charm and with the effect the ceremony had on her (she was both radiant and serene), and on Jack's seriousness about the whole event. In spite of her sore feet and a headache starting, she knew things had gone well even before the high-fives from her champagne-drinking friends. And when she got home, Finn helping her bring in the bakery boxes of leftover cake and puff pastries before he settled in with a drink and book in the guestroom, she found a bouquet with a card on the kitchen counter: *Mom, Thank you. Thanks for absolutely everything. You've been terrific and we both love you, Sylvie and Jack.*

The note had touched Clare. It also surprised her. It wasn't just Sylvie now. It was Sylvie and Jack. It felt very new.

Clare had sniffed the flowers. Then she studied the card for a long time. She wondered if it was a truce—if Sylvie had started to forgive her, if she'd talked with Jack, if he'd nudged her toward a real reconciliation. If he would be that kind of a husband. She thought it seemed promising, though she wasn't sure.

Clare still wonders what would have happened if she'd lied. Bad as she is at it, she thinks she might have if she could have ever come up with a story that lacked the self-destructing loose ends or other details that might have wounded Sylvie. What breaks her heart over and over is that, for Sylvie and her, there were the seeds of alienation right from the start. Clare torments herself over this. What could she have done to prevent this distancing and, now, to repair it? Should she have told Sylvie her story from infancy, risking what she thought was most dangerous—that Sylvie would be defined by it the moment even a single friend broke her confidence? And wouldn't Sylvie have struggled in all sorts of ways if she'd grown up believing that Luc killed himself because of her? Clare knows Sylvie would see this second argument for silence as far more protective of Clare than of her, but she's always eyed it coldly herself, considering its heavy implications. Still, she wonders. Is there any possible way she could have made Luc's story part of who she and Sylvie were from the start? And what might it have meant if it had been settled history when Sylvie met Jack?

This is very uncertain territory. Though Sylvie and Jack were a couple and all but married before Sylvie learned who her father was, she had always known what her father wasn't: someone who had been a part of her life and provided another set of relatives, someone her mother felt free to talk about. As beautifully as Sylvie had grown up (and as close as Clare knows the two of them were), they had both understood there was something looming ahead of them to navigate, a no-man's-land, as Clare—not unironically—had called it to herself. Clare wonders how Jack became part of this story. She wonders what she doesn't know.

In its broadest outlines, she has talked about this very matter with the therapist she's still amazed that she has. She's posited questions: Anna, do you think there was something about Sylvie not having a father—and then not knowing who he was—that might have made her a sort of prey? Anna, if you consider Sylvie objectively at twenty-one—and even if I am her mother, she had essentially no flaws—could a person maybe take advantage of this missing father thing to make her feel less than? Crazy question, Anna, but could someone "win" Sylvie by making her feel bad about herself and then making it clear that he, generous fellow, could overlook it all?

Sometimes Anna has turned the questions back on her, but the last time she didn't. She'd been very pointed. "I could ask, of course, if this is a mother blaming her rejection on somebody else. Are you sure that isn't coming straight from Sylvie? They've had other things in their lives. Seven years of marriage. You said all the miscarriages. I know rejection is a stronger word than you'd like. But, Clare, do you have any real evidence for this—that he's undermined her sense of herself?"

Clare was careful. "You might not think so. It's happened over time." She paused. "Whatever's happened," she said, balancing Anna's clear suggestion that there were other things "besides her" with the mental picture of Jack and Sylvie after the last miscarriage—Sylvie pale and devastated, Jack devastated but an absolute rock. Clare hadn't known at all how to help.

She changed the subject with Anna, not ready for the very long sidetrack her smoking gun would mean. But she has one. She'd called Sylvie and, when Jack answered, he'd only half-covered the phone before he'd summoned her. Clare had heard what he said: "For you, Sylvie. The priest-fucker."

Stunned as she was, Clare hadn't commented when Sylvie picked up the phone. But the next time they met for lunch, and before or after Sylvie told her Jack had a job offer in Dallas and that she'd given her notice (it doesn't matter which, Clare thinks, though she's tried remembering all year), she'd brought it up. "I heard what Jack called me. He must have thought the receiver was covered. It wasn't."

She remembers the exact expression on Sylvie's face, though even now she finds it hard to describe except to think it was something between a sort of smile and an appearance of total and abject misery. She looked found out. She looked defiant. She was defensive, and Jack was the person she was defending—Jack and his rights to their story, hers and Sylvie's. "So?" she said. "It's not like it isn't true. It's not like I wouldn't tell him. Of course I told him."

"I know. But the characterization, the disrespect—"

"Do the crime, pay the time."

"Not the disrespect for me. The disrespect for you."

"That's your opinion." Sylvie picked up her menu so it blocked her face. "Are we having lunch? Fortunately, there are some people who can recognize teasing."

And I'm one of them, Clare had wanted to say. However, she didn't.

———

Clare pulls a fleece vest over her sweater as she takes a step down the basement stairs. The neighbors haven't called and it's cold enough in the house that she's almost decided to launch a furnace investigation on her own, though she never comes down here. She spots cobwebs on the slanted ceiling that rises above her and reminds herself she should paint the railing. She needs to sand the spindles where they've chipped and then paint them with a good enamel, which she's been thinking about forever, though she knows she won't do it.

Clare pushes the door open farther behind her so she doesn't miss the phone ringing. She sinks down on the upper step, collapsing her shoulder and back into the door frame. There's a low whistle of air from the furnace vent where it's strapped to the high ceiling before it angles out the window, covering it, blocking the light. On a windy day, she always thinks the whistle seems more like a musical saw, but either way, either sound, it's a part of things down here: the dank floor, the black tangle of pipes, the dividing brick wall that is dry in the winter with its faint, lingering odor of salt. The scent reminds Clare of the seashore of her childhood where the sand hardened with cold, which is what she always told Sylvie.

This is a secret she's kept, but she bought this house in part because of the nearly cinematic quality of this basement. It was like purchasing her own catacomb, an idea that disturbed her, but was still compelling enough that she managed most of a down payment from the bonds her Grandpa Wheatley left her, and cobbled the monthly payments together, sometimes renting out a room. Sylvie was a baby when they moved in, and Clare can't begin to count how often she paced back and forth down here, touching the walls, leaning into them, gripping them with her fingers, the door open at the top of the stairs so she would hear the cry from the nursery. She thought about Luc.

It was an obsessive thing. Clare knows that. She thought of him as a young priest, an almost priest, she doesn't know which. She imagined him when he was in Rome, enthralled by the city. In thrall to it. She put him in all sorts of settings: Luc descending the dusty rows to the lion ring in the Colosseum (Clare always hears the ancient lions roaring); Luc in the line of tonsured clerics passing quietly through darkened hallways; Luc at a picnic on a Roman hillside with other young priests in their cassocks and their shallow hats, round and flat-brimmed.

Clare sees him as happy in these scenes, though it's not an easy sort of happiness. It's something eerier and mysterious, which is maybe why this space has always had such a power to conjure him. Something in the air and in the sound. Something in the walls and the bricked-up arch where it's closed off from the neighbors' side. It evokes subterranean Rome for her, which is as close as she could ever get to understanding her own need to be here. It gave her Luc when he was all about discovering another world, Luc when he was all about hope. It gave her Luc before her.

Clare feels a shiver that starts in the small of her back. She stands up. She brushes her jeans off. She pushes her hair back, and shakes her arms, shakes her whole body. Forget the basement. Forget the furnace. She has to get out of here, out of the house, and she takes the steps up to the hallway and closes the stairway door, jamming her back against it while she tries to remember where she put her running clothes. The ones she didn't pack.

When she finds them and changes and heads to the kitchen, Harold thinks he's going, too.

"I'll walk you later," she says, and he tugs at her shoestring, untying it.

"No. Bad puppy. But you're grown, Harold. Act like a grown-up. What kind of a mother raised a spoiled dog like you? Me? No, dog. I'm Sylvie's mom. Just Sylvie's." Down on one knee, Clare pushes her face into his neck, thinking she can hold on here, that maybe she can keep herself from losing it entirely. She sneezes, her nose itching from Harold's wiry curls, and she reaches up for the half-eaten sandwich she left on the counter. She gives Harold the slice of beef with her mouth-print in it. Then she remembers something from the long ago past—her mother blowing on the thermostat in their house in Delaware. Clare goes into the hallway and fingers the top of the thermostat. She leans over and mouths a puff of air into it. There's a pale and tiny flight of dust. She thinks she can hear the click of ignition, a sound from the basement transmitting through the radiator pipes. She waits, and then waits longer until she's sure that the furnace is actually running.

She goes back to the kitchen. "High fives, Harold," she says, swiping at each of his front paws, relieved and very pleased with herself. "We're not going to freeze to death," she tells him. "And, hey. My phone's charged."

When she's reversed the call forwarding and picked up her running cap, Clare heads outside. She shields her eyes as she stands on the porch. Breathing in the fresh air that always makes her feel, for an instant, as if she owns the whole universe, she sees her elderly neighbor who lives on the corner. He's in his red and black jacket, and he's methodically sweeping a walk that someone has already shoveled. Clare thinks she could tell him that Sylvie has a baby, though maybe not. She's not certain he even knows Sylvie, not even sure he knows she's a mom, though she thinks it's written all over her. And grandmother. Is that going to show?

She heads down the steps and starts off running. When she passes the neighbor, she waves and says hello. She realizes from the look on his face that he didn't hear her coming, that she might have surprised him into something serious like a heart attack. But she's safe. He's OK. He nods back with his narrow, jowly smile, and she's tempted to stop. They could talk about anything—the snow, the weather, the fact he's not watching a football game.

Instead she keeps going, dodging snowbanks and crossing the street to avoid uncleared walks, though the sun has melted most of the new snow. She's going past houses and bars alive with football and the noise of men shouting in unison. She wonders if there's a football game on in the ward where Sylvie is, if there's this connection, although she knows Jack doesn't share that particular sort of male bonding. His interests are more esoteric. He's a kayaker, and he plays the mouth harp, something Clare has always found interesting about him. Surprising, too. Maybe she wishes he liked football.

A half hour later—a half hour of running and walking and slipping but not falling—Clare stops at a corner and pulls out her cell. No missed calls, but she knew that. She wonders if she should try to text Sylvie. She has no idea how to do it, though she thinks she could learn. But not now. She waits for a light. She has an eye out for baby carriages, and she knows she's looking for Sylvie. A Sylvie look-alike. Sylvie the mom. Sylvie and a baby. Mother and child.

When the light changes, Clare crosses to Starbucks and stands in line to buy a Grande and picks up a copy of a *Tribune* that someone has left on a table. She pulls her cap off and unzips her collar. Sitting down in a burgundy chair covered with faux velvet and staring at the front page, she wishes she could add her own headline: *Sylvie McHenry Jacobs New Mom.* She'd like to read that story; she'd like to know if it says Sylvie Jacobs believes her own mom was good at the job. What she'd like is the cross-stitch: *Mom, You're a Really Great Mom.*

———

On Monday morning, the furnace still working and her day's meetings canceled and an early appointment wangled with Anna, Clare is on the way to the office off the redbrick path. She wants Anna to tell her what to do. Or to have an idea. Or at least to listen. It surprises her again: after so many years of resisting even the idea of a therapist, she's become such a convert. A part of her thinks she's just starting to get cheap.

"What a deal," she'd told Elizabeth after only two visits. "Her office is like a beautiful cocoon. She's always supportive. She has these ideas I think might actually work. At the very least, she's helping me be more resolute. And my insurance pays! Or it will eventually."

Elizabeth had nodded. "Quite the deal," she agreed. "I quit mine. He decorated his office with urinals and bedpans. I thought it was hostile."

Clare had laughed. She laughs now, though for only an instant. She knows she didn't tell Elizabeth the more intense parts—that she'd felt she'd recovered something like the sacrament of Penance with Anna and that she'd made the first appointment because of Sylvie. She'd been afraid not to, afraid that the background tension that had existed between them for Sylvie's whole marriage was turning into a real fissure. And she hadn't said what she'd told Anna, that she found Jack baffling and that when he and Sylvie moved to Dallas a year ago, Sylvie had become not only absent and cool, but she was born again. "Don't ask me in what church," Clare said. "I mean I'd tell you, but I've really no idea."

"So you feel an estrangement?" Anna had asked, and Clare recoiled at the word. When Anna went on, pushing her to explain what was baffling about Jack, Clare had answered she couldn't, although she's certainly tried enough since. In her mind, she tries again now. Aloof is another word she could use. Aloof from her. Suspicious of her. She'd thought once he was only being protective of Sylvie, but she's decided that's wrong. He has a religious temperament, and she believes it's what makes him both rigid and generous with Sylvie, though generous in an essentially condescending way. But the fact is she keeps feeling farther and farther away from Sylvie and she doesn't understand why. She's been to see her in Dallas, though just once. It was in May for Sylvie's birthday, and Sylvie had filled the schedule so full—she'd even invited *Finn!*—that Clare doesn't think they had two minutes alone together. Sylvie had been distant, and Jack seemed to hover. Clare had left early, flying home with a bug she'd caught from Finn that turned into pneumonia, and Sylvie was largely silent and on bed rest for most of the fall. And no, Sylvie had said, she didn't need Clare to help. She had friends at the church. Clare had work. Their place wasn't finished. Jack was taking very good care of her.

Clare parks and hurries through the chilly morning to Anna's office and finds her, diminutive and clear-eyed and waiting for her with a cup of tea. Clare sits in the familiar chair across from her rocker.

"Congratulations." Anna is smiling. "How's Sylvie?"

Clare shakes her head. "I haven't talked to her yet. It's why I wanted to see you. Jack said she'd call and she hasn't."

"And you haven't called her?"

"Not exactly. I called her cell." Clare puts her own cell phone down on the table in front of her. "Last night. I left a message saying I was thrilled and I hoped everything was fine. And I forwarded calls from the house to this."

"Do you think she has her cell phone at the hospital?"

"Maybe. Sometimes they have signs you can't use them."

"And you didn't call the room?"

"I called the nurses' station. After I found out what hospital she's in. They were going to ring the room, but I said not to. I was afraid they'd wake her."

"And you haven't called Jack's cell?"

"No."

"So it's a day and a half since the baby was born and you haven't talked to Sylvie?"

Clare nods.

"This isn't good, Clare."

"I know, but he told me she'd call. I've been trying to do whatever they want. What's easiest for them. I guess that's what I'm doing."

Anna is quiet, turning her pen in her hand. "Are you afraid of something in all this?" she asks, and Clare takes a sip of the tea and looks at the carpet.

"I'm afraid she won't want to talk to me. I'm afraid she doesn't want me there. I'm afraid that I've lost her. Anna, I've told you this."

Anna opens the pad on her lap. "Clare, let's talk about the men in your life."

Clare looks up and stares. "What men?"

"I mean any men. Any men in your life. Did you want to stay single? We've never really talked about that. We haven't talked about Sylvie's father."

"We haven't. But what does it have to do with my talking to Sylvie?"

"Maybe nothing. But maybe there's something there."

"Anna, I've come here to figure out where I am in my daughter's life. I'm at a loss about what I can do. Isn't this maybe . . . a little frivolous?"

"She's had a baby and you don't know how to call her. Why is that?"

"You think I'm jealous she has the baby and husband both and I didn't? Am I supposed to say here that I gave her everything, that I kept nothing for myself and now I'm basically nowhere? That she's abandoned me for Jack?"

"Is that how you feel?"

"No."

"Just no?"

"I've had boyfriends. Men friends. I've told you that. But paying for everything for a child, and yada yada yada . . . being the only responsible—Anna, you know all this. Or not wanting your child to find some stranger in the house if she gets up at night."

"You mean the example?"

Clare starts to nod and then shakes her head. "For lack of a better word," she says, putting her cup down and clamping her arms between her knees. "The point is I wanted her to come first. It was never a sacrifice. It was what I wanted. No regrets."

"But she's been grown and gone—basically—for how many years?"

"I said I've had boyfriends. I've had fun, and I love my job. You do get used to being alone."

"If your daughter's an easy phone call away?"

"Yes."

"And now that phone call is hard."

"Yes."

"And what would make it easier?"

"I don't know. It's why I'm here."

"You've got your cell right there on the table. You know the number at the hospital?"

"I programmed it in."

"Then it's simple, Clare. Hit the button."

"It's not even eight o'clock."

"It's a hospital. She'll be awake. Look, I'll step outside. You won't have an audience. But it's a call you have to make. It's been thirty-six hours, Clare. She needs to hear your voice."

"Do you think Jack told her I was going to call?"

"Whether he did or didn't, you need to talk to her. For both of you."

"Right, but this feels something like drowning."

"What else does it feel like?"

"Cowardice. Like avoiding making everything that's wrong— that might be wrong—real. You know. Shut your ears to the news and it's not news . . ."

"I'll be in the hall."

Clare pulls her coat on. "No, I'll do this outside. Sylvie likes winter. I want something to tell her. About the air. About the lake."

"If it's past the hour when you're done, leave me a note?"

"Right." And a check, Clare thinks.

In the parking lot, stopping at a tree on the far edge, Clare draws her coat collar up and looks in the direction of the lake. She can't see it, but it's out there beyond the buildings and bare branches, out there by the marina where, in other seasons, the tops of sailboat masts jab at the horizon. She takes two deep breaths and then presses a button and another on her cell phone, watching the numbers pop up and spread across the screen. She holds the phone to her ear while it rings.

The nurses' station. The call being transferred to the room. The rings again and in a moment a hoarse voice. But not Sylvie. It isn't Sylvie.

"I'm calling for Sylvie Jacobs?"

Clare can hear the person shifting in the bed. "Jacobs?" A throat clearing and maybe a tray being knocked into a bed rail. "There was a Sallie," the voice says. "She checked out. Jerry, was her name Jacobs?" A pause and a man's voice in the background. "He thinks so."

"Sorry." Clare's nose is running and her eyes tearing from the wind. She brushes at them with a gloved hand. Two Jacobs in one maternity ward? What are the chances of that? Or has Sylvie actually left? Not much of a possibility with a caesarean. "I'm really sorry I bothered you," she says, ending the call and stuffing the phone into her pocket. She's relieved and unrelieved, annoyed and disappointed. And she's cold. Pulling her collar tight, she hurries back inside.

The door is still open to Anna's office, and Anna is at her laptop, her glasses in hand and her mouth closed shut on the end of one temple. She looks up expectantly.

"I didn't get her. Wrong room. Wrong Jacobs. I need to go home and hunt on the Internet more. Maybe I imagined all this."

And maybe Jack didn't call. Maybe Sylvie wasn't pregnant. Maybe she and Jack weren't even in Dallas. Maybe they'd become missionaries in South America or wherever the island was where Damien cared for his lepers. Molokai? Hawaii? "God, Anna!" Clare says, pulling the phone out again and staring at it. "Why doesn't she call?"

"You'll keep trying until you find her?"

"Sure. *Yeh-yeh. Yeh-yeh-yeh.*" Tearing the check out of her checkbook, Clare is surprised to hear herself, to realize she's borrowed the phrase Elizabeth brought back from London six months ago. "Anna, thanks. I'm a little owly. The last two nights I slept in the chair."

Anna is looking at her. "But Jack actually did call you, right?"

"Yes. He called . . ." Clare stops and then nods. "Yes, he did."

Anna twirls her glasses once. She folds them and puts them down on her desk. "Clare, I'm taking off my therapist hat here. We've talked about this. You're not in her marriage and you're not in her faith. But, Clare, if Sylvie's your daughter, you not only should trust her—and I really do believe this—I'm certain you can."

———

When she hears her ring tone again, Clare is in mid-argument with herself about whether Anna—if she ever told her the full story—would agree she has a smoking gun about Jack, or instead look dubious. She is driving down Lake Shore Drive, and she makes a fast check in the rearview mirror and turns onto a side street. Then she snatches the phone from the other seat. She is so ready to say *Sylvie* that it's almost out of her mouth before Finn's name pops up on the phone. The echoey sound tells her she's on speaker.

"Finn, what?"

"Are you on the way to the airport?"

"I'm on a street off Lake Shore Drive. It's the middle of morning rush hour."

"The kid sounds pretty good."

"Who?"

"Who do you think? Sylvie. Your kid."

Clare is silent—wounded and furious. Still, she realizes that, if she is careful, this is an opportunity. "I thought I asked you not to bother her. I'm surprised you had the patience to find the hospital."

"Hah! In Dallas you figure Parkland. JFK's. But Sylvie picks Baylor."

"Finn, I'm double-parked."

"I'll talk to you."

Clare snaps the phone shut. Then she leans forward on the steering wheel, her fingers pushing into her hair. She thinks she ought to be exhausted, but she feels agitated instead. She looks over her shoulder, makes a quick U-turn, and pulls back onto Lake Shore Drive. She guns the car into the line of traffic, and she's on her way home. No work at all today. Not even a token appearance. She's made up her mind about that.

In her kitchen, she lets Harold out on the patio and then stares at both the phone she's holding and the one she put back on the wall. She wants to take the call forwarding off (less chance of a bad connection with the wall phone than the cell), but she's blanked on which numbers to use. She eyes the settee. She has options. Find the phonebook, wherever she left it, and look for the unforwarding directions. Make coffee or take a nap. Instead, her heart beating faster, she takes a pencil from the drawer and pulls the newspaper over to write a number on. She picks up the cell.

There's a grid out there. Something to do with fiber optics or phone poles or buried wires or satellites. Something connected or something in the air. Clare has no idea. But the link from her brownstone in Chicago to an information operator and then to Dallas and a hospital switchboard—are there still switchboards?—to a nursing station to the phone by Sylvie's bed . . . it all seems so hypothetical. Really, it wouldn't surprise her if she winds up talking to somebody in Alaska or the Sallie Jacobs she'd called by mistake. But no. It's Sylvie. She's hearing Sylvie's voice.

Clare isn't sure she can speak. She swallows. "Oh, Sylvie, sweetheart, a little boy! How are you doing? And how is he? I wish I could hug you. Both of you. Did you get my message? I called the wrong hospital. I thought that—but how do you feel?"

A tick of silence. Another. "Like I was hit by a truck."

"You sound . . . I'd say you sound fine. And Damien?"

"He can be loud."

Clare laughs. She sounds a little nervous to herself, although she certainly doesn't want to. "Yes, well a baby . . ."

"I can't really talk now. I have to feed him. If he can figure out what he's doing. Or if I can. Jack just got here."

"Wait. Sylvie? Sylvie, do you want me to come? I can cook, I can clean. I can change diapers. And I can always make myself scarce if I get in the way. I can do laundry. There'll be so much laundry. I can rock the baby."

"I'll call you. Later. Thank Uncle Finn for his flowers?"

"Sure," Clare says, trying her best, which isn't really that good, not to feel one-upped. "Take care of yourself. Love you."

"All right."

Clare puts the phone down. She hugs her shoulders and realizes she's still rattled, but hugely relieved. She goes to the door and calls Harold. When he comes running, she hugs him, too—the cold fur, the damp nose that, to the touch, is like something between tar and a fine grade of sandpaper. She feels at least ten times better just having heard Sylvie's voice, but she still has no plan. She has this silly picture of herself in mind—Clare in her workout clothes and up on a tightwire between buildings, balancing rod in hand, and the open window she's headed toward suddenly slammed in her face.

She closes the door against the nippy wind. "What can I do, Harold? Should I find a street corner where they're handing out religious material and try reading it? Think I should meet Sylvie halfway at least on that? Not that she wouldn't see right through me. Probably she's got church women ready to take care of her again. I'm sure they're very nice. Texas church ladies when her mother doesn't even know whether y'all is singular or plural. Harold, my bad."

Clare stands looking at the kitchen while Harold goes over to his dish. He starts to drink. She is listening to his sloppy water-lapping and wondering, as she has lately, if it's time for a change. In so many ways, this kitchen was the center of her life with Sylvie. She has always assumed she'd keep it familiar for both of them. But Sylvie doesn't live here any longer. Hard as it is for Clare even to think about, Sylvie lives far away, and it isn't likely she'll be coming home often. Clare doesn't know when. Clare doesn't know if.

So this is her question. She can keep Sylvie's clothes in her closet, but does she really need to keep the kitchen as if it were some sort of time capsule? She could spend a lot of money here. She doesn't want a designer who'd push a stylish, fruit-based color scheme she wouldn't really like. (Lime. Yellow-orange. Rosy peach.) And she doesn't want stools and chairs with skinny, chrome legs and backs shaped like artists' palettes. She's seen very beautiful kitchens with mahogany cabinets and deep green soapstone counters lined with white veins. She'd want that. She could cover the floor with ceramic tile and put a wooden table and chairs where the island is now (she imagines the table with a bowl of fruit and then decides on a tall vase of flowers). She could finally really learn how to cook. It would all be a statement that even though she is closing out her fifties, she still has a life. Or that she's thinking of acquiring one.

Though what kind of life, exactly, would it be? Pottery courses? A promotion out of a job she's good at and really likes? A man who's on the right side of seventy? Courses in Gaelic or Portuguese and ethnic dinners for her classmates in her remodeled kitchen? Maybe ladling out meals in a soup kitchen instead? What would be the added value that could take the place of what she's already had? Of her daughter. Of Sylvie.

Clare is weeping again. She's like a faucet. She knows she's a total disaster, and she assumes she's flirting with dehydration. She pours herself a large glass of water and finds a cucumber that is starting to get mushy. She cuts off slices until she has two that are good enough and then pastes them on her eyes. What she wants is not to look like somebody's grandmother. She wants somebody who can tell her what to do. Is she maybe going a little crazy?

She's had so many conversations with Sylvie when Sylvie isn't here. They are variations on a theme: Which is it, Sylvie? Did I embarrass you about Jack? Did you hate it that I quoted that scurrilous name for me? Are you still incensed that I kept my secret so long? Or is it that you can't stand what the secret actually was or, even more, its dreadful finality? I know you went from being defensive to being angry, but are you the one who believes you shouldn't forgive me? Is it Jack? Is it both of you? I'm a little at a loss here. Obviously, I don't know what a marriage means from the inside out. You have to tell me, Sylvie. Is a marriage like an ink blotter that soaks up all the other parts of your life so there's nothing else? What part is you? What part is some sort of amalgam—maybe a gestalt?

It comes to her then in a blinding instant. There are people she can talk to. People besides Anna whose silence is guaranteed. People who, by the very fact of her existence, would have loved Sylvie. People who already have.

———

When she's gone through security at the airport, Clare tucks her boarding pass in the back pocket of her suitcase and runs over logistics again.

She has a folder of everything she printed out from MapQuest. She has a list of names and places and the dog-eared notebook where, for years, she's jotted down important things. She has motel reservations; she has a car booked. And she also has the numbers to cancel everything on a moment's notice if Sylvie—if Sylvie or Jack calls. She touches her pocket. Her cell phone is there. When she's boarded the plane and it starts down the taxiway, she nods quickly to sleep.

A light snow is falling in the early darkness when they land in Minneapolis. Clare turns her phone on. No messages. She's a little logy from her nap and still worn out from her day. She knocks her head when she stands up to get her suitcase down from the overhead bin.

"You OK?" the man in the window seat asks her. "I can get that for you."

Clare manages a laugh and a nod. On another trip at another time, she might have chatted with him. He looks engaging. He's younger than Sylvie—a boy really—and very stylishly dressed. But Clare has slept the whole flight, and when she awakened at the bump of the plane's wheels on the runway, this boy was still reading the GQ he'd opened at O'Hare. "Thanks," she says, touching her head as discreetly as she can to make sure she's not bleeding.

Out in the terminal, she's alone in the crowd. It's years since she's flown here, and she's unsure about the signs. She hesitates between guessing and asking someone which way for rental cars and then asks. Dragging her suitcase behind her, she thinks about food but she doesn't stop. She wants a hotel with room service, a book, and an early night, but that's not an option. She's on a schedule. She doesn't know what the schedule is. But she knows what she wants to fit in between here and Dallas, whenever Dallas is.

By the time she's organized herself and a coffee and banana from Starbucks, and a marked-up map in her rental car, Clare feels remarkably alert. Not actually alert. But all things considered, alert enough to find it remarkable. She's headed north and a little west and, once she gets out of the city, if the snow stays light and she stays on course, the evening trip ahead of her will be maybe an hour and a half, a little more. In fact, if her parents hadn't moved thirty miles to a lake-front house in a sleepy village thirty years ago, her trip would be even shorter. But she isn't going home. She isn't going to a town where she's ever lived. She follows the entrance to the freeway, the layer of melting snowflakes on the windshield blurring the lights of the city.

Once she's left the city behind and the snowflakes have thinned to almost nothing, Clare sets the cruise control and fiddles with the radio. Jazz. She hears Kenny G and, though she knows Sylvie would groan at the schmaltziness—that she would have, too, as her younger, Mozart-playing self—Clare doesn't care. She can feel the tension draining out of her. She reaches for the banana and peels it back. She sips at her coffee and drives.

The winter night surrounds her, the sky so overcast there isn't a single star. She travels in a stream of headlights and taillights, listening to the rumble of trucks, seeing billboards and the signs for casinos and strip clubs, noticing the hill clusters of townhouses that look oddly like cliff dwellings. Then, finally, and for mile after mile, she is in near blackness until the looming green signs of the Interstate point the way to a deeper, tree-shadowed dark.

She assumes she'll get lost. It's the way she usually does things. She's a slow study for finding things. She can just hear Sylvie: "Spot my mom three really wrong turns and an extra hour and she'll show up exactly where you want her. Or close enough to call for more directions."

But there it is. The motel.

"Wrong, Sylvie," she mumbles, the folder from the motel clerk clamped between her lips after she checks in. This time no problem. The exact exit. The correct turn onto the entry road. Here she is in the actual place where she booked a room. "Kiddo, I kid you not."

Clare carries her suitcase up the stairs. When she's opened the door to 218, she puts the suitcase down and hangs up her coat and then goes to the window and stares out at the dying light on the motel sign that, like a little star, caught her eye from the road. Then she closes the drapes.

When she wakes in the morning, it's still dark, and a semi-truck is idling in the parking lot. She was OK with an evening meal of tea and a small bag of peanuts and she fell asleep before finishing even a page of her book. Now, though, she's hungry and ready to go. She's brought a dress—it seemed the right thing to wear—and when she showers and puts on what Sylvie calls her day makeup (in fact, it is her only makeup), she pulls the dress on and goes down to breakfast.

For a person who can still wear her daughter's clothes (and not the maternity ones, which she hasn't seen), Clare is ravenous. She pours herself juice and fixes cereal. She spreads a bagel with an entire packet of cream cheese. She picks out a miniature Danish and a muffin and, when she's eaten them both, she goes back for an orange and hard-boiled egg. In the meantime, she has two cups of coffee. When she's added cream to a third cup to take to her room, she stuffs her purse with another egg, a container of yogurt, a banana and apple, and a second bagel wrapped in a napkin. She starts to leave, then changes her mind, and goes back for a spoon and a cinnamon roll.

Provisions. She has no idea what her day will be like, but she's certainly protected herself against starvation.

When she gets in the car, the sky is a thin wash of pink at the horizon. Clare puts the phone down on the passenger seat and takes out her glasses. She fumbles for the reading light and studies her directions once more. If this were simply a sentimental junket, she would find the road along the lake and drive into town to look at her parents' house. But it isn't, and the cemetery is the opposite way.

Driving, it's easier to find than she expected. "See, Sylvie?" she says. As the sun slips up above a row of tombstones, she rolls the car to a stop in front of the cedar tree just beyond her parents' graves. She thinks of looking at herself in the mirror, of checking the glints of gray her stylist generously calls highlights. She opens the car door instead, thinking the whole time how strangely old she would seem to her parents.

Her legs are cold. She buttons her coat as she makes her way across the patchy snow. There is so little of it for January. She stops in front of her father's grave first.

"Hello, Daddy," she says. "We've got this thing called global warming." Clare squats down and scrapes the stone clear with a gloved hand, and then stands up again. "It means I knew I wouldn't need a shovel. I didn't go to the lake, but I'm sure it's frozen so it's not *that* warm. But New Orleans got flooded; it's basically gone. A lot of it. Tennessee and Arkansas keep getting wilder and wilder tornadoes. The Arctic ice cap and Antarctica are melting. We had a summer like Dallas. Which is where Sylvie is. Sylvie and Jack. They have a baby. Two and a half days old. He's Damien Gabriel. So a great-grandson. Congratulations, Great-Grandpa. I'm going to see him. I wanted to tell you and Mother first. It's why I came. That, and I love you."

Clare stands a moment longer. She touches her nose with her glove and feels the stiff leather. The wind is ruffling her hair, baring her neck, and she wishes she'd brought a cap. She wishes she'd kept her hair long. She looks out across the graveyard. Such a gathering of gray, although there are bouquets of plastic roses scattered about, their petals coated with ice.

"OK," she says. She shifts her eyes to her mother's grave and then kneels on the edge of her coat and brushes the stone clear so it matches her father's. She runs her finger through her mother's name. The *Madelyn*. The *Wheatley* and *McHenry*. She'd intended to stand up, but it seems easier just to stay on her knees. Reflexively, she turns her back toward her father's grave and keeps her voice low.

"I'm sorry." She swallows before she goes on. "For all the ways that I made you sad. I'm very sorry. *Truly, Madly, Deeply*. A movie title, but . . . I know I could have told you more. Everything really. It was Father Étienne. From St. Francis de Assisi. How strange that I even met him again when I was grown. But you shouldn't blame him. I never wanted you to blame him, though I did wonder if you knew it was him, if you understood there was something about me that was that angry, that vengeful. Against St. Francis. Though I believed that I loved him. I did love him. The convoluted thing is it felt nearly like retribution at first, that I was actually making something up to you. Because I believed them—what the nuns told me, what Sister Immaculata said at St. Francis—that you wouldn't be saved. That you had to be Catholic. Did you know she told me that? Did you know I actually believed her? It started out with that betrayal—of you—and never came right. Except for Sylvie. She was the miracle. I always expected one. What a naive child I was. What a ridiculous woman I am. You could say I'm foolish just to be doing this. But I can't say how comforting it is that you're still here in this way . . .

"And Sylvie has a baby. They didn't think she would. All the miscarriages. Did I ever tell you I almost lost her? You never said, but didn't you lose a baby when I was young? I remember you in the bathroom for the longest time and washing out blood. But Sylvie and Jack have this baby. Damien Gabriel. A little boy. I always thought she'd have a girl, that it would be you and me and Sylvie, and Sylvie's little girl . . . She's fine. I'm fine. And Finn's the same. He sent Sylvie flowers. I'm not crying, which is very good. Not that you saw me cry so much. Not when I was older. Maybe it's new. It's a lousy idea. It makes a person feel dreadful. Hacky and prunelike. But I'm fine. Like I said."

Clare is quiet. She tightens her eyes. She is trying to see her mother, and her mother's face is almost there. But what she sees more clearly is her mother's housedress. It means she is young.

Clare looks back at the stone. She leans over and touches the *Madelyn* again, and then she traces the rose she had cut in the corner of the stone. She is shivering, cold. She wants to be back on the road, but it's hard to leave. It isn't sad—not really—but peaceful here. Almost a refuge.

Clare gets to her feet and steps back so both stones are in front of her. She makes a little cross in the air for her father, a half wave for her mother. "So I'm going," she says. "You're my father and mother. Bobby and Maddie. *Man-Bap.* What the Indians say. In India. I should leave this," she adds, remembering her father's sweet tooth. She reaches in her purse for the cinnamon roll and puts it down on his grave. "You can share with the sparrows."

Back in the car, Clare panics at the sight of her phone. But no. There aren't any messages. She hasn't lost her chance of a live voice by leaving the phone out of earshot. She uncaps her water bottle and takes a quick drink. She's had too much coffee. Too much of everything, and her stomach feels queasy. She studies her map and directions once more. She looks out the window at the cemetery as she starts toward the road. The ridgy snow. The cold sun. The slopes of tombstones that stand up or, like her parents', are lodged discreetly in the ground.

Eyes on the road now: she is heading farther north.

⁓

Other than the man himself—his being, his presence—Clare knows very little about Sylvie's father. About Luc. *Luc-Cristof Étienne.* She has remembered the few things he told her—the bits that lay outside the frame of who they were together. The stepfather from Minnesota with the French Canadian ancestors and the mother who was French from France (as Luc was himself). The two had met when the stepfather was in the army, and the mother, a French soldier's widow, in the Resistance. Clare was struck by the romance of it.

"Luc, what did she do?" she'd asked him. (By this time, they'd renegotiated the question of names: "Luc," he'd said, "though it could be startling to hear my name on a woman's lips again. But pleasing. I don't mean that it wouldn't be.") "I'd like to know. Luc, what did she do?"

He'd shaken his head, his hands raised in a brief gesture that meant he knew nothing. His mother had kept her secrets. He assumed she'd done whatever dangerous things had earned her the *Croix de Guerre.* From General de Gaulle himself. She kept it in a case at home, and wore it pinned under her blouse on Bastille Day. On Christmas Eve, she set it in the center of the table. "The family jewels," Luc said.

Clare had forgotten this. Or she'd not thought about it in any real sense for ages, which is essentially the same thing. For a long time, it was too painful, and then, later, she'd pushed it out of her mind. Still, the demographer in her occasionally, if idly, set to work. She found the settlements of the *Quebecois* near the Mississippi. She enumerated the Minnesota towns that had French settlers dating from the voyageurs, and studied pictures of the Church of St. Louis, King of France in St. Paul. (Sometimes she thinks she could never have given up being Catholic if beautiful St. Louis had been her church.) Though she couldn't find the name Étienne in directories of the town Luc and his mother had moved to with her new husband, Clare, who never assumes, in this more speculative matter does. She believes it's likely that Luc kept his Franco-French father's name. She thinks it's very likely, though she doesn't really know. It wasn't something she asked. It didn't come up, though perhaps now she'll find out.

In the late morning, bagel crumbs on the car floor and an interest in many things French on her mind, Clare spots yet another lake with scattered houses for ice fishing. This is the lake she is looking for. On her map, it curves along the edge of the town she knows was Luc's. Once, in her office, she came across a picture of this very town dated nearly a hundred years ago. It was charming then with its turn-of-the-century buildings—comfortable large homes in the prominent foreground, stores and industrial buildings behind them, all of them mining-related. She'd never in her wildest dreams imagined she'd come here. Now she has.

Clare pulls into a gas station and fills up the tank. In the restroom, she looks at herself in the fluorescent-lit mirror and decides she's aged ten years since she left Chicago. She needs a run. She needs a nap. At the moment, neither one is an option and she buys a paper and asks the clerk for recommendations for a café. She isn't hungry at all, and she still has food in her purse, but she has an impulse to sit at a counter and chat with somebody while she drinks a cup of tea, or maybe slide into a booth and pick at a sandwich while she reads the paper and gets a sense of the town. It's hardly necessary. The town is exactly like all the others she's driven through—bland, with scarcely any old facades, and dingy, with a thin and dirty cover of snow and in a far too treeless setting for what was once the Great North Woods. Clare supposes she could find vestiges of its more vital past, but only that. And anyway, she has her plan. She has her bookings. And she still has her phone that could change her mind about everything in a single instant.

Clare puts her map on the counter, and points at it. "Am I right?" she asks the waitress. "Do I stay on this highway and turn here to go to the library?"

She is pleased when she finds it: a Carnegie library. Temple-like. Temple of Learning. She has two missions, and she starts at the reference desk. Or what serves as the reference desk. From what she can tell, reference and checkout are the job of just one person.

"Do you have high school yearbooks?" she asks. She laughs to acknowledge that she's asked something essentially trivial or maybe to deflect the obvious questions. She doesn't really know why she laughed, but just that she did. She waits. The librarian nods, busy putting cards in the backs of a stack of books.

"Over here," she says when she's finished. She leads Clare to the oversized shelves.

A drift of weariness spreads over Clare. She's put her glasses on, and she reaches under them to rub her eyes. She isn't entirely sure of the dates, but she's almost sure. She thinks 1949 is the year that she needs. It's simply a matter of taking the volume from the shelf, and that's what she has to do. Her eyes follow the numerals down the row.

Yes. *1949*. Clare gathers herself. She reaches up, hooking a finger over the spine, and then pulls the book free. It's so slim. The pebbly back. The year engraved again on the cover. Clare opens it to the middle and flips her way to the front and the pictures of seniors. She starts turning pages.

And there he is. There's Luc. The black hair, already close-cropped, the nose narrow at the bridge, the three-quarters pose and eyes focused on whatever spot they'd been directed to by the photographer.

The Cristof is missing. This Luc is Luc Étienne. He is wearing a jacket and tie like the other boys, but Clare knows she would have picked him out of the lot even if she hadn't had him in mind. He looks handsome. He looks thoughtful. He looks French.

She closes the book, startled at her own reaction. At its body-shaking intensity. But she's well aware she has to set the feeling aside. This is strictly about Sylvie.

Clare reaches into her purse. She digs through the cough drops she dumped in loose until she finds the camera she packed. When she pulls it out, her hand is gooey with banana. The camera is covered, too, but it's closed and, of the important parts, only the viewfinder is sticky and slimed. Clare wants very much to swear out loud. Instead she sets to work with Kleenex and discreet daubs of spit. Then sneak-ily—is there a policy here against copying old yearbook pictures with a digital camera?—she opens the yearbook again and finds her page. She looks at Luc through the viewfinder and studies him a moment, thinking how much he's already like Father Étienne and the older Luc that she knew. Then she pushes the shutter button and, checking the light and reflections and the location of the librarian, snaps the shutter several more times.

When she's finished, she puts the book back and goes to the desk.

"You find what you want?" the librarian asks.

Clare says that she has. "And if there's a plot book for the cemetery, I'd like to see that as well."

"You're in luck."

Half an hour later when she goes back outside, cemetery diagram in her hand, Clare hears her ring tone. Quickly, she flips the phone open. She sighs. "Finn."

"So where are you?" he asks, and Clare freezes, thinking she's forgotten to forward her calls. She tracks back quickly. She'd called home from her motel room and, after two rings, her ring tone had played. She's all right.

"Outside," she says.

"How's Sylvie?"

"Fine. Tired when I talked to her."

"You're not in Dallas?"

"No." Clare considers whether she needs to say more and then makes sure that she doesn't.

"You're more patient than I am."

"Yes," Clare says, not adding that it's partly illusion.

"You need any airline miles, I've got some."

"I'm covered," she says quickly. "But I appreciate it," she adds, not mentioning that she's already sacrificed her new kitchen plans (if they actually were plans) on the altar of last-minute travel prices.

"Clare, remember when Sylvie was born you didn't want the folks there even when you got home? Maybe it's hereditary. The independent McHenry women. If it's like that, I wouldn't worry too much."

Clare is silent, surprised—almost touched—that her brother has both this memory and this insight. If that's what it is. Mostly, she feels exposed, though she isn't so sure how independent the McHenry woman they're talking about actually is, though of course, in many ways, independence has always been Sylvie's hallmark . . . Clare stares at the overcast sky and at the lake beyond the library. "Finn, I'll talk to you. You at home?"

"Shanghai."

"The one in China?"

"Right. So I'm nowhere near Dallas, and I won't see your grand-kid before you do."

"Finn, I wasn't . . . Oh nothing."

Back in her car, phone in one coat pocket and camera in the other, Clare regroups, resetting her guard against Finn and all his years of being in and out of marriages and her life and so many foreign countries that she'd once actually believed he was in the CIA until she realized it was simply what he wanted her to think. She eats the apple. As small as this town is, she still needs to get her bearings. She thinks about going to the Catholic church, or even to the rectory if there is one. Somebody would likely know about Father Étienne and be able to tell her his mother's name. His stepfather's. Yet Clare suspects their plots are close to his in the graveyard, and that she can identify them herself. It would be more discreet not to ask, and she owes him that. She owes it to Sylvie.

And, anyway, she is limiting what she does here. She could have searched more in the yearbooks—hunted to see how Luc had changed throughout high school. It had startled her how much he looked like Sylvie when he was seventeen. She might have traced the resemblance back to his freshman year. She could have checked to see when he'd gone from looking like a boy to the young man he clearly was as a senior. And if she'd wanted to, she might have scoured the indexes and found every team he was ever on, every office he'd held, whether it was him accompanying the Homecoming Queen. She knows none of these things.

But she doesn't intend to stalk his past. She has no rights to him. Sylvie has rights, but Sylvie, as far as Clare knows, has no interest in learning anything more. And as far as making inquiries at this church goes, Clare, seducer-apostate, has no rights at all.

Earlier, when she'd driven past it, she'd told herself it would be simple enough to find it again and to go inside. She's curious about it, this church Luc attended before he left for the seminary, although she knows he'd decided to be a priest when he was still in France—when he was still a child and his father had died in the Ardennes and his mother had joined the Resistance. Does she have that straight? There was someone who'd been killed in the Netherlands near the bridge at Maastricht early in the war. Was that Luc's father? She's no longer sure, but she's made up her mind. She's skipping the church.

Easy drive. It's just a few blocks' drive to the cemetery, though long enough for Clare to grow nervous—nervous and excited, a stage fright sort of excitement, both apprehension and eagerness. This is a reunion she's opted for. She's here on a whim and, yet, with a kind of compulsive intent.

In an earlier time, and before Sylvie knew about Luc, Clare knows she and Sylvie would have had great fun coming up with a name for an imaginary woman on just this sort of mission—*The Very Grave Graveseeker. Lady of the Tombstone. The Cold Stone Voyeur.* Sylvie would have thought of something better, something that was actually funny that would have sent them both into paroxysms of laughter.

But this: *Luc Gravewalker*, Clare thinks, pulling the car off the road. That's me, searching for Luc.

She looks at her notes and the scribbly sketch she made in the library. The sun is trying to come out, and Clare holds the paper up, trying to read without her glasses. She can't. She digs in her purse again, wary of encountering more squashed banana. But once she has her glasses on, she gets herself oriented. She has the plot number for Luc's grave and directions that place it a dozen yards off the path if she heads straight west toward the lake. If she passes a very large monument for a family named Thorenson, it should be just a few stones south.

Walking, Clare eyes the names. If she were here for any other reason, she knows she would have been curious about everything. Polish names definitely. English and Scandinavian. But French is what she is after. *Luc.*

A new thought strikes her out of the blue. This isn't sanctified ground. Not in the Catholic sense. Father Luc-Cristof Étienne, suicide as he was, would not have been granted a Catholic burial. His priestly career—all twenty years of it—would have been discounted with the ringing pronouncement of a single canon law.

The rational and family part of Clare (is this an oxymoron? she wonders) thinks *good!* He should be buried here close to his mother and his stepfather.

The emotional part of her thinks something else. *Guilty, Clare. Guilty of one more hanging offense. You're headed to an even deeper circle in hell than you imagined. Guilty. No appeal. You're guilty as sin.*

Then she turns and she sees it. Luc's gravestone.

———

Heading to Duluth, Clare is well aware she is part of a delusion. The car hums along as if the world is all right; the road rises to meet her as if she's been handed the answer to an Irish prayer. How wholly irrelevant it all is. If she could just stay focused on the trip: the hotel booked for the hours of sleep before her flights to Minneapolis and Chicago. The room with a promised view of the giant lake (Superior!) and tomorrow's dawn over Canada. This car, which she'll leave in Duluth with a penalty for not returning it where she started out.

Her mind, though it flutters over these things, is mostly elsewhere. Earlier, she'd turned on the radio, hoping the voices would draw her in. They didn't. It was all so much annoying chatter, an irritating, chirpy buzz that ran in her head. Still, she kept it on, afraid to lose the sense it gave of company. Of mooring.

It had been so very devastating. To stand there in front of that grave. To see the date engraved so decisively after the dash—1976.

The End. Nothing more.

But there's Sylvie.

She had told him that: *Sylvie.* As lovely a daughter as a man could have. She favors you. She's very bright, very creative. It seems she has an interest in religion, though it's late blooming. And now she has a child. In a few hours, he'll be three days old. Damien Gabriel. She's married. They live in Dallas, and it's where I'll go to meet the baby. It's Sylvie and Jack. They were married seven years ago in June. This child . . . it's amazing that they have him, just as it's amazing I had Sylvie, though how could we, either of us, be sad that she exists? And if there's no way I can thank you, I can tell you this. I've loved her as your daughter. She's always been your daughter. There was never a man I allowed to take your place. Nobody could have. Nobody has.

Nobody. Driving, Clare pushes her hand against her forehead. She wonders if Sylvie feels about Jack as she did about Luc; she wonders, too, if her mother felt about Luc—even in absentia—as she does about Jack, if her mother blamed him for the distance between them when she should have blamed her daughter instead.

Or those long-ago nuns. Ghosts, as Clare thinks of them now.

Or no one at all.

None of it is anything Clare wants even to consider now. She is crying again. An unanchored sort of crying. It isn't for any particular one of her sorrows. It merely is.

She'd found the other graves, and far more readily than she'd expected. They flanked Luc's grave. Odd, she'd thought. But touching. Or maybe revealing. Albert Jacques Bissonette, born in 1904, lay not beside his wife but next to his stepson, having outlived him by four years. A good life, if a longish life is the same as good.

The surprise was Luc's mother's grave: *Janine Fournier Étienne Bissonette*, 1904–1997.

Clare was stunned. Really that long? *Really?* What a confounding thought. How could Sylvie have had a grandmother she didn't know or even know about for almost twenty years of her life? A grandmother who'd never known her. And how could Luc's mother have lived with his death for those same twenty years without knowing at all why he died? Clare can't imagine it. She can't fathom the magnitude of such a loss. What she does see is the extent of her own culpability. It reaches so far beyond what she's let herself think. And now—what about Sylvie? Has the retribution arrived like the turning of a wheel? Has it come from Sylvie directly to her?

At the grave, she'd stood very quietly, incapable of considering such bitter implications. Now, though, she can hear Anna tucked away in her office off the redbrick path, prodding her with this: "Since I've known you, Clare, you've experienced this so acutely. But it's always there. Believe me. This mother and daughter thing. This conundrum. It's always the chicken and the egg. Whose love is the one that wounds first?"

"I don't know," Clare said, talking back as though Anna's words were loud in the car and the one clear voice from the radio. "I assumed it was mine. And go ahead. Tell me how not to put myself in the center. If it's what this is all about."

Silence. Anna has closed up her shop.

Clare assumes she is running on empty. Not the car, but just her. She tries remembering what she's eaten and when, and all she can think of is what a hard time she had leaving the cemetery. She'd walked up and down the rows. She took pictures of the gravestones and then sat on a ledge and watched how the afternoon sun fell on Luc's name. It was quiet and heartbreaking.

Later, she'd had just as much difficulty leaving the town. Her legs still cold—blotchy cold—she'd wandered the main street, looking in windows, checking her reflection and thinking she'd grown shorter since morning, thinking she was collapsing in on herself, yet still noticing her smart coat, its dark copper coloring the windows as she passed, the air she had of the city (an oddly reassuring excursion into vanity). And all the while, she'd kept the sense she was missing something, that there was something, in spite of her limited mission here, she still needed to find.

She had passed the same store maybe five times without really noticing it, when a young woman, older than Sylvie, but still young and pretty, opened the door and called out to her. Clare stopped and looked at her. The woman was wearing jeans and turquoise beads and her hair was in a shiny braid that fell down her back. In spite of the effect, she didn't look Indian.

The woman smiled. "You're not lost, are you?"

"I don't think so." Clare laughed, trying to dispel her embarrassment. "Maybe I am a little," she added, "though I do know what town I'm in."

"This is my store. Laurie's Rag and Bijoux. So I'm Laurie. Come on in. You look cold. Can I get you some tea?"

"I'd love that." Clare followed her inside. She looked around and then grinned a little. "You don't sound—you know—*Fargo*," she said.

"I'm not. I'm from Montana. I met my boyfriend in the army and he's from here, so now it's home. Five years. My kids like it."

Clare picked up a copper pitcher shaped like a dragon. "Intriguing," she said, wishing she had Sylvie with her. "My daughter would like this. In fact, I need to buy her something. She just had a baby. A little boy. And I should get her husband a new father gift. I already have things for the baby."

"Does she live around here?"

"No." Clare shook her head, not ready to get into the Dallas part, and well aware she lacked a decent cover story. "Hey, look at this," she said, intending to change the subject, although she liked what she saw. She held up a cream-colored jacket with jungle animals made out of wood. They hung from the bottom edge. "Sylvie would go for this. And she'd look great in it. At least I think she'd like it now." Clare hesitated. "Hard to be certain."

"It would be great on you."

"Right. I could give it to one of my friends if Sylvie doesn't want it."

"Here's your tea. Want me to wrap that?"

Clare nodded.

"There's a stool over there by the vintage jewels. Hah." Laurie switched the tea for the jacket. "Her guy into military stuff? Over there, too. My boyfriend's like a pawnshop. His pals are always bringing him stuff. We can deck the dad and baby out like four-star generals."

"I'm not sure." Clare took a sip of the tea and moved toward the stool. She was almost warm, almost comfortable. She was thinking she wouldn't mind adopting this girl. Especially, if it meant she could stop all this awkward courting of Sylvie. "I think he's more into boats. I like that little ship."

"Man-o'–war. I like all the rigging."

"So do I. I didn't know shopping could be this easy."

"You want it then?"

"I do, but . . . oh . . ." Clare was looking in the case with the antique jewelry and the military insignia and medals. There was a bronze cross. It had two swords, which intersected behind a profile of a head, and it was attached to a ribbon that was a faded red with green stripes.

Laurie came over to look. "I don't have a clue about that. It came from the other junk dealer here. I know it isn't American."

"I've seen pictures. It's French. It's the *Croix de Guerre*."

"There you go."

"May I look at it?" Clare waited while Laurie got it out and handed it to her. Then she smoothed it out on her palm. "This, too," she said. "Add this."

———

In her hotel room, picking at nachos from a Mexican restaurant and rubbing her hair dry, Clare looks at the medal, which she's laid on a pillow. It's the one thing she knows she wasn't crying about in the car. There's no name on it. Nothing like Janine Fournier Étienne. No Mme. Janine Bissonette. But Clare is sure it belonged to Luc's mother. Anything is possible, and so it's possible that it didn't, but the odds that it was hers seem overwhelmingly high. She could do the math and research in her office—the approximate number of French in the area, the number and type of *Croix de Guerres* given out that had even a possibility of migrating to a small Minnesota town, and a variety of other factors as well. It wouldn't be such a difficult thing to figure the probability. But, to Clare, the persuasive detail has nothing whatsoever to do with statistics. It's the fact that Luc's mother died an elderly widow with no survivors. Or none that she knew about. How else would the "family jewels" turn up in the junk man's stock?

Clare sets the clock for her early flight and then goes over to the window and holds the curtain back. It's too dark now to see the lake, but it's there. She spotted it in the snowy dusk as her car crested a hill that gave her the expanse of the harbor and two towns in two states. After she'd gone to her room, she walked out to the boardwalk, which in places was almost drifted in, and she looked at the snow blowing past lampposts and dusting the ice-encrusted rocks that covered the shore. She saw the lighthouse, blinking its green light, and eyed the lake, which was frozen at the shoreline but, farther out, had to be simply deep and icy cold.

Yet it's a way out. Here in the interior, far from the oceans, Clare knows that these giant lakes with the ships that will come once again in the spring are a promised, safe way out.

The phone by the bed rings, and Clare drops the curtain. On the run, she gets there by the second ring and answers yes, that the room is fine. Then she looks at her cell phone and sees the missed call. Ten minutes ago. She was in the shower. It's less than a heartbeat before she sees it wasn't from Dallas. Elizabeth. Clare lies down on the bed and calls her back.

Elizabeth goes straight to the point. "I've heard from Jack."

"You did? Is Sylvie OK?"

"He said so. He thanked me for my flowers. He said Sylvie wanted him to. And then he said she's going home tomorrow—did you know that?—that he's getting off work early in the afternoon to pick them up, and that's it's cold there. She'd like to borrow my shearling coat."

"She needs your coat? To go home tomorrow?"

"Obviously I can't get it there in the morning. Unless you take it, of course."

Clare is quiet.

"Clare, are you still there?"

"Yes." Clare waits a second, thinking she could mention the yoga knitting phone call or Elizabeth's clueless last boyfriend, though either one seems like a weak counterpunch. "So what aren't you telling me here, Elizabeth? I can see Sylvie liking that coat. I can hear her telling Jack she wishes she had a coat that's like it—loose, you know, but stylish." Clare laughs. "Call me skeptical, but Sylvie wanting your actual coat sounds a lot more like your idea than hers."

It's Elizabeth's turn to be quiet. "Not entirely," she says after a moment. "I was maybe channeling you. But listen, Clare. You know how many women get post-partumy? I did. Other people do. For all I know, you did and Sylvie might. I think you're crazy to wait for an invitation. Go down there and see her. Decide she's dandy, if she is. If she really doesn't want you there, which I doubt, you can always get back on a plane and come home. But what if she needs you and she's too proud to ask, or too hemmed in or whatever it is? Do you want to take that chance?"

"You're very meddlesome, you know. I could say you're conniving. What exactly's the truth here? Did Jack really call?"

"Did I say that? I think I said that I heard from him. What he had to say."

"Which was what? So you called him."

"I called Sylvie. I got him. He asked if I was the one with the coat that she likes. And he said she was going home tomorrow. Which is what I said."

"So you didn't talk with her."

"He said she was sleeping."

Clare lifts her legs up from the bed and stares at her feet, which hurt just like the rest of her. "OK. I'm going," she says.

"You mean hanging up, or going to Dallas?"

"Dallas," Clare says, surprised at her certainty, but certain nevertheless.

"I'll bring the coat over."

"No, no. I'm not at home. I'll go straight from here to the airport."

"Where's here?"

"Here. I took a road trip so I could think. Near international waters."

"My God. You're in the U.P."

"No. But if I'm getting a flight in the morning, I need to get off now. It's actually been a very long day."

"You want me to call anybody for you at work?"

"I'm covered. I'm good. I'll call you." Clare is already rebooking her flight in her mind as she clicks the phone shut. Then she opens it again and quickly hits redial. "Elizabeth, can you put your coat in a box and take it to FedEx? I'll pay you whatever. I'll buy the coat. And send it express."

"You're not going to Dallas?"

"I'm going. But if you'd send the coat. They're open another hour. On Green Bay Road."

"So maybe I got myself into this, but Clare!"

"I'll owe you something really humongous."

"Right. Like dinner for starters if I'm abandoning mine for FedEx."

"Whatever you want. If I can bribe Sylvie, I can bribe you, too. Go. I'll give you my house."

When the alarm clock goes off, it's still the middle of the night. Clare isn't sure that she's slept, though maybe she has. She has an image in her mind of a whole herd of sheep posing in shearling jackets with buttons at the throat and standup collars. She dresses quickly, scanning the room to make sure she hasn't forgotten anything. When she closes the door to go down to the lobby, she has her suitcase, her purse, and the bag with the gifts from Laurie's Rag and Bijoux. Except for the medal. The *Croix de Guerre* is wrapped in tissue and stored in the zippered purse pocket, banana free.

By the time Clare has found the airport and dropped off her car, she is stumble-footed and yawning. She buys coffee and sits at her gate peeling an egg and eating from a box of cereal that was left out on the hotel buffet. Then she sleeps on the plane.

At Minneapolis, she feels cross-eyed. The nap, however, has made her coherent enough to change her flight, and by 9:15 she's on her way again. It means a longer nap, flying to Dallas. More than once, she catches herself jerking upright when she topples over in her sleep. But by the time the pilot has announced their approach, she's awake enough to wipe her face with a napkin and run a comb through her hair. She puts on some makeup, imagining Sylvie's comment: "Mom, you never look bad, but your face is a little gray."

Clare has her answer ready: "It's probably newsprint."

The fact is she's started running on a very large surge of adrenaline. She buys flowers at the airport. She gets a cab and watches for the skyline as the cab speeds along. She talks to the cabbie. "I'm a grandmother. My daughter's had a baby. A little boy. I'm going to see them," she says, and the cabbie turns around and gives her a large, toothy grin.

"You happy, mum," he says, and Clare nods an emphatic yes. At the hospital, she gives him a big tip.

Terror sets in only when she's gone up in the hospital elevator, the flowers crushed against her, and steps into the hall on Sylvie's floor. She is clutching her purse tightly, clutching the bag, clutching her suitcase handle, and suffocating the flowers somewhere in the midst of all that clutching. She stops at the nurses' station and asks the way to Sylvie's room.

"She's probably not there yet," one of the nurses tells her. She looks at the clock. "She's on her way back from the bath demonstration. She's still slow walking. But she's dressed the baby and he's ready to go. He's been hanging out in the nursery. They just took him back to the room."

"He's alone?" Clare asks, alarmed.

The nurse laughs. "For maybe thirty seconds. He's a little pet. We'll miss him. You need a cart?"

So no church ladies yet. "Thanks. I'm OK." Clare starts up the hall, thinking maybe she should have said yes. She passes the open doors of rooms filled with mothers and babies, fathers and visitors, and it occurs to her that, in all the happy sounds she hears, there are all these stories. The shocking physical pain. The abrupt change from life as a person who sees herself untethered, to the life of someone in perpetual tandem with somebody else.

She keeps walking. Doors and more doors. Another door, and then the room she is headed for. *Sylvie's room.* Clare stands in the doorway and looks around. No Sylvie. There's a FedEx box by the wastebasket, and Elizabeth's coat is lying on the made-up bed. Clare nudges her suitcase against the wall. She puts the bag and flowers and her purse down beside the coat, and then takes her own coat off and adds it, too. Then, as quietly as she can, she makes her way to the small crib beside the window.

He is wide awake, this baby, looking at her from the deep navy of his baby eyes. He is dressed in a tiny sailor suit, swaddled in a light blanket, and covered with the baby shawl that Clare's Great-Aunt Sophie made at the beginning of time.

"Oh," Clare says, her eyes filling with tears. She grips her shoulders to calm herself and then takes a step closer. "Hello, baby." She touches the blanket, feels the pokey foot beneath it. "Damien," she says. "Aunt Sophie's blanket. What a pretty boy. What a handsome fellow." She smooths her hand across the blanket to find the other foot. "I've brought you something. Hold on a minute." Clare hunts in her purse and comes up empty. Then she remembers the side pocket, and unzipping it and unwrapping the tissue paper, takes out the medal. "Damien, just for you. You'll be a little like a mixed metaphor, but here you go." Carefully, Clare pins the medal to the baby's shirt. She feels the amazing ticktocking of his heart.

"Your very own *Croix de Guerre*. It means you're a hero. Or at least that you look like one. And I know what we're telling your mother. I thought about it a long time last night. There's your father— you have a father—and I don't know what we'll say to him. I'm thinking that's up to your mother, and I don't need to say anything. That I shouldn't. But what we'll say to your mother is that she's given you a French name, and so I've given you a French medal. She'll like the whimsy. She's fun that way. And then I'll tell her the real story. The whole story and not whatever it's gotten to be. She'll want to know now because of you, Damien. And because of you, I can tell her how sorry—

"Oh, big, big yawn!" Clare holds her finger out for the baby to grab onto. She feels the sweet warmth of his grip. Better than Kenny G—totally and absolutely better, she thinks, though she stops herself from saying it out loud.

She shuts her eyes, thinking of other babies. Boy babies. Moses in the bulrushes. Jesus in the manger. Mohammed and his mother given shadow by angels who covered the sun. A new Dali Lama traced with the help of a star and stretching his hands out for the gifts that belonged to the old one. Is it such a surprise that a boy baby, hero and savior, lies at the heart of all these stories? Clare can't think of an idea more hopeful or, she realizes suddenly (wondering if it's a lesson from Luc), a being more defenseless.

"Little boy, such company you keep. So many new pages started by someone like you. Think of the stories we tell that boys like you help us believe. Damien—"

Clare is instantly quiet, hearing the footsteps that stop at the door. She catches the baby's other waving hand. She holds her breath, back in the larger moment and terribly afraid to turn around. She is listening for the one word she is desperate to hear.

Then it arrives. Simply. The exact sound, just lilting and imprinted so deeply in her brain.

Sylvie's voice.

"Mom?"

THE BEAUTIFUL SHIPS

It was the summer of the tall ships. It was the summer when the beautiful ships with the intricate riggings crossed the oceans or came down the St. Lawrence and through the Bras d'Or Lake and descended the East Coast to lay at anchor in New York's harbor. They had come to celebrate the Bicentennial, and their arrival and subsequent parade across the water in full sail had colored the summer with romance. When the Norwegian *Christian Radich* sailed on alone through the Great Lakes, Clare McHenry, on a day trip with friends, eyed it from a perch on the Indiana Dunes and laughed that she felt susceptible. She was ready for adventure.

Clare was pleased that the Bicentennial had been a cause of general celebration after so many roiling years of war in Vietnam. A page had been turned. She still had her poster of Gene McCarthy with the breeze lifting his hair above his forehead. It hung on the inside of her closet door, but she hardly noticed it except to remember that he was a poet, that he was almost her kind of Catholic (and would be if he bailed), and that he reminded her of her father. She rarely thought any more of the fact that his run for president—and against the war—had pushed Lyndon Johnson out of the race. Clare had moved on.

The Ann Arbor apartment where the picture hung had muslin curtains and was cluttered with cartons of Clare's things her mother had finally insisted she take when she was home earlier in the summer. It was a graduate student apartment. The desk was made from a hollow door and two file cases, the bookcases from boards and bricks. The bedspread, which was Indian, could as easily have been a tablecloth. Clare had inherited it from a former roommate, though for the last two years, her assistantship had meant she could live alone. In a bottom dresser drawer, there were sticks of incense she didn't plan to use and a joint a friend had pressed on her that she'd kept, saying she would smoke it later though she knew she wouldn't. She owned a flea market wooden table, but took pleasure in the fact that three of the four chairs actually matched. She hoped to find a fourth. She had two drawings from another friend, and a small oil, and there was a good place near the window to hang something else. More than one person had said it was the right spot for a Che Guevara poster.

"Not me," Clare had said, laughing. "Not Che."

Of the photographs she'd excavated from the boxes, one had particularly caught Clare's eye. She'd stuck it under a refrigerator magnet where she could glance at it when she dried her dishes. It was a photo of her: five feet six, 118 pounds. Skin pale from a summer spent working two jobs—one in the bookkeeping department of a bank, and the other tutoring a fourteen-year-old in math. Blue eyes. Streaks of blonde in her hair. Natural streaks, and she looked good. The picture was convincing evidence of a pretty girl. But Clare, looking back at herself at almost nineteen, didn't remember having a single date that whole summer.

She'd been in a stubborn mood. One year of college under her belt, and it counted as a light year. She knew the physical distance from Minnesota to the Long Island Railroad, but the emotional trip had been something else. She'd returned to the Midwest and family and friends and her new summer jobs with a sense she'd left her real self behind her, the one with the dawning pretensions of independence and an intellectual life, notwithstanding the fat D in biochemistry that had stunned her parents into silence and that at times, while she stamped checks with the cancel mark in the bank's basement, reared up in her thoughts, gripping her with panic. But the fact remained: she had been in the process of becoming somebody new. The dateless, windowless summer was both an interruption of that fact, and a confirmation of it.

Ten years later, Clare felt a real tenderness for her younger self in the photo. How serious and sad and thin she'd been. How eager with anticipation, though about what Clare wasn't sure. Something about the looming promise of the future. Or something as immediate as the summer baseball players and the DJs at the radio station. Had she been more confident of the prettiness, which was so clear in the photograph, or had she been even slightly carefree, she might have veered more in their direction and never made it back to the life that was waiting for her then. Or to her life now. Or to the possibility of adventure that had suggested itself when she'd looked across the Dunes at the glorious ship.

The fact was she was at another transition point in her life. It scared her enough that she wanted a diversion. She was close to finishing her dissertation—so astonishingly close she could scarcely believe it—but though she had looked for teaching jobs, she hadn't had a single interview. She knew why. Even if she'd finally gotten an assistantship, there were hardly doors open for women in history, unless of course they'd piggybacked on a husband's career (think Mary Beard, think Ariel Durant). And even if there'd been a real clamor for women (fat chance!), there simply weren't any jobs. From what Clare could tell, the entire junior ranks of the academic world were shoehorned tight with men who'd spent their twenties pursuing degrees and jobs that gave them deferments from the war. It was a done deal. It was a complete lockout for the people who were next in line, and this obvious fact suggested that the passions attached to the war were simply being replaced by the war's practical fallout. In thirty years, Clare thought, this would all mean material for somebody else's thesis.

"So it's just bad timing?" her mother had asked before Clare had left to come back to Ann Arbor, her VW so packed with boxes that Clare thought one hard slam on the brakes meant her certain decapitation. Until the last box went in, she'd managed to avoid the subject of jobs.

"Sort of," she said. "Though it's hard to know when the time would have been good."

"But don't they give you counseling or something? Don't they tell you you're studying for a field where there isn't any work?"

"That's an interesting idea," Clare answered, and she kissed her mother good-bye, trying to ignore the look on her face that Clare knew was alarm that her daughter was approaching her thirties with no husband, no real job in the offing, and apparently no future. Clare had wanted to say that she'd learned a great deal and made some good friends—that she'd written practically an entire book. But she knew nothing she could say would stack up against her mother's concern, and so she went out to the garden to tell her father good-bye (she was very relieved he didn't ask if she was still going to Mass), and started her trip back, doubting that she'd make it through Chicago in one piece.

She had, though. Trusty little Bug.

(Trusty little rebuilt engine.)

⌣

In her first years in Ann Arbor, Clare had found a campus so politically alive that, political junkie as she considered herself, she still felt like a neophyte. The thing was, she wasn't an activist. Though she sometimes marched or signed a petition, she mostly observed and thought about things. Or she discussed them with friends. If she had a political gift, it was to understand context, which was hardly an ability that was useful for organizing—or even for participating. Still, she was grateful she was where she was. She liked the ferment. She liked the strongly held beliefs. To her, the history was palpable: *Angell Hall and the nation's first teach-in against the war. March 24, 1965.* Five and a half years after that seminal moment, during her second fall in Ann

Arbor with the protests still in full swing, Clare had heard Jane Fonda make one of her most controversial remarks: *If you understood what communism was, you would hope, you would pray on your knees that we would some day become communist.* Clare remembered the words; she remembered the late-night arguments that resulted. She remembered what she had thought.

"She assumes communism means real socialism—fairness for workers but no carnage," she'd said to her friends.

Now, in the warm and busy Bicentennial summer, her skirt swinging above her sandals, and the billowing sails and scent of the Dunes still with her, Clare walked down the paths and streets of the campus and thought how much she would miss it when she'd gone on to whatever job she might find. She had friends who criticized the eclecticism of the buildings, but that had always been part of the charm for her. And she loved the fact that, among all the warring styles, there was the small gem of the law quadrangle with its ivy and gray stone. It reminded her of college and New England, and that was good. It was also her church. To her, it was a peaceful cloister even during the school year with the preoccupied law students hurrying by. Clare congratulated herself on not being one of them. Not that she'd ever really thought of the law. She hadn't. She'd been definite about history.

"It interests me. I like knowing the things that affected the people who lived before us," she answered if anyone asked.

Her dissertation, which needed only a boffo ending and the laborious trip back through the footnotes she'd intended to complete by fall but now suspected would take until Christmas, had been just that sort of exploration, though narrowed to an actual point. She'd plowed through directories and newspapers, and through voter and draft and parish lists until she'd identified a specific shift in urban, Irish American politics that occurred between World War I and John Kennedy's election. (Her back thesis, which intrigued her for its controversial character, but which she'd left unexplored at her advisor's direction, was that politics and culture had shaped the stated religious principles of the Irish Catholic communities; they'd come first.)

Since she'd started writing, she'd been ready to talk about her subject with anyone. Now, though, she'd grown reluctant, concerned that any challenges might send her back into what she thought was finished. "I'll talk about footnotes," she said, laughing. "Footnote form."

It was her automatic comment when anyone new joined the dozen or so friends who met for drinks at the end of each week. "Clare McHenry," she'd say, looking through the loops of smoke that turned the air blue and, with her hand stuck out, identifying herself by program and progress, which was what they all did. "I can discuss footnotes. Anything more might be a jinx."

On the balmy Friday the week after she came back from the Dunes, Clare saw the newcomer at the far end of the table and felt an unexpected silence descend on her. Like fog. Like snow or sand.

"I told you about the seminar you're missing," her friend Anthony said next to her—awkward Anthony with the large, fleshy body and the milky tan skin and the glasses that were like an advertisement for contacts. "We brought the teacher with us. The visiting one. He was at Catholic University during the strike. Come on. I'll introduce you."

"It's after my time. My dissertation time."

"Then you're free to talk."

Clare stared at the mirror over the bar. She was having the oddest swirl of emotion, assaulted by both chagrin and excitement that stretched all the way back to childhood. Taking a sip of her margarita, she hunted back through her memory to see what part of that particular past she'd divulged on evenings like this.

Not him, she thought. He'd not been part of her stories.

"I actually know this man," she said in a voice just loud enough for Anthony to hear over the noise of the bar.

"Somebody's already introduced you?"

Clare glanced quickly down the table, wondering how she could be so certain after so many years. She was. It was the same handsome, Gallic-looking face: the nose thin at the bridge, the black hair that was cropped close.

"I knew him a little," she said, turning back to Anthony. "Years ago."

"You did? He's a priest. In spite of that shirt."

Clare nodded. "Unless something's changed, yes, he's a priest."

"You want me to re-introduce you?"

Clare shook her head. She felt the night air through an open door. She thought of the blackness that lay over oceans and lakes, over ships quiet at anchor or moving like clouds. "That's OK," she said and, feeling far calmer than she expected to, she looped her bag over her shoulder and picked up her drink. She moved to an empty chair at the end of the table and waited for a break in the conversation.

"Father Étienne," she said when his glance rested on her. "Clare McHenry. I remember you from St. Francis de Assisi."

Though it lasted only an instant, the silence after her words was a thing Clare felt as a lightness just above her eyebrows. A moment of unreality. A sense of herself reduced to being a child once more—a child who was both frightened and fierce. Clare knew that when she spoke again, it would likely be with an edge of hostility.

The answer she heard, though, was disarming. "Weren't you the May Queen? But sorry. What was the name again?"

Clare had the sudden feeling she should touch her lip, that it might be dotted with margarita salt. "Clare McHenry. Actually I was. The May Queen, I mean. I was ten. I'm amazed you remember." She hesitated. "Or perhaps it's a safe assumption that any woman might have been a May Queen in childhood."

There it was—the borderline rudeness she had thought she could curb, having decided it was unwarranted and out of place. If the Father Étienne seated across from her was the same priest who had drawn her keen interest as a child and the very same priest to whom she'd once made a bad confession, it was also the case that he had had nothing directly to do with her old wounds from St. Francis. It was hardly fair to make him a surrogate for the nuns who did. But, still, there was what she'd always considered the situation, the particular ethos represented by St. Francis. In the larger sense, Clare couldn't separate him from that. And, for that matter, would what she'd just said have seemed curt if she'd addressed it to someone besides a priest—if she'd said it to a man she might have expected a different kind of interest from?

She waited while Father Étienne ordered a beer. When he looked back at her, he didn't address her comment, but focused on St. Francis instead. "It's not a place I think of often. I was there just a year. It was my first parish assignment."

"Mine, too," Clare said, and she laughed. "My first Catholic school. Anthony says you were at Catholic University. During the student strike."

He nodded. "A person moves on to the next thing," he said, and Clare didn't know if he meant the strike or being in Ann Arbor. He rolled his fingers back and forth across the table edge, and she wondered if it was a gesture she remembered. It seemed familiar. It seemed impatient, and it made her curious in a way that was different from merely opening an unexpected window on the past.

"If you'd be interested, I'm having a small party next Saturday," she said. "A couple of professors. Some students. There'll be a few from your seminar. I'm not a great cook, but you're certainly welcome to join us."

And we can discuss the sinister aspects of St. Francis School, she wanted to add, wondering if he'd been aware of them. However, it was a moot point now. He couldn't come, he said. He told her that he'd be out of town and, for a second, Clare thought he meant to request a rain date, but Anthony came over and bummed a cigarette from him. The conversation changed.

Alone in her room, Clare lay in bed, staring at the ceiling. The far window was open, and she heard the sound of cars a street over and the bands of students heading home after the parties ended. She was feeling odd. The summer and her general excitement that her research grind and its frequent trips to Chicago were nearing a finish had lulled her into a sort of easy equilibrium. It had seemed almost physical, like swaying in a hammock. But now, with her sense of coming adventure and tonight's reminder of past ghosts, she was once again feeling like her complicated self. Unsettled Clare. Uncertain Clare. The person who shook her head when a friend in college said she was the best-thought-out person she knew.

"It's only that I chart a course," she'd answered. "More often than not, I meet an emotional push. It's like a strong gust of wind. It changes the heading."

It was still true, she thought. Her mind had been racing from one thing to another since she'd said her good nights and come home to her toothbrush and the jar of Noxema she'd never outgrown. Father Étienne was the catalyst. The gust of wind. She remembered him in a long-ago dusk watching her run home and, the next day, asking if she was afraid of the dark. Seeing him had stirred up all sorts of thoughts of St. Francis and its scary nuns (Sister Immaculata, first and foremost) who'd introduced her to a dismal brew of Catholic guilt and fear. Clare thought of the commandments she'd kept and those she'd believed, as a child, that she'd broken and those that she eventually had. Her mind flashed from grade school to high school and on to college and finally stopped at her junior year and Cody Dawkins. Her mother was there, too, for she'd met Cody on Parents' Weekend (the only one either of Clare's parents had ever been able to make) and asked if he didn't seem troubled. Clare had bristled at the idea, in part because she thought her mother suspected they were sleeping together, which they weren't (she was a single boyfriend ahead of the game), and in part because she was sure she was wrong. Yet the very next week, Cody had stunned her with a story of a priest raping him when he was an altar boy. For Clare, it was the violation that became the hanging offense for the church she'd always known was her first real love, and the reason the next boyfriend, unaware of her furious but muddled desire for some sort of payback, found her easy. Determined and, perversely she thought, easy.

Tonight, everything was linked. It all seemed to spill from the same Rorschach blot. Yet in spite of her flurry of emotions, Clare had still placed herself as observer. She had watched Father Étienne—Father Luc, as the others called him—defining the careful space between being one of the crowd and someone who was, of necessity, aloof. He smoked but didn't chain-smoke. He ordered a second beer but didn't finish it. He played a game of pool and won easily. He knew about the Tigers' hot streak in June and Mark Fidrych. He discussed Jimmy Carter's campaign while avoiding a question about the appropriateness of Father Drinan of Massachusetts serving in Congress. He was smart and witty but slightly reserved. He didn't flirt.

When they'd all left the bar—they were noisy and laughing and some of them were a little drunk—Clare noticed that Father Étienne had distanced himself from the scrum. She thought he must have his car keys out, and that he was waiting for a moment when he could nod good-bye to the people he'd arrived with. She was drawn into a conversation about bats flying through apartments in August. Then she looked up, and he'd disappeared. She was left staring into the night, music blaring from an upper window and the faces of her friends tinted red from neon and drink, and wondering why this particular priest was in Ann Arbor and why he was teaching a course here, and how in the world she would ever find out.

In her bed, Clare pulled a pillow into her chest. It was something she was going to obsess about. She knew it. She'd already begun.

———

The next week was hot. The heat was a familiar sort of August heat without any rain. To escape the kilnlike temperatures in her apartment, Clare deserted it early in the mornings for the library. On Wednesday, she was cross-referencing sources when a flushed and panting Anthony came up to her in the stacks and, catching his breath, asked if she'd teach his Thursday section. His mother was ill. His mother was in the hospital in a diabetic coma and he was driving to Flint as soon as Clare said yes. Clare took the notes he handed her and searched for something reassuring to say.

"She'll be all right," she tried, thinking what a lame and baseless claim it seemed, although Anthony hardly noticed. He left and she had to run down the stairs after him and ask where the section met.

She spent the rest of the day doing teaching prep and occasionally doodling revisions on her party menu. She x-ed out anything that meant she had to use the oven. When she got home, she set up her window fan and made a quick call to her mother for a recipe for a frozen dessert.

Whipped cream (Clare remembered that, and that, in a pinch, Cool Whip worked). *Pecans and macaroons. Sherbet.* She wrote down proportions and directions and realized, listening to her mother's voice, that she'd called for more than the recipe. And then she heard herself saying there'd been the oddest coincidence, that she'd run into Father Étienne from St. Francis. That he was teaching a seminar with one of the history professors, and he looked a little bit older, though not much. He seemed really very much the same.

Her mother sounded vague, and Clare wasn't sure at all that she remembered him. It irked her a little. Just what had been on her mother's mind that miserable year when Clare had gone to bat to save her Protestant soul? Exactly what all had her mother missed?

Then her mother clicked back into focus, returning from the recipe file she'd been sorting through. "I thought he was the best of the lot. And very bright," she said.

Clare let it end with that, aware that in spite of the fact Father Étienne and the shades of St. Francis had been swirling in and out of her consciousness with the waves of summer heat, she'd thought of him and of St. Francis less than she might have. In the suffocating nights, her memories had gone back to Cody Dawkins and to the rest of the boys and men she counted as part of her love life, for count them she did. It was one way she combated insomnia, although it was charged and so considerably less effective than counting potatoes in a drawer, the method she'd stumbled on more recently. She included the church in her list of loves, but only when she was being metaphorical, even if she'd never forgotten the actual physical allure of the first church she'd gone to with her father: the wonderful windows and stone, the airy quiet, the rituals of incense and bells. It had been exciting and mysterious. It was deeply stirring in a way she'd been too young to understand, but wasn't that love? Falling in love? Falling?

There was no one now, and Clare thought it was at least in part because, from the earliest beginning, she'd been careful. She couldn't have been much more than three when she'd watched the neighbor child climbing steps two at a time and, in spite of the head-long intensity of her feeling for him, been unable to say hello, though it was one of her words. She'd watched invisibly from her porch. It amused her to think of it now, but it was not so different from high school when she navigated dates thinking more about what she would and wouldn't do with a boy than about how much she liked him. If that had changed in crucial ways as she got older, her basic caution remained. She didn't want her life spinning out of her control. It wasn't really a feminist thing (she wasn't a movement anything though she kept a low-level anger at how she felt the world was rigged against women), but it was certainly the way she felt. She'd listened as her friends touted the importance of free love (*absolutely free*), but Clare always thought there was a piper waiting somewhere to be paid. Or at least when it came to the fraught world of men. Women and men.

In his annoying way, her brother had tagged her exactly. "Meet Clare. My sister's one of the girls who always looks in the rearview mirror."

With Cody, though, there had been more reluctance on his part than on hers. Clare knew that now. She'd known it then. By Cody's time, she'd had all the conversations with her friends about what they were doing and when they'd started and how simple it was since they had the pill. Clare wasn't sure there was anything that simple about any of it. Though she knew girls who slept with every date without batting an eye (and had been doing it happily since high school), and girls who held out longer but still saw losing their virginity as not having much more significance than getting a first period, she was sure there were girls who felt bad about it. They'd maybe been drunk or cornered when it happened. Or they worried about their parents finding out. Or it didn't go well. Or they were the seriously Catholic girls—she knew just a handful in college—who assumed they were going to hell and so worried a lot. There were even possibly the girls like she was—she didn't actually know if anyone felt as she did—who weren't so much afraid of sinning, though there was that, but of giving up what they'd been taught was a positive ideal. Clare, who'd been well into the mental process of quitting the church (hedging her bets, she'd still never missed Mass), had laughed when she told people about Sister Mary Andrew, her fifth-grade nun, who claimed that heaven had a special choir for virgins who sang songs in a language nobody else understood (and who would *want* to understand it? one girl had asked). Though Clare didn't believe a word of it, the image had stayed with her like the threat of seven years of misery brought on by a broken mirror. This was the calculus: add carnal knowledge to your life; wind up in the cheap seats for the whole of eternity.

Yet with Cody, things had seemed to proceed on a different and quite independent path. She really loved him. When they met, she'd been dating two men off and on. One was a seriously smart grad student in biology with a beard and wittiness that almost leavened what she'd begun to suspect was a mean streak. Clare was aware of his lust for her (his lust for most women?), of a particular clock ticking, of his breathing down her neck both figuratively and literally. Looking at things as clearly as she could, she decided his attention flattered her— he was so smart and so much a New Yorker—but nothing made up for his basic creepiness. She didn't want to see him anymore.

The other man—he was a boy really—was her own age and a skinny six foot three and so wired with energy that he seemed to be still growing, and right in front of her eyes. He had wild hair and a grin so endearing that she considered him the perfect incarnation of the little brother (nothing like Finn, her real and older brother) she'd always wished that she'd had. They made each other laugh, and Clare hoped she could keep him as a friend, though when she was being completely fair she knew he needed a girl who considered him a good deal less maternally.

Then Cody appeared. Clare fell immediately and hard. He looked exactly the way she thought a man should look. He was tall, but not distantly tall. He had an athletic build and large hands. His nose was a little off center in the middle from a break that had healed wrong. His eyebrows were straight and close to his eyes, and his eyes were blue, though not so light that you noticed their color right away. His hair was shortish and brown. He had a cleft in his chin and whiskers that made him look particularly appealing when he hadn't shaved for a day.

Clare had had the advantage of observing him carefully before he saw her and, if she hadn't noticed all this at first, she'd experienced the effect of it, the feeling that he was someone she wanted to look at more. They'd been in the crowd streaming out of a football game, and one of Clare's friends knew the group of opposing fans Cody was with. There were digs and banter about the game and then a question about the best place to eat. It meant everyone went to the same place. Clare had seen Cody notice her and, by the end of the meal, they'd started talking and she'd learned that he liked the same rock bands she did, that he had younger, twin brothers, and two older brothers, one in Vietnam and one who'd played minor league baseball until he blew out his knee. His only sister was finishing high school, and his dad had died when he was twelve. He liked history, but he'd just graduated with a degree in zoology, which meant he was still running a forklift at a lumberyard. He was mostly interested in marine animals and intended to go to graduate school in oceanography when he'd saved enough money and if he didn't get drafted first. For two summers, he'd worked in Maine building lobster traps. Clare told him that she loved the ocean, that she'd lived near it as a child until her family moved to Minnesota, that as close as she was now, she rarely had a chance to see it.

This was their first real bond: the ocean (and the fact that they'd noticed each other).

"Really? Cody Dawkins asked you out?" the friend who knew him said when they got back to the dorm, and Clare told her he had.

"Is that a surprise?" she added, and waited until her friend said no, that it wasn't really. It was just that Cody Dawkins sometimes seemed wary when it came to girls.

They drove to the ocean in his rusty car. Watching the boats out on the water, Cody said he'd like to sail around the world alone. Clare told him about the seashells she'd taken with her from Delaware to Minnesota, and added that her Delaware relatives were gone, that they'd all moved away or died of old age. Standing beside him at the water's edge and watching the smooth swing of his arm as he skipped shells out into the waves, she remembered her mother's old comment—not quite a jibe—that she'd always been in love with somebody. Clare knew it was true, but there was something unexpected about Cody, something about her initial attraction that made her feel that falling in love with him—and she already was—would be entirely different from anything she'd known. Amazed, she realized she actually believed that whatever happened was only about them.

Autumn had Cody written all over it. Clare lived in a state of discovery. She was eager for his voice on the phone, for the sight of him in his windbreaker when he came to get her, and for all the small things they would talk about. She had no sense that he was troubled, as her mother said later, but a feeling perhaps of an old wound that lay below the surface and let him see farther and weigh things more carefully than most people did. She assumed it was about his father dying.

They went to the movies and a play. Laughing, they rode a bike, Clare's arms around Cody's waist, her face pressed against his back. She bought yarn and tried to mend the worn-through elbows of his brown sweater. She asked him about things like stingrays and Portuguese man-of-wars, and he showed her a letter from his brother about fighting in Vietnam. It was a lot about getting drunk or stoned; his brother could take his pick. Then they discussed the war and how they felt about it, and how it was turning into something really huge for their generation.

Clare had known for a long time that she loved to French-kiss. With her last actual boyfriend, she'd also discovered that having her breasts fondled in a dark entryway was its own sort of addiction, though she'd felt strange when they broke up and that particular knowledge of her was cut adrift with somebody she'd never been sure should have had it in the first place. She still remembered that boyfriend and Sister Immaculata in the same thought.

Cody went slow. Though she had a trace amount of impatience, Clare liked the sense of the careful game of cat and mouse. She felt as if she were in the '30s movies her parents watched, with the love story circumspect, but with an unmistakable seduction in progress. She didn't feel toyed with. Lying on the mattress in the warehouse loft that Cody's friend vacated during working hours, Clare felt herself caught beneath a camera lens, the slowly circling eye tracking from above while the sun fogged the dirty windows white. Cody, half in shadow, touched her face, touched her lips. He kissed her. She memorized the flicks of black in his irises that made them a darker blue. A sensation of being warm and terribly alert started below her cheekbones and spread all the way through her body.

Clare felt shy about saying what she wanted. On the afternoon when they'd kissed so deeply that they were both thoroughly aroused, she was sure Cody knew. They'd begun more serious fumblings and then, to her surprise, she felt him pull back. He leaned against a pillow, his breathing rough and his arm crooked over his head. "We should stop," he said.

"Is it her? Is it my mother?" Clare asked quickly, a fast anger boiling up that her mother, on her visit, might have said something to put him off.

Cody looked puzzled. He closed his eyes and shook his head.

"I'm OK with this. Really," she said, wanting to tell him she'd been practical, that she'd gotten condoms from a girl she knew would have them. She was ready whether he was or not.

"Cody, what?" she said. She sat up on the mattress and dug in her purse. She put the condoms in their wrappers on the bed without looking at him. "I won't get pregnant. We haven't talked about this, but I won't feel guilty. I won't feel Catholic. This is just about us. Isn't that how you think about it?"

"*You* won't feel Catholic," he said. Then he told her. He gave her the disjointed bits of his horrifying story.

She was slow to piece it together, and then she cried. "I've never . . . I can't even imagine that," she whispered, trying to sort it out, and suddenly fearful in the falling light of the day, with Cody so close to her, that by telling her, he was both trusting her and saying good-bye.

"I'm sorry about this. It messed me up," he said, and he didn't touch her again. He wouldn't. And he wouldn't talk anymore but waited while she got her clothes back together and, shivering, zipped her jacket all the way up to her chin. Then he drove her back to her dorm. For days Clare tried calling him and haunted every place they'd been together, but it was the end of things except for the message he left the next week in her post office box that said he'd enlisted.

Clare, floundering in the deepest shock of her life, called her mother and told her he was gone. "Are you happy now?" she asked, knowing she was being terribly harsh, that she wanted someone to blame and—in the moment's bitterness—had settled on the person who'd been so oblivious in the days of Sister Immaculata but had understood immediately about Cody.

In the stifling Ann Arbor heat, Clare felt once more how unfair she had been, though she suspected she would do it again: fault her mother for sensing too much. (And for seeing too little.)

———

It was still hot on Thursday. Clare planned ahead. She had her piano music with her, and she headed for an air-conditioned practice room when she was done teaching Anthony's class. The class had gone well. She was animated; the students were animated. She took the energy with her and practiced for two hours, winding up with the flourish of the "Revolutionary Étude" and playing it, she thought, flawlessly. She was exhilarated, remembering the adventure she'd promised herself. She felt like a person of multiple talents. Walking home in the airless, ninety-degree heat, she entertained two fantasies: Clare McHenry at Carnegie Hall (sterling reviews); Clare McHenry, full professor at Harvard or Princeton (jam-packed lectures and a list of awards).

At midnight, she was still buzzed and awake, one sheet rumpled beneath her and the other in a knot at her feet. In a while, she heard the quiet beginning of an unexpected rain. She listened. It was striking harder at the sidewalk below and the air was growing cooler.

Then it was morning and the phone was ringing. Clare stumbled to her desk. It was foggy outside, and foggy in her head. Anthony was calling. "You OK?" she asked when she recognized his voice. "Your mom?" she said, and she pictured Anthony's big, soft body. She thought of his stained shirts and rumpled pants and the stacks of his books on the desk the two of them shared.

He wasn't OK and, from his voice, Clare was sure his mother had died until he said she was out of the coma but had gone into surgery. They were cutting off her leg.

Clare was instantly full of sympathy and offers of help. She'd cover his section. She'd talk to people and check on his cat. He should call her whenever. Call her collect. What else did he need?

She listened for the answer, suddenly afraid it would be a trip to Flint.

Instead it was his Dvořák quintets and Louis Armstrong and Stones albums he'd meant to bring to her party. "When you feed Chester, you can get them if you want. And can you talk to Father Luc and tell him our chess game is off? It's already canceled for this week, but tell him next week, too."

"Of course," Clare said and, when she'd put the receiver down, she sat quietly, staring out at the drifts of fog that had draped themselves across the morning.

An hour later, she was slipping into a booth for the monthly breakfast she hadn't made in a while, the token history person among the literature girls: Alice, who was their star, and Jennifer, Imogen,

Daphne. Lara, the brunette who might have been a model and was engaged to Father Luc's friend, the professor Clare had heard was the one who'd invited him to teach here this summer. They were all Anthony's friends, too, and Clare told them about his mother. She passed around a card to sign.

"Is he a mama's boy?" Lara asked, finishing her note with a perfect "*L*," and Clare said she didn't know. "Poor guy," Lara went on, and then she told a story that was new to Clare. Her first year, Lara and Anthony had sat at a bar and gone through every drink they could think of. They'd ended with Galliano, which Lara said seemed marvelous at the time, though she hadn't been able to touch it since. She added that there must have been food involved since she found gravy on her blouse the next day. She had a vague memory of Anthony eating dangerously and crying and calling himself a faggot.

Clare didn't like the story. She didn't like the laughter at Anthony's expense that followed it. She looked for the waitress to ask for more coffee. "Oh," she said then, turning to Lara as though she'd just remembered something. "Will you see Father Étienne? Father Luc. He and Anthony play chess, and Anthony wants him to know he can't make it next week either."

"Jake sees him. You want me to tell Jake?"

Clare nodded. She leaned back as the waffles arrived and wondered if she actually had this base covered, wondered if she should say that Father Étienne had told her he'd be out of town, but hadn't said how long. She decided against it. "Thanks. I thank you. Anthony does."

The conversation went on. The weather. The rain in the night. The London fog, as Daphne called it. Their students and classes. Their prelims or dissertations. Their love lives and Lara's comments about Jake in bed. Clare had had too much coffee and too little sleep. She had a headache.

"It was great seeing all of you," she said putting her money on the table and then, doing a quick head count, she invited them all to her party.

When she got home from the post office, her downstairs neighbor was sweeping the stairs. Clare chatted a moment and asked if she could borrow her vacuum cleaner. Then she heard her phone ringing. She ran up the stairs. She unlocked the door and, pushing it open, got to her desk. When she picked up the phone, she heard Anthony's throat-clearing cough.

Clare waited a moment. "Something happen?" she asked then, and she heard him inhaling, trying to compose himself. "I'm still here," she said.

There was a longer pause, and then Anthony spoke in a raspy voice. "Can you come to New Orleans?"

Clare pulled on the phone cord where it was twisted. "You mean Flint? You asked if I'd come to New Orleans."

"I promised I'd take her home."

"Home? Whoa. I thought Flint was home."

"My dad made cars in Flint. My grandpa played a horn in New Orleans. Can you help drive? And just . . . I guess be there?"

It was Clare's turn to be silent. She couldn't think which was worse—Anthony wanting to drive his sick mother home or Anthony planning to take his mother's body to New Orleans. "Umm . . . Anthony," she said. "Louisiana? In August?"

"They do something with the body. The embalming. It should be OK."

"I'm so sorry," Clare said.

"You won't go?"

"I'm so sorry she's dead."

She heard his voice breaking. ". . . yeah," he said. "It's funny hearing it, but yeah, she is dead."

———

Three days later, Clare was weary and staring with amazement out the open window of Anthony's noisy Ford Fairlane. They were on a causeway approaching New Orleans. It was almost dusk and a fat, rose-colored sun was ready to glide down a blue sky into a sheen of glassy blue water. Clare was mesmerized. Earlier, they'd driven past houses on stilts, and now this beauty. The horizon itself was surprising. It looked like a taut, navy blue string.

"I've never seen an alligator," she said, still staring out the window into air that had become relentlessly hot.

"They're out there in the bayous."

Clare nodded. She glanced back at the U-Haul following along behind them, bouncing and jouncing dangerously where the road was bad.

"She's still there," Anthony said, and Clare smiled a little and thought that he was doing all right. He'd gotten better in the three days they'd been driving south. She thought it seemed he was heading *toward* his mother. Her turf maybe. Her beginnings. Maybe something comforting like the shape of her life.

In Ann Arbor, Clare had thought she'd signed on for a mess. She'd looked despairingly at the freezer of frozen dessert and the jug wine she'd bought and stored in the broom closet. She made phone calls to cancel her party, worried she'd forget somebody and her neighbor would find some random guest at her door like the owl-eyed mourner who showed up at Jay Gatsby's funeral, his glasses dripping with rain. She managed to find another sub for Anthony's class. Then she packed her black skirt in her suitcase and, trying to cheer herself up, put in both of the outfits she'd thought of for the party: her jeans and her sleeveless, copper silk shirt (and, on second thought, her chain belt); her white top and brown peasant skirt and the agate pendant her father had made. After that, she met a weepy Anthony and his coffin-carrying U-Haul by the curb in a hailstorm and remembered it was Friday the thirteenth.

In spite of what had looked like an impending disaster, the trip had really been all right. Anthony talked about his mother, and his stories were more funny than sad. He told Clare there was nothing like a New Orleans funeral, that she was headed to the choicest of destinations. They listened to his tapes. They searched on the dial for radio stations. When Clare drove, she felt like she was driving a bus. They crossed a river so misty she thought its crosshatch of girders looked hung with a series of billowy scrims. Both times when they stopped for the night, Anthony insisted on paying for a separate room for her.

"An unkept kept woman," Clare had said laughing, and her joke fell flat—Anthony didn't really react—but she didn't think he was offended.

"There it is," he said, tapping the steering wheel, and Clare saw the start of the New Orleans skyline. Anthony looked in the rearview mirror and made a small but triumphant wave. "Mama, we're here," he said.

Clare tucked her feet up on the seat and hugged her knees. "Maybe this is it. I promised myself an adventure." She glanced quickly at Anthony. "I don't mean how that sounded. I just mean . . . well maybe New Orleans."

⌣‾‾‾

Shotgun houses in mint and yellow. The airiness of bread. In spite of the mix of greens and spices and seafood or sausage, the opaque taste of gumbo. Following behind Anthony on one of his hug-filled catch-up visits, Clare had listened to a recipe that included cayenne and dandelion tops, and things she was unfamiliar with like arugula and pepper grass (if you could get it). Anthony had an astonishing number of relatives, their skin tones ranging from almost light like his to nearly black. Clare couldn't define the local accent. It was something eastern, something southern, something that was something else. It was a mix of things like the gumbo and the music that seemed to be everywhere—in the neighborhoods where Anthony's family lived, in the houses and corner bars, on Bourbon Street in the French Quarter where Anthony met a friend and Clare looked in the open doors to the smoky air and the bands playing.

She had fanned herself throughout the funeral service. It was so hot. Humidity laced the air. She felt immersed in it and in the beautiful hymns. When the coffin was closed, the church bells rang, and that was another sound Clare logged into her brain. Anthony had told her they'd follow the hearse to the cemetery, that he'd be with his uncles, and that she should watch the man in the tuxedo who took the lead. She had. She'd been listening to the somber, pure notes of the horns as they left the cemetery when Anthony's young stepniece stuck a damp hand in hers. Clare looked down.

"Gonna strut?" the child asked, pulling at the frilly hem of her small white dress. "You gonna shake it?"

Clare had laughed. "I'll watch you," she said, and she'd done that, too, after she heard the drummers starting a new beat. She felt the pulse of the music growing stronger and stronger until it broke into a sound like the jazz she'd heard on Anthony's records. There was no rain in sight, but umbrellas had opened everywhere and people had started to move with the horns and drums. They were dancing, the music and party attracting people along the route as though they were joining a parade of pied pipers.

It was all this that had preceded Clare's arrival at the Hotel Monteleone on Wednesday night. After the funeral, she and Anthony had had an awkward, laughing moment at his aunt's when they'd both realized their evening plans were diverging.

"Go ahead and go with him. Go," Clare said, tilting her head toward the man who had blond curls like a surfer's. He was waiting in a crowd across the room. "Don't worry about me. I won't be here tonight anyway. I can tell you about it later. It's a *Breakfast at Tiffany's* thing. A kid thing."

Even as she spoke, Clare wasn't sure she would actually explain herself. Since arriving in New Orleans, she'd heard various interesting rumors. One was that Truman Capote had been born at the Hotel Monteleone. "Really?" she'd asked, and a scornful dissenter piped up that his mother had lived at the hotel, but he'd been born in a hospital like anybody else. Another person said he still frequented the Monteleone's bar when he was in town. People nodded, nobody disputed it, and the possibility of an actual sighting had seriously piqued Clare's interest. Yet she didn't think Anthony or anyone else needed to hear what a fan she was, that even if she'd never read *In Cold Blood* and didn't intend to, she'd read everything else that Truman Capote had written and seen *Breakfast at Tiffany's* four times.

Drumbeats from Bourbon Street were punching the air, and a hot and damp wind was chasing a paper bag up Royal Street when Clare got out of her cab. The hotel doorman held the door for her. She nodded her thanks and shook off the bellboy who'd started toward her, his eyes on her suitcase. "I've got it," she said. He hovered, and then he backed off and stood with his hands folded. Clare wondered if she should give him a dollar anyway. Instead, she reached up and touched her hair, which was stuck to her forehead. Then she pushed it back and walked through the cool air of the lobby, certain she was in as fancy a hotel as she'd ever seen. She looked up at the leaded-glass windows of the mezzanine and decided they were mirrors. She looked at the chandeliers and the dark, reddish walls and the marble floors with stretches of burgundy carpeting. There was a giant grandfather clock. There were leather chairs and blue velvet couches that were so deep she thought the people sitting on them looked lost, sunk inside them. Behind the desk clerk, rows of keys were slotted into cubbyholes.

"I called for a reservation," Clare said and then waited for the clerk to check the book, thinking the whole time she had one last chance to save her next month's budget—October's, too—and knowing she wasn't going to. "If you have something with a view of the river. An upper floor . . ."

In the elevator going up, she gripped her room key and felt the hotel crest pressing into her skin. She looked at the mark it made. Two lions.

An hour later, Clare felt transformed. She'd napped a few minutes and taken a shower in a bathroom that was maybe a tad dated, though who was she to say. The room had an exceedingly comfortable bed, and she'd sat against the pillows and looked out the window while she dried her hair. There was a view of rooftops and a regal white church. There was a ship on the river, or maybe a ship in the canal. In either case, it was a real ship, with the right proportions and the perfect, long and clean lines. Down there with the other boats, it gleamed in the evening sun.

When she'd laid out her clothes, she'd stood in her slip considering what to wear—what she had with her that was most Holly Golightly-like. Nothing, of course, though she'd mugged in the mirror, and held up her hand, pretending she had a foot-long cigarette holder. She'd mimed a quick puff of smoke.

Now, in her peasant skirt and white top, she paused in the open doorway to the hotel's Carousel Bar, taking it all in. At first, she saw only a smear of crystal and gilt, the lighted center of a darkened room. Then, as her eyes adjusted, she felt the distinct suggestion of theater. She thought circus. She thought carnival. Colors emerged on an actual carousel, its top painted and fitted out with mirrors that were studded with lightbulbs in the style of a marquee. There were jesters' caps and ruffs on carved heads, which jutted forward like figures on the prow of a ship, and heads of frowning cherubs with their wings mounted like big ears. Tiers of stemmed glasses and bottles ringed a center pole. The bar circled, too. It was actually turning, its pace so slow it might have been pushed by a determined snail. Instead of prancing merry-go-round horses, there were bar stools, each one sporting a carved back that was gaudy with a painting of a jungle animal. Rousseau-inspired, Clare thought: a fiercely tusked elephant ready to pound its way over lush plants and right out of the picture. A raccoon-faced monkey.

Clare walked to a table by the wall and sat down, aware there was no hurdy-gurdy sound of carnival music, but only the murmur of the bar crowd. She checked her bag for her billfold. She flexed a sandaled foot against the table leg. A waiter paused with his tray of drinks to put down a napkin, and Clare ordered a bourbon and water, thinking the choice seemed very New Orleans, that the idea must have popped up in her mind from the street name. "Make it a Jack Daniels," she said, looking up at the waiter. She smiled at him.

She tapped her toe and waited for her drink, her eyes on the bar. It was an odd way to watch the world go by, people in their summer clothes, alone or in pairs, drifting past in a slow rotation, backs to her but faces caught for a long moment in the tilted mirrors beneath the cherubs. The intimacy of her position amazed her. The people never looked up, never caught her studying them. She'd already scanned the room. There was no Truman Capote, which didn't surprise her, though it left her feeling slightly deflated. But the portraits in the mirrors were entirely intriguing as people made their languid progression in and out of the frame. Her drink came and she was gazing at an Indian with a turquoise pendant who might have posed for the nickel. She was half-way through the drink and a half dozen other faces of varying types when she realized she was looking at someone she knew.

She froze, staring at a nose thin at the bridge, at close cropped black hair. The skin was tanned darker than it had been a week and a half ago. Two weeks ago. Twelve days ago, to be exact. But it was the same face that had hovered on the edge of her consciousness for every one of those days. Clare touched her throat and averted her gaze. Then she turned her eyes back. Father Étienne was looking at her in the mirror.

She put her hand over her drink and tightened her fingers on the rim, holding on to it. She was trying to find her breath wherever it had gone in her body. She wasn't light-headed. Her head felt as though it were expanding—sponging up the room's voices and the light from the bulbs. She thought maybe she was hallucinating. Maybe she was having a delayed heatstroke. Even a real one. At the least, she was going to blush, and the idea of that, the silliness of it, helped her regain control of herself. Father Étienne's right ear had disappeared behind the mirror frame by the time she stood up and walked to the zebra chair next to his tiger.

"Father Étienne?" she said, and she realized when she spoke that she was actually turning a page on a script that was already sketched out in her mind.

"I thought you looked familiar," he said, turning toward her, and Clare made a quick decision not to offer her hand.

"Clare," she said.

"Right. McHenry. So we're both in New Orleans. Pleasant surprise."

Clare rested her hands lightly on the chair back as it registered, like the clink of a coin in a slot, that he'd remembered her name. "My drink's at my table," she said, gesturing behind her. "I'm here with Anthony from your seminar. I don't mean he's here in the bar. We came to New Orleans for a funeral."

"I've heard about New Orleans funerals."

"They're a real send-off. If you like music. And dancing . . . And of course the bodies are buried aboveground, though poor Anthony. It was his mother's funeral."

Father Étienne stubbed his cigarette out and picked up his drink. "How is he?" he said, leaving some change on the bar and then starting toward the table with Clare as she'd hoped he would.

For a split second, Clare was ambivalent, uncertain she was doing the right thing. Then she shook off the feeling and smiled, though she grew more serious as they sat down. "I think he's OK. Hard to tell. You'd know this better than I do. Aren't people a little numb at first?"

"I have no idea. My mother's alive."

Clare laughed. "But isn't it the sort of thing that a priest knows?" she said, and she noticed that Father Étienne still wasn't wearing a collar. There was something very precise about him. There was an angularity to his features that reminded her he was French. Too, she felt an unhappiness in him that she hadn't noticed in Ann Arbor.

He looked toward the bar and out toward the lobby, and Clare wondered if he was expecting someone. "Could be," he said when he turned back to her. "I only had three years as a parish priest. The funerals I'm part of are usually full of priests." He'd begun rolling his fingers slowly back and forth on the table edge as she'd seen him do in Ann Arbor. Clare wondered briefly if he was a little drunk. She didn't think so. She didn't want him to be.

She was eager to know why he was in New Orleans, but Clare stayed with the parish priest part. "If you started at St. Francis, how did you get to be not a parish priest?" she asked. She was sorting back through her information about religious priests and secular ones and the old definitions she'd trotted out for her Protestant mother, who'd said it was a strange way to divide them. She wondered if she'd remembered wrong, if maybe a Benedictine or even a Jesuit had been detoured to the rectory at St. Francis. "You're not in an order, are you?"

"I'm not." Father Étienne shook his head, and Clare saw him seem to consider what to say next. She knew he had a choice to make. He could tell her something more about himself, or he could take the safer route and ask her about a neutral thing like her dissertation.

"I'm not trying to pry," she said quickly. She pulled at the napkin under her drink so it separated where it was wet. She was very aware of Father Étienne's physical presence, and just as aware that the fact of their conversation here in a bar in New Orleans could seem transgressive to him, and to anyone else. "It's just that St. Francis is stamped on my brain. St. Francis was a very odd place."

He looked interested. "Odd how? I hardly remember it."

Clare shook her head and then laughed. "Would you like to hear about my dissertation? I'm writing about a shift in Irish Catholic urban politics in America."

"That's actually an interest of mine. Or my interest is related— how the Irish clergy make the church here so different from the church in Europe. We can trade notes. McHenry's an Irish name?"

"Right. My dad's Irish."

"You've come to the perfect city for research."

"No, no. I'm done with research. Completely." Clare made a quick pretense of stuffing the wet napkin bits in her ears.

Father Étienne looked amused. Or maybe bemused. Clare wasn't sure which. "They've got a wonderful diocesan archives here," he said. "There must be some Irish names on the books since New Orleans has everything. You'd certainly strike a find if you were hunting for Spanish baptisms. From the colonial period."

"You're well informed."

"I am. I spent an hour being well informed by an owlish fellow who must be the dustiest and driest person in New Orleans. It's why I'm having a drink. Would you like another?"

"Go ahead," Clare answered, still feeling the slight effect of the first one. "Thank you, but I'm saving my chits. I have the whole night to enjoy this city."

Father Étienne glanced at the bar, but he didn't motion to the bartender for another drink. "So how do you plan to do that?" he asked. He took out his cigarettes and offered Clare one. When she said no, he lit one himself.

She was careful, thinking out loud. "Dinner somewhere. Listening to jazz. Probably on Bourbon Street. I'm staying here, which is kind of a long story. I thought maybe I'd walk down and look at the ship I can see from my window." Clare paused. "Are you meeting someone?" she said, trying to sound casual.

Father Étienne had put his cigarette down in an ashtray. The smoke rose in a straight line as he crossed his arms and leaned forward, resting them on the table. Clare counted silently to herself. She looked at the smoke and then shifted her gaze back. Father Étienne was staring at her with an expression that so transparently told her he was taking a leap it made her feel as if she were stealing something. "You told me Anthony's here," he said. "Except for him and the fellow at the archives—and he was headed home somewhere out in the bayous—I don't know a soul in New Orleans except you."

⁓

What is the story of a night? Of a few nights? Of a week, and of more weeks that unfold as a single, inevitable narrative? In the persistent evening heat of New Orleans, Clare had no real sense she'd launched herself into anything more than a moment. An interesting moment certainly—a moment that felt a little dangerous and exciting and that appealed to the part of her that liked having all the questions answered. What had Father Étienne done in the years between St. Francis and

New Orleans? Had he actually lived in France as a child? Was it unlike him to be sad? Was he cynical? Did he feel she was safe?

If she'd stopped to think about it, Clare would not have denied there was something about the whole situation that stirred the more complicated part of her—the darker side that had never gotten over being angry about Cody Dawkins or about the nuns of her childhood and that wanted some kind of payback. But she didn't think about it. Why should she? She found the city intoxicating. She was ready for the holiday she'd promised herself. No responsibilities. No deadlines. No worries about things like finding a job. The singular bonus of an interesting man.

She had one quibble. She thought the streets of the French Quarter should be cobblestone. It was the subject of conversation for the better part of a block. She argued for a change in look. Father Étienne said the dingy asphalt was the right anchor to the painted buildings and storefronts—that they made a perfect metaphor for a city whose tarted-up exteriors couldn't hide the underlying poverty. Clare disagreed. She said that if illusion was the point, nothing should detract from it. Father Étienne countered that music was the point. And seaminess. And food. Was she ready to eat?

Since she wasn't, they wandered awhile. Clare felt she was breathing in some sort of particulate matter, the air was so heavy. It was full of scents. Beer and fried food. A garbage smell from bags that were stuffed into bins in the skinny alleys. A recurrent odor of cat pee. They walked farther past trees and mossy walls and climbing vines. Clare thought the whole world was dripping. At the Ursuline convent, they turned around and headed back toward a noisy crowd of pot smokers who were listening to a street band. It took Clare a minute to realize the musicians were all transvestites, but Father Étienne, who said he liked the heat, seemed unfazed by them or by anything else. It occurred to Clare, and not without interest, that Father Étienne had spent a part of his life in a dark cubicle listening to people talk about their sins. And anyway, it was the Big Easy. He was French. It was a summer night.

When they decided to eat, they found a courtyard with dangling flowers and two hummingbirds. Clare watched them, smitten. After the birds flew away, she told Father Étienne what she'd learned about New Orleans food. Then she ordered the barbecued shrimp the waiter suggested. They had another drink, and Clare felt happy. The conversation was easy. Meandering. They were in France, and Father Luc—it was what he preferred to be called, although Clare didn't think she would call him anything—was a child in Bar-de-Luc, which was only a real pun in English. He'd been a street rat, and his friends rode bicycles wherever they went unless they climbed onto the running boards of his grandfather's car. His grandfather was a corset maker and his father worked in a foundry.

Everything changed with the war. His father died in the Ardennes. The Germans were in charge, and life was full of secrets since his mother had joined the Resistance. When the war was over, General de Gaulle gave her the *Croix de Guerre* and she married an American soldier who whisked both mother and son off to America and northern Minnesota where, as far as Clare could tell, the son's schoolboy English had lost any trace of an accent. If he'd had any wish, it would have been that he could have taken his mother back to France to see de Gaulle sworn in as president of the Fifth Republic. At the time, he'd been in Rome on the first of two assignments at the Pontifical North American College. Clare had never heard of it, though she nodded her head when he said the name. There was a whole universe of priestly things she knew nothing about. But Rome . . . *Roman Holiday*. Another Audrey Hepburn film. Clare wondered how frivolous it would seem if she talked about Holly Golightly and Truman Capote. On the second glass of wine, she did, and they both agreed it was serendipity they'd met in the Carousel Bar. Cheers to Mr. Capote. Absolutely. They ordered the crème brûlée, and Clare broke the praline in two and ate her half with her fingers.

It was hardly any cooler, but stars were scattered across the sky when the waiter brought the check. Clare took her billfold out, and Father Luc shook his head and said that he'd get it, that she'd very nicely saved him from a dull evening. Clare wondered if that was it—if they would nod good-bye, if they would shake hands so there was a record of formality for the people at the tables around them who, to tell the truth, she'd barely noticed. To her surprise, she felt tears in her eyes. "Just a gnat or something," she said, quickly blinking and putting her hand to her face. She leaned over to get her napkin, which had been blown under her chair earlier by a moist wind that had come and gone. She quickly wiped at the tears, hoping she wasn't going to make a fool of herself.

She laughed when she surfaced, trying to cover her embarrassment. "You have to let me buy you a drink. I think it's illegal to leave New Orleans without listening to live music."

Father Luc's gaze was steady. "We certainly don't want to break the law."

He had beautiful eyes, Father Luc-Cristof Étienne, and his sports shirt made it impossible not to notice his forearms. Clare had the strong desire to touch his wrist. It was the same feeling she'd had as a child when he'd waited for her to run home. She had thought if she touched him, he could rescue her.

She picked up her bag. "It's settled then. I'll buy you a drink."

If she'd been pressed to sum up New Orleans music, Clare might have said that it spoke to the stereo-listening dancer in her and the shower singer, the playing-by-ear piano player and the tabletop drummer and whatever else there was in her that liked a groove. It was the captivating rhythms mostly—the insistent beats with the cagey overlay of lyrics and melody. It felt like 5/4 time, though it wasn't, or three against two. Or maybe poetry with iambs punched up with unexpected dactyls and anapests, if she remembered the words right from her high school English. She loved it. It was funky. It was unbelievably smooth.

But the fact was she was in no position to think it through when she was actually hearing it. She'd walked with Father Luc down Bourbon Street past windows with gyrating girls who beckoned to them to come inside, and past knots of loud and inebriated people in every sort of costume and hairdo. Someone had yanked her bag from her shoulder, and the next thing she knew, Father Luc had collared the fellow and retrieved the bag and was steering her out of the crush of people and into a bar with a band that was playing in an oscillating beam of light.

He found them a table. "Are you all right?" he asked and Clare told him she was. She knew how she felt: she'd had a brief sense of intrusion and surprise, and her shoulder hurt a little, but it wasn't really pain. It was more of an aftershock. And now there was this terrific music.

Father Luc was rolling his hands on the table edge once more as he looked toward the street, and Clare decided it was a reflexive gesture that accompanied his thoughts of something he was uncertain about. "I might have looked for the police," he said. "It could have meant a mob scene if he had friends with him."

"It's OK," Clare said. The band had taken a break, and it was suddenly much quieter. She could talk in a conversational tone. "It's not like I haven't been mugged before," she continued, thinking of the two mugger exhibits in her grab bag of old stories. She wanted to tell them both in a way that made them funny so they lightened the mood, though the more they came back to her—the more she said—the less they actually felt that way.

"So you're a veteran of street attacks," Father Luc said when she finished, and Clare wasn't sure of his tone. They'd both started on their drinks.

"In a sense," she said, remembering the part she hadn't mentioned—how the boy who'd been on a bike had grabbed at her breasts before taking her purse and speeding away with it. She shook her head, ready to move on. In spite of herself and its being hot in the bar, she shivered a little. "You haven't told me how you happen to be in New Orleans."

"No, I haven't. I'm glad you weren't hurt," Father Luc said. "Not then. Not now." He reached across the table suddenly and covered her hands with his. "I remember you, Clare. You were the pretty child who looked so wounded when the crown you put on Mary slipped down crooked over her eye. You're not as earnest now."

"And not a child."

He'd moved his hands back as quickly as he'd moved them forward. He'd withdrawn them to the table edge, but Clare could still feel the weight of them like a charge running through her. "And it wasn't the wreath I was wounded about," she added looking up at him, still aware that, of the many things she'd felt desperate about that morning, the most immediate was that she'd believed she'd just made a bad confession. And to *him*. For years afterward, it haunted her. She'd thought she was going to hell.

Clare took a careful sip of her drink. "Do you remember my mother? Sister Immaculata told me my mother was going to hell for being a Protestant."

He looked uncertain. "Sister Immaculata?"

"The principal. She taught at the high school the next year, so she left St. Francis when you did. If you don't remember her, you're lucky, though if you remember my mother, that would make you lucky as well."

"I get a mixed card. I don't remember either one of them. Sorry."

Clare was quiet a second. She was trying to add things up, but she couldn't. She hadn't been able to do it since she'd encountered Father Luc in Ann Arbor and he'd asked if she'd been the May Queen at St. Francis. It made no sense to her that he remembered that—that he remembered an essentially miscellaneous child. There had to be more to it, and she considered pressing him, but she knew it would seem confrontational and, right now, that was the last thing she wanted. She looked at the band. They weren't at all young and she liked that. They had a look as if they'd been here forever, like the Spanish moss and the giant oak in the cathedral courtyard. She particularly liked the skinny guitar player in his overalls and felt hat. "There you are," she said. "They're starting again."

It was why they were here: the music, the drink. Clare wanted to separate out everything else that wasn't about that. She wanted to close her mind down, to stop thinking about St. Francis and the other scars she'd accumulated in almost twenty-nine years. And she felt that she could. She'd gone back to the Jack Daniels after the wine at dinner and was settling in with the woody taste and the slight sense she had that she was floating.

A gorgeous, dark-haired woman of indeterminate race had stepped into the spotlight and Clare, looking at her blue spangled top and the confident way she held out the microphone waiting for her entrance, thought how cool. She didn't know if this was the New Orleans sound. She checked the muted trumpet, the electric guitar, the piano and drum, and now the throaty voice slipping into place with the instruments. Close enough. She felt like dancing. She wanted her own turn with this sassy—this perfectly put-together music.

"Such a far cry from Ann Arbor," she said, leaning toward Father Luc, who'd shifted his chair closer to her when someone sat down behind him. He inclined his head for her to repeat what she'd said, and when Clare shook her head and smiled that she didn't need to say it again, he was right there, his face inches from hers, millimeters. She might have laughed, and then everything would probably have been different. She might have pushed her own chair back to make more room. Instead she looked at him, at that angular face, and the small cleft in his chin she hadn't noticed before, and when she thought he was going to say something, she put her finger to his lips.

It was a test. He might have drawn back right then before she took her finger away—and he still could have when she tipped her forehead against his and closed her eyes in the half dark and felt the rumbly sound of the crowd following the band. But he didn't move away, and though Clare knew she could stop what was happening if she wanted to, she didn't.

"We forgot to look for the ship." She felt the solid bone shape of his forehead and smelled the close scent of tobacco on skin, which she didn't really mind. In fact, in a purely physical sense, she didn't believe there was a thing about this man that bothered her.

"That's true. We didn't," he said, and Clare lifted her head to look at him. This time she put her finger on his lips not to silence him, but to touch them.

"I can still show it to you," she said. "The view from my room is pretty amazing."

<hr/>

When she'd finally made this night in New Orleans a more or less set memory piece, Clare sometimes made adjustments when it came to the alcohol. She had a very clear picture to draw on. It was the two of them, easily arm in arm, walking down the cross street from Bourbon to Royal. They were pointing out constellations to each other, and Clare was charmed to hear the names in French. At the time, she had considered what they'd had to drink and thought it was just the right amount. It was exactly enough to really hear the music that still played in her head. It was enough to open the soul—to open the heart. The body.

But later on—when was later on?—later Clare had assumed a level of intoxication that, at the very least, had affected the judgment of both of them. There was hardly a question about that. Yet in spite of it, she never doubted that something would have happened in any case. Everything was aligned: there was their intense attraction to one another; there was their fraught, though tenuous, history; there was the fact that both of them had reached a point in their lives that was drawing them to something as unexpected but certain as, say, an unavoidable train wreck. There were also their own particular demons that, in the town of carnival, presented themselves not only as something alluring but as something essentially innocent.

Clare considered such things in the later period when she allowed herself to think about them rationally—or, more accurately, in the time when she actually was capable, once again, of reflecting. But the Clare who accompanied Father Luc when they turned onto Royal Street and walked the last block back to the Hotel Monteleone, was a more headlong sort who was both dizzied with the day's impressions and beset with an acute longing.

"It's the sixth floor," she said when they got into the elevator. Father Luc stood next to the door, and Clare felt suddenly awkward. She busied herself digging for the key in her bag. When the doors opened, she went out first and started down the hall, listening the whole time for the steady footfalls behind her. They'd reached the room before she turned around. "Two lions. See?" she said, showing him the key. "The hotel crest." Then she put the key in the lock and opened the door.

She had intended to dazzle him with the beautiful room, the beautiful view. She'd been imagining the moment ever since they'd walked back into the lobby, but the reality she'd forgotten confronted her through the open door. In an excess of modesty, she'd closed the curtains when she was getting dressed, and now the room was dark and the bed covered with black huddles she recognized as a bunched up pillow and the damp towel she hadn't put back in the bathroom, her extra clothes and her hair dryer with the cord dangling.

"Uh-oh . . . sorry. I should have asked you to wait." Clare had started to scoop things up. She stretched across the bed to get the towel. When she'd managed to grasp everything in her arms, she stood there feeling exactly like a washerwoman. "I'm not usually this messy. Well, I am. Sometimes. And today, apparently . . . If you'll let me just put these things in the closet."

Father Luc laughed. He stepped away from the closet door and, even in the dark, Clare registered his thoughtfulness—the fact that he didn't glance over his shoulder to see what else she might have put in the closet. And, too, he didn't do the sort of annoying thing some of the men she'd known in her life would have done—explore the room uninvited, staking out territory. It meant she could ask him to open the curtains, which she did, and it meant there was the smallest bit of light in the closet when she fumbled her clothes and the towel onto hangers and then closed the door.

He was looking out at the city when she walked up behind him at the window. "It's more beautiful at night," she said. "I love cities at night. I like flying into them. Nighttime changes everything. All the orange and blue lights. But where's the ship? Don't tell me my ship's gone."

"I've been looking for it."

"I hope you don't think I got you up here under false pretenses. It was a beautiful ship. Or it was a ship, and I tend to think they're all beautiful, though I like the old ships with riggings even better than an ocean liner. It was very sleek."

"They're more romantic—ships—if you've never been on one."

"And you have?"

He nodded. "The entire harbor was full of ships when my mother and I sailed from Marseilles. Military ships. Troop transports. And Marseilles itself was full of sailors and soldiers and the girls they'd met. It's one of my most vivid memories. The whole port smelled like France. The fish. The food and the wine. I thought I'd never in my life get to smell it again."

"But you've gone back?"

"I have."

"And it was the same?"

"No, it wasn't."

Clare had moved so her shoulder was against the window. She was standing so she could see his face, which was half illuminated and half in shadow. "That's sad," she said and, for all the buzz of alcohol left in her, she felt particularly articulate. "You mean that some things, once they're changed profoundly, can't be restored—that maybe they're changed so much you can't even truly miss them?"

"Yes. Exactly."

"Then I need to tell you this." Clare turned back toward the window. She settled her gaze on the cathedral spire in the night sky. "I not only have my own father, but I couldn't be in a room with a man this way and intend ever to call him Father again. That would change."

"A small price to pay."

"Not so small. It means I wouldn't recognize his station. Or his elevation above me. That closed-off world. Whatever it is. Just so you know."

"As I said. A small price. Go ahead. I'll call you Clare. You call me Luc. It might be startling to hear my name on a woman's lips again. But pleasing. I don't mean that it wouldn't be. I might even welcome it."

"Might?"

"Would. I welcome everything. About you."

"Luc then."

For both of them, she knew, it was words as foreplay. He had moved one hand to her shoulder as they spoke and begun lifting her hair with the other. She waited for the kiss at the nape of her neck and felt it as a little starburst beneath her eyelids. Slowly she reached up behind her and locked her arms around his head and wondered if they would dance this way or if it was more like skating, this kind of controlled extension of the body and the firm way he placed his hands on her waist and then turned her toward him as if he could twist her into a spin and then catch her.

Though that was a child's idea of sex, which was not what was happening. Not what they were doing, which was a good deal more intense and closer to what one might expect of animals with the wild look of the creatures that had circled their meeting in the bar. Blatant fellows. Blatant. Nothing subtle about them. She could almost hear them panting, feel their teeth sinking into flesh. Hear the long rip of fabric rent with a claw, though there was the remnant of superego here that meant Father Luc—that Luc (she had to call him Luc, think of him as Luc) would be careful of her clothes if not her body, and she of his so that when he left her room, if she ever let him, her mauling of him wouldn't show. How very good it was that her body was smooth and taut—skin like silk—*soie,* he said—and wasn't it wonderful that being French meant staying lean and muscled whether you needed to or not? She'd guessed his age as forty-five, but he didn't seem old to her. He seemed strong and so eager and—where had he learned all this?—so stunningly good at what he was doing—what a *waste!,* what squandered talent—that she didn't know why she would ever want to do anything else. Or why he would. She crawled up the bed, and it was the perfect, exciting way to make the four-legged beast—was that *it?*—no, no, no . . . the beast with two backs. But oh . . . *omigod.* What was happening? She was gripping some part of the bed frame and it seemed as if all the cherry rockets from the long-ago summers at the Delaware shore had been set off inside her.

When they'd finally flung themselves on the bed, gasping for breath, she thought she might be embarrassed. That he might be. Instead, as they reached for each other's fingertips, she felt the most extraordinary happiness. She could feel it on her face. She could see it on his face, and she logged it in: the blood rush of alcohol and sex = happiness. Or sex with this man. And the right sort of drinks. What had she had? She would have to remember.

He reached up to touch her cheek. "I'd give you champagne . . ." he said, and Clare caught his hand. She chewed on his fingers and knew there wasn't a way in the world she was finished yet. He'd half buried his face in a pillow, but he was right here. He was absolutely, entirely here.

It was some time around two when they found the ice bucket. Or Clare found it. She considered putting her clothes on to go look for the ice machine, but settled for getting glasses of water from the bathroom. It felt domestic. They were both thirsty and Clare looked in her suitcase for the package of pistachio nuts Anthony's aunt had given her, and didn't say what she was thinking, that she'd read somewhere they were good for the liver. Detoxifying or something. That maybe they'd ward off a hangover, although she didn't know if Luc (*Luc,* she practiced to herself, *Luc, Luc*) being French—raised in France—even ate between meals.

He did. They lay on the bed prying the shells open. Luc placed the pistachios on her tongue or caught them out of the air like a puppy when she tossed them to him. He complimented her on the pitches. She praised his catches. It was all play, and Clare didn't let herself think how long they could keep it up—this easy intimacy.

By three, she was lying crosswise on the bed, her head on Luc's chest and his arm draped across her. It was his turn to answer a question, and he was telling her he'd been at a conference and a retreat in Houston before driving to New Orleans. He'd left the retreat before it was over, rented a car without knowing where he was going, wandered into the parish archives here, and then been in the bar downstairs for half an hour before she came in.

Clare was curious. It sounded provocative to her—that Luc had abandoned a retreat and been drawn to New Orleans. A part of her felt a rush. She wanted to believe he'd somehow known she would be here, that he'd actually guessed she would be with Anthony in New Orleans, that he'd intuited what she hadn't known—that she would arrive in the Carousel Bar at just the time he was waiting there. She thought of saying all that—of confessing what at best was an alcohol-tinged fantasy, something about a half-conscious magnetism drawing them both here—but a slight edge had crept into Luc's voice as he spoke.

She turned her head to look at him, considering what she should say, and then she decided on a more careful course. "We don't need to talk about this. I know now how you happened to be here. More or less. But you'll be back in Ann Arbor?"

He nodded. "For a little while. Probably. Your turn."

"Yes?"

"Tell me—where did you get that chip on your shoulder? A charming shoulder to be sure." He tilted his head down to kiss it. "I've been curious since the night in Ann Arbor."

"Only my right shoulder? It's a long story."

"They all are," he said, and Clare fell quiet, wondering what the long parts were for him—what it really was that had caused his early departure from Houston and arrival here, and whether he'd intended all along to find someone to be with—not her, but somebody.

"I was an oversensitive child," she said. "You could say it makes me an overcompensating adult."

"That's not that specific."

"I guess not. But you were at St. Francis. Even if you don't have a strong memory of it, you could guess what an ordeal it was for a child who took it all seriously. It loomed so large, maybe out of proportion for what it was, but still. Then later I lost . . . I lost a friend, college friend, boyfriend, in a way that felt related. He died in Vietnam, though I didn't know it for a long time. I didn't know until last year when I looked at a list. But you have to say how you could possibly have remembered me. Just one random child."

"One child, yes, but a child who actually asked Monsignor Evans if flagellation was necessary for faith. How could I forget that? It's maybe the one thing that year I do remember."

Clare felt the ping of recognition, explanation. "When I think about her—that child—she was an absurd creature." Clare sighed. Then she yawned.

At seven, they were out in the city, feeling the slight breeze that pushed through the heavy air. They were going for coffee and beignets, and Luc had pulled her hand over his arm. It moved Clare. She wasn't quite sure what she'd expected—that maybe he'd shy away from her in the daylight. Instead she felt happy and cosseted, which was an odd word but apt. The other words that had flitted through her mind described the situation more than they described her. They were words like ephemeral and fugitive and iniquitous, and those words she was keeping at bay.

———

Clare felt as if her life had a sound track. Wherever she was, her mind played her version of the New Orleans sound: muted trumpets and electric guitars with a bit of slide, saloony pianos, walking rhythms, easy voices. A little gospel. The sound was an insistent accompaniment to everything that she did. Driving back with Anthony, she didn't want the radio on, and Anthony, who might have had his own sound track, didn't object. They traded driving and sleeping and, in the moments when they both were awake, they were both preoccupied. Clare was reliving the Hotel Monteleone and Luc-Cristof Étienne. *Luc.* Anthony, she assumed was thinking about his mother and reliving the surfer.

When she'd met him back at his aunt's house on Friday morning, he'd looked like a complete wreck. Clare didn't ask questions, though she gathered from his aunt that he'd been to Baton Rouge. She, on the other hand, had not set foot outside of New Orleans. She and Luc had managed a walk to the French market and the ship canal, guidebook in hand, but they'd spent most of their time in the hotel room. It was some time in the middle of Thursday afternoon, with the curtains drawn, when Clare had learned that, in twenty years of being a priest, Luc had never before broken his vow of celibacy. She was surprised, though not entirely. Yet more than surprising her, the disclosure impressed her with the gravity of what had happened. Of what was still happening. While the intellectual part of her had decided the vows priests and nuns make are up to them to keep, and not to the rest of the world, which as far as Clare was concerned had no particular stake in such a public abnegation (wasn't it, in some way, even a little weird, a little silly?), it was impossible for her not to be affected by the fact that Luc's underlying sadness hadn't disappeared. If anything, in spite of his moments of ebullience, it had become more pronounced.

Clare wondered if she could make light of things, maybe offer to start calling him Father Luc in spite of what she'd said—even to revert all the way back to Father Étienne. But she knew it was nothing to joke about and, by the time they'd said their good-byes, she was feeling her own sort of sorrow and the leading edge of what she was all but certain would become a serious case of guilt. Yet he made no accusations or excuses. He didn't say they wouldn't see each other again and he even asked if she had more research planned for Chicago, which she instantly decided she did. He was sweet with her, helping her to repack her suitcase. When they were ready to go, he smoothed her hair back and thanked her and told her she'd been lovely, which had left her entirely unable to speak. All she could do was push her head into his shoulder and hold on to him.

By the time Anthony pulled up in front of her building on Sunday evening, Clare thought she'd never missed anyone in her life as much as she missed Luc-Cristof Étienne. It hit her particularly keenly after she'd given Anthony a quick pat on the hand and told him she could manage her suitcase and then started carrying it up the stairs to her apartment. What exactly was she coming home to? The stairwell was airless. The stairs were steeper than she remembered. There was a stack of newspapers she'd forgotten to cancel lying in front of her door.

Inside, she opened the windows and started the fan. The last time she and Anthony had stopped to eat was for lunch and, while Anthony had snacked on Cheetos all afternoon, Clare wouldn't eat them. She wasn't really hungry even now, but she did want an apple or maybe an orange—something to at least banish the smell of the Cheetos that, after inspection, didn't seem to be in her hair. There was nothing edible in the fridge. It reeked of spoiled deli meat, and Clare considered helping herself to some of the frozen dessert and then opted for the wine in the broom closet. It made her teary. Luc must be back. He must be somewhere out there in Ann Arbor, maybe thinking of her and game to join her if she only knew how to reach him. She imagined various tableaux: the two of them drinking wine on the floor of the kitchen with the soles of their feet together the way they'd sat in the hotel room when they were eating Luc's leftover clams. Or maybe she could perch on the window ledge as if it were a fire escape and wait for him to arrive and to call up to her—her own Stanley Kowalski moment, which she'd actually thought about in New Orleans when she'd seen a bus with a destination sign for Desire. (Desire Street? Avenue? Talk about a city being up front about itself.) Clare was considering the proximity of her bed to everything in her apartment and trying to remember how long it had been since she'd changed the sheets when the phone rang.

She was up in an instant, the wine splashing out of her glass as she ran to her desk. She stood still a half second to make sure she was breathing normally, and then picked up the receiver.

There was a man's voice on the other end. Her father, to be specific, and Clare wondered what had happened. Her father never called, and it was alarming he was calling now, though, in a flash, she realized what was wrong. "Oh! I missed her birthday. I completely forgot. It's good to hear your voice, Daddy. But is she there? I need to explain."

And she could explain, couldn't she? Certainly, her mother would understand about Anthony, about her need to help a good friend, and even about Clare's forgetting what day it was, given the traveling and being in New Orleans. Could she even go as far as saying she'd been to the Carousel Bar, where Truman Capote sometimes went, that she'd actually been there on her mother's birthday? Probably not.

"I didn't want him to call," her mother said when she got on the line. "I told him you were preoccupied with your party and probably still cleaning up. It was yesterday, right? Your father thought it was a week ago."

"He's right. Sorry. It would have been a week ago." Clare launched into her explanation and apology for tardiness—gift forthcoming—and said how sorry she was she'd worried them, which she was certain she had.

"You were a friend in a time of need. It's all right, sweet," her mother said. "Your brother calls New Orleans Fling City, though of course a funeral's quite a different matter. And Anthony—"

"Finn's been to New Orleans?"

"Don't you assume he's been everywhere? If you reschedule your party, couldn't you invite Father Étienne? I remember him as being quite nice, and you liked him. If he's just in Ann Arbor for the summer . . . even a priest must get lonely."

Clare swallowed. She thought she'd developed an air pocket in the middle of her head. Just what had happened to the Madelyn McHenry of her childhood that she'd become so uncanny? "I suppose," she said.

Her mother went on chatting. She said she'd been canning all week, and they talked about that and about her garden. Then Clare promised again to mail her birthday gift right away (while she talked, she scratched down *BUY GIFT! MAIL!*)—and then spoke with her father when her mother put him back on. She was distressed when she hung up the phone. She stuck her finger in her glass and pushed the last drop of wine around the bottom and wondered just how she'd managed to give her mother another chance to be generous and forgiving.

It meant the scales were tilted even more than usual, and she hated it. She wished she had a cat. She missed Anthony. She missed Luc.

She startled at a knock at the door and was taking a wild, quick look at the mirror when she heard her neighbor's voice. It settled her down, and when she opened the door, the neighbor was standing there in her pink bathrobe, holding out a thin stack of mail. "I thought I heard you. I brought your mail."

Clare made her thanks. She took the stack, which looked like it was mostly circulars and bills. "Anything happen when I was gone?" she asked, and it wasn't really that she wondered. She was just trying to be polite. Well, really to be polite would mean offering her neighbor a glass of wine, but she just couldn't do that tonight.

"You told me somebody might show up looking for you."

"Right. For the party. Was somebody here? Did somebody not get the message?"

"Not for your party. There was somebody who left an envelope. He was here earlier asking for you. Tonight. It's there with the mail."

Clare felt a head rush. It was nearly blinding, though she could actually see. She could see but it was something like looking up from a well. She held on to the door frame, trying to be inconspicuous about it and trying to seem normal. "Well great," she said. "Something besides ads and bills." She steadied herself. She watched the black spots that floated over the hallway, starting to clear. "I didn't bring back any souvenirs—"

"Don't worry about it. You must be exhausted. All that driving."

Clare nodded. "I really am," she said. "Thanks—" She gestured with the mail in her hand.

When she'd closed the door, she leaned against it, listening to her neighbor retrace the steps. She heard the door close downstairs. She stood a second longer and then walked to her desk and set the mail down. Very carefully. Deliberately. She'd read once about English sappers starting to disable a bomb, and she thought they must have experienced a sensation like the one she felt now. A plain white envelope was sticking out from the pile, the last letters of her name visible in the exact tidy script she'd observed when Luc had signed for their dinner check. Clare stared at it. She knew she had to gather herself before she could open it—circle it a little mentally before she picked it up and made the small, jagged rip line with the letter opener. And when she actually took the message out, she knew she would learn what came next. She would see the new card from the hand she'd picked when she eyed the tall ship that day on the Dunes, and decided she was susceptible.

———

Clare had never kept a diary, but the re-entry of Luc-Cristof Étienne into her life meant that she did now. She was intentionally cryptic: *August 18th—Ran into L unexpectedly in New Orleans. August 22nd—Went to L's to let him know I'm back in Ann Arbor after he left his address for me. August 23rd—Snuck L up past the neighbor's. August 25th—Have taken to disguises. August 28th—Met L for the weekend in Chicago and showed him the city research ropes. Walked out on Navy Pier. September 4th—Chicago again. September 10th— Will my dad believe I like fishing? Went by ourselves (of course) to L's friend's cabin. September 19th—Semester well underway. L has leave (not sure what that means for him) to work on a book. Here and in Chicago. September 29th—I can't believe this. Oh my God.*

The entries stopped there, not because she had stopped making them but because that was all Clare allowed herself to keep. Once in the dead of winter, she read over the pages that followed and then burned them. Until the saved page had to go as well, the entries for August and September stood as the skeletal remains of . . . What? There was no way really to characterize what the "it" was. The defining part of her life? Maybe. A love story? Yes, but just as truncated as the diary was. Wishful thinking? Yes. A terrible thing?

Clare had settled on a leitmotif for what she kept, and that was "hiding," for it was what she and Luc had done (the freedom of their time in New Orleans felt so unexpected in retrospect that she sometimes wondered if she'd imagined it). She came to think of their furtiveness as an existential thing. There was no single person they needed to avoid. There was nothing like a suspicious husband or jealous wife. Instead, there was an idea—an idea and an institution. And there was a collective mind that could materialize at any moment from the very first whisper. On one level, it felt very exciting. It was more daring than anything she had ever done. But on another, Clare experienced a slight but growing feeling of claustrophobia. Hadn't she already shed the institution part? What exactly was it that was going on here?

She could ask questions of that sort that went to the bigger picture, and she did ask them. But the stories that lay behind the entries were essentially inviolate, for she could pick a date and play it in her mind with results as predictable as the sound from a record.

August 22nd. Pulling the note from the envelope, she'd recognized the clear invitation in the address she read. It was scary but electrifying. There was a phone number, but it seemed almost an afterthought. It was the address that was underlined, and she thought it might be safer than a call. Whose phone was it anyway? And why hazard calling when Luc's address would take her right to him? The note itself was short. It was barely a line that told her he wanted to know she'd gotten back safely, but the address said everything. He wasn't suggesting some neutral location. He wasn't telling her they'd made a mistake but saying, *I need you, Clare. How can I possibly survive another minute without you?*

She was savvy enough not to take her car. She rode the bus, tapping lightly on her bag to the sound of air brakes and the bus shifting and accelerating. A little night music. Did she have New Orleans with her? She hoped so but, for all the ways the people of Ann Arbor were drawn in on themselves, even this city felt wonderfully drummy. Clare headed down the bus steps. On the street, she guessed she had maybe five blocks to walk, though she wasn't positive. She wished she'd looked at a map before she left or had brought one with her. When she spotted the right cross street, she felt like running, though she restrained herself. She knew she had to be careful. There had to be something businesslike in her approach in case someone noticed her.

She was almost there. She was sure of it now. One more streetlamp. An alley. The below-street-level door with the right address. A bushy shrub with heavy-scented flowers nodding into her shoulder when she lifted her hand to knock. She wanted to tell Luc she'd come as quickly as she could, but not to say that she'd dragged her brush through the knots in her hair in a panic and scrubbed at the wine on her tongue with her toothbrush and two teaspoons of baking soda, that she'd worn her jeans and the silk blouse with the chain belt she'd left out on the bed in New Orleans, though she'd almost thought better of it, almost rushed back to change. She waited, a buzzy sound in her ear, an impudent, talky trumpet, and then Luc had opened the door of the place he was house-sitting, but how shocking. He was wearing his collar. He was in his shirtsleeves, yes, but the collar was there, the white notch in the clerical garment—and what was it? It was black, but was it some sort of bib? Maybe a type of vest? Should she know the name? For a second, Clare was overwhelmed by this new sense of him. He was Father Étienne, looking very official, which left her just where? From the look on his face, she knew he'd registered her surprise.

He touched the collar. "This startle you?" he said, and it was him, it was Luc—his face and voice. He'd filled in for the chaplain, giving Last Rites. He'd just gotten back and had been afraid that he'd missed her. Well he had missed her. He hadn't really thought about anything else. He was saying all this in the dark hallway with the door closed behind her. There was a faint, musty scent, and his body, too, the scent of him, the just rough feel of his whiskers, the starchy feel of the collar and now his mouth traveling her face and her neck, his hands on her blouse, which she opened so he could touch her breasts and easily trace the path of the tucked-in shirttail. A fan was blowing behind him, and Clare could just sense the air stirring on her arms and on the right side of her face. On her eyelid. The moving air was part of the whole feeling and, oddly, a thing she knew she'd remember.

Of the occasions in her diary, Clare preferred the ones when she and Luc hadn't talked about anything personal. Or the ones when they hadn't talked of anything that wasn't essentially playful. (Or maybe playing. He liked it when she played the piano, stationing himself at an anonymous distance from the practice room door, which she would leave ajar if no one was in the next rooms. How many times had he listened and said how much he enjoyed it? Two? Even three?) In Chicago—*August 28th*—they'd had a perfectly neutral discussion of the neighborhoods and the architecture and the hot wind tunnel of the downtown sidewalks. Surrounded by Japanese businessmen at a restaurant in Water Tower Place (they'd decided to order only a drink when they couldn't find prices on the menu), they talked about the Indian sepoys in the King's regiments in World War II who'd gone over to the Japanese. Given the differences in their background and age (and, for want of a better word, their careers), it was a rare bit of very miscellaneous information that they both knew. Clare welcomed it. She liked the click of recognition. And it was the sort of thing that was so much easier to talk about than the fraught subjects they had in common like St. Francis and the business of being Catholic, though of course she knew they were headed there sooner or later.

It was on Navy Pier that they had the first of what she later considered the inevitable conversations. It started out lightly. They were talking about New Orleans because Clare knew the pier had had a carousel in the 1920s. They both wondered if there'd be another one built with the new construction they'd seen. Then they moved on to Truman Capote and *Breakfast at Tiffany's*, Clare saying how much more she'd liked the end of the book than the end of the movie. Luc asked her why, and she told him the movie had a silly Hollywood ending, that Audrey Hepburn, who was nothing less than perfect in the whole movie, wound up with George Peppard, who was dreadfully wrong. In the book, "Fred," the Peppard character, was in large part an observer like Nick Carraway in *The Great Gatsby* (Luc hadn't read *Gatsby*, so this, too, required its own side trip of explanation). Holly, amoral little sprite that she was, was meant to be looked at, and perhaps aided, but not married. Or at least not to Fred.

"Is that your general opinion?" Luc asked, and Clare wasn't sure if he was serious or teasing.

"That women should only be looked at? Or that they shouldn't marry people named Fred?"

Luc made a slight shift of ground. "I was wondering how free-spirited you are, how much Holly Golightly there is in a girl like you."

The question, if it was that, rankled Clare. Her first thought was to ask what he was suggesting. After all, she'd paid for the room in New Orleans, and she couldn't imagine that he actually saw her as the sort of woman (girl?) who might do things for money, though of course he didn't know about Holly's fifty dollars for the "powder room." He hadn't read the book, hadn't seen the movie. It bothered her to think she might be put into some category—seem an interchangeable woman in any sense, in spite of the fact she knew she'd been remarkably available when they'd met in New Orleans, though if you counted the days since they'd reconnected in Ann Arbor and added in something for Luc's being somewhere in her mind ever since childhood, it seemed less glaring. She was feeling defensive, shamed by even the possibility that, from Luc's point of view, she might have been anyone in New Orleans, that she'd merely been in the right place at the right time. There was also the fact that she felt guilty for making him feel guilty, which she was sure that he did. And there was a further matter just as troubling—the question of whether there'd been an element of payback when she seduced him. Take that, St. Francis. Take that, church. Take that, Father Étienne.

Had she seduced him?

"I don't know what you mean," she said. A swirling breeze was blowing strands of hair into her face, and she held them back while she looked out at the water. "I guess maybe I would know if I could just understand better why you were in New Orleans." She placed her hand over his, curling her fingers through his fingers until her fingertips touched the gritty brick of the wall they were leaning against. "Luc, if I hadn't been there, would there have been somebody else?" she asked, knowing how much it still excited her to say his name, which was maybe its own kind of issue.

He took as long to answer as she had. "I don't know," he said finally. He wasn't looking at her, and Clare realized there was something about his profile that reminded her of Cody Dawkins when he'd pulled up the collar on his windbreaker. "I'd like to think not."

She considered the answer—the ambiguity. Did it mean he didn't know what he'd intended when he went to New Orleans? Did it mean that he wished he could undo everything that had happened between them? More than that, why did his answer hurt her? What right did she have to want this to be about something more than it was, and what exactly did she want it to be anyway? It wasn't as if they'd started with a clean slate and limitless possibilities. She tightened her fingers over his. "I hope you don't mind," she said. "I'm sorry about this, but the fact is I'm falling in love with you. I have. I've fallen. I'm in love with you."

She was waiting for his answer—not for him to say he loved her, too—she had no expectations about that—but for the more obvious thing, the play on her words to tell her he'd also fallen, but in a larger, more metaphysical sense. But he didn't say it. She should have known. He was too much of a gentleman for that sort of j'accuse.

Of all the inevitable conversations, there was one that Clare felt brought them closest to clarity, even to a sort of equivalency, if that was what she meant (a sense of being in the same place? a congruence like the kind that comes with humming the exact pitch of a machine so the two sounds become indistinguishable?). It was the conversation that brought the answer to her question of why. Why New Orleans? Why the sadness? Why her? *September 10th*—They'd driven to Luc's friend's cabin, which was well secluded: hidden in the woods. No other cabins in sight. A private dock. Clare had brought groceries, which she felt offered an opportunity for feeling domestic once more—a pistachio-and-water moment as she thought of it. She'd shopped carefully, hunting for fare that was a bit sophisticated, and a lot genuine camp food. She was particularly picky about the beer (she'd read about lagers in the library) and the cheese—it was imported— and about the s'mores ingredients. The revelation, though, was the fish. Clare caught it herself, a beautiful lake trout that jumped onto her hook when she was trolling the line. She almost lost it reeling it in, which made Luc laugh (she loved hearing him laugh), though he said afterward he would have rescued her if she'd lost her footing and spilled out of the boat.

"I can swim. I would have rescued myself," she answered, watching as he filleted the fish when they'd gone back to shore and he'd started the grill. "But I'd like it if you cook that. It looks as if you know what you're doing."

He did, and Clare wondered if it was a French skill, or even a priestly one. She put out the salads she'd bought, and the pasta one she'd made herself (she'd correcting the seasonings several times until the lucky moment when she realized she could save it by adding lemon juice). They had what she thought was a perfect meal. A fat sun sunk toward the water, smudging chalky pink on the sky, and Clare tried to describe the sunset she'd seen on the approach to New Orleans with Anthony. They hunted for the baseball game on the transistor radio and, when they couldn't find it, Luc hoisted his beer like a microphone and did five minutes of play by play, partly in French. Clare listened, sharpening sticks for the marshmallows. He was very good, very funny, and she even understood some of the French. He was almost boyish and the happiest she thought she'd seen him. She decided she'd done an excellent job of picking the beer.

They roasted the marshmallows, and Clare's caught on fire, which meant the air smelled of pine and scorched sugar. She peeled away the blackest part and squished the rest of the softened marshmallow onto a chunk of Hershey bar. "It really is like camp," she said. "My parents want to move to a lake. I'll have to get used to it."

When they'd cleaned up after their meal, they sat on the dock with their feet touching the water and watched the afterglow of the sunset behind a patch of red sumac. Clare listened to the crickets, which were loudest where the woods were already dark. She allowed herself a moment of fantasy, wishing they were sitting sled-style with Luc clasping his arms around her, and that she was leaning back against him, her cheek against his, and feeling very contented. But that wasn't quite Luc. There was something. He could do the relatively casual parts and the intense ones, but there was a formality to him when it came to what she thought of—aptly or not—as the boyfriend things.

"My stepdad has voyageur blood," he said, slapping at a mosquito on his ankle. "If he were out here, he'd want to explore this lake and take it as far as he could. Link onto other lakes. Maybe portage."

Clare nodded. She liked it when they learned more about each other that was useful, though she wasn't sure what anything could actually be useful for. They were quiet a moment, and then they talked about what they would do in the morning, whether they would fish or swim, and she thought of teasing him about skinny dipping, which suddenly seemed very appealing to her. She didn't, however. They weighed whether they would hike into the woods and look for berries or spread blankets on the thin bit of beach and read.

When the mosquitoes started biting in earnest, they headed into the cabin. Clare looked around again when they turned on the lights. It was more spiffy than rustic with big window views of the lake, but when she searched for identifying marks—a snapshot or something—she couldn't find anything. Luc opened another beer. It had grown a little chilly, and Clare fixed herself cocoa from a packet she found in a cabinet. She waited for some kind of cue from Luc, but he seemed a little distant, or at least quiet, and so she tried the chairs until she found one with a comfortably chintzy cushion and settled into it with the *New Yorker* she'd brought along. Luc stood at the door drinking his beer and looking out at the lake. It worried her a little. She wasn't sure why.

Waking alone in bed in the middle of the night, Clare had no idea where she was. Then she knew. It was another place she and Luc had made love, and this time he'd carefully removed a piece of marshmallow he'd found in her hair. She could faintly smell the smoke from a cigarette. She waited a minute and then she got up. She didn't want to go naked looking for him in a strange house, so she took his shirt from the chair and put it on as she went out to the living room. Discounting coloring and her not really gaminelike look, she decided it made her Audrey Hepburn. Holly Golightly. It made her Holly.

He was standing at the door again, and he had on his pants and T-shirt and was holding a glass this time. He'd just put his cigarette out and a thin waft of smoke was still filtering up through the screen. It was dark in the house except for a spill of moonlight through the windows. Clare thought she could see the stars in the sky.

"Hey," she said softly, not wanting to startle him. She paused a second. Then she walked up to him and put her arms around his waist. "Can't you sleep?"

"Right." He didn't turn around, and Clare decided that if he was maybe a little drunk, it certainly wasn't in a sloppy way, which wasn't his style. It was her brother's. It was Finn's style. She wondered about asking him what he was drinking but she didn't for fear it would sound like a request. Or an accusation.

"There's a light over there." He pointed across the lake. "About your question . . . I've decided you need an answer. I owe it to you."

Clare was quiet, her arms still around his waist. She didn't agree. He didn't owe her anything, and she was feeling more than reluctant to hear any answer he might give her tonight, though his mood seemed improved. She closed her eyes. "I suppose you mean about New Orleans."

She felt his hands close over hers, the heavy glass against her fingers. "It's a fair question," he said. "I've been thinking about it—"

Clare interrupted him. "But you were thinking about it—whatever it was—before we ever met in New Orleans. After all those years of being the faithful priest, you left that retreat and drove to New Orleans and found me. Why? I can't bear to think it was all a mistake and my doing. But the truth is I can't bear to think that it wasn't. I mean that it didn't have something to do with me."

Clare stopped. She knew her face was burning. She was honestly startled at what she'd said. They stood without talking, just touching. His body was so familiar to her now. She tried to think of what she might say to make things seem lighter: *Do you want your shirt back? We should take this lying down. I can sing you a lullaby.* But, really, she was in the farthest-away place where the child she knew best had lost her deepest trust in her mother and was praying intently for a miracle to save them both.

Clare worked her hands loose. She took Luc's glass and tasted the watery, medicinal Scotch. "I had a crush on you," she said. She gave the glass back. "Sister Immaculata—she was evil, she was so crazy, and she had me believing I had to be this spotless vessel of constant prayer so I could save my mother's Protestant soul. Some little boy made it impossible for me to stay pure. A minor sexual assault, though I heard he later moved up to rape. No, that's not right. It was Rocco Muletto who was the rapist, not Timmy Porter. I thought it was all my fault. But I was too ashamed to confess it to you on May Day. Crazy child. I lied to you in the confessional. I was fourteen before I told another priest the truth, and he sorted things out, but it meant four years of me thinking I was going to hell, which I totally believed, totally. It was hell in itself. And now I'm here wearing your shirt and I'm afraid you're going to tell me what you think I've done to your soul. And we're not getting any sleep again. Don't you think it's probably bad for us? Healthwise? You don't have to tell me anything. You don't owe me a thing. Really."

Clare looked down at the floor. She felt a little unsteady. She wanted her sweater or a robe, though maybe Luc himself worked just as well. She pushed her cheek against the pocket on his T-shirt. She felt like a puppy listening to its mother's heartbeat, though more sentient than that, which was hard not to regret. Impossible really. She knew Luc was still going to tell her why he'd gone to New Orleans. All her ammunition wouldn't stop him. It had been her question after all.

"I can give you the shorthand on this, which I gather is what you gave me, but it might take longer than that."

Clare wished he didn't look so serious, but she nodded. She wondered what the etiquette was for a moment like this. Should they really be standing up? Should this be a conversation they were having across a table with Gregorian chants playing in the background? Or would it be wrong to make it pillow talk so they could blurt things out and be emotional if they wanted—if she wanted—and have their perfect way to distract themselves again. She wondered if Luc maybe needed a cigarette. It occurred to her that he needed a confessional, that maybe that would be his default position for something like this, but she kept herself from making the joke. She wasn't going to cry, was she?

"Come on," he said. "There's a coat in the kitchen and I saw some bug spray."

"We're going outside?"

"If we're going to talk about eternity, I could use a lake."

For an instant Clare was alarmed. It occurred to her what a leap it was to believe there were people to trust above anything even when there was something essentially untrustworthy at the heart of who you were together. But she did trust Luc. She followed him into the kitchen. "Is that where this is going? Talking about infinity? You're not trying to scare me, are you?"

"No. Here you go." He had a raincoat in one hand and the bug spray in the other. "If you want, I'll get the back of your legs when we're outside."

It was *his* domestic moment, she thought when they were out the door. She felt the cold spray on her legs. "Do we really want to smell like this?" she said, taking her turn and spraying his back.

They made their way over the ground. It was damp and full of pebbles and Clare wished she had her shoes on. "So the dock again?" she asked and Luc said yes, and it was different in the dark with the small waves lapping against it and, farther out, the spots of moonlight on the water. She took a few steps out on the planking and then stopped, pulling the raincoat around her. Luc went ahead to the end of the dock. He put one foot on the corner piling and leaned forward on his knee, and Clare thought if he'd had a spyglass, he'd be the captain of her ship.

"There's eternity," he said, and Clare felt his words as much as she heard them. "Out there. Up there."

Clare tilted her head back, looking up at the stars and the dark streaks of clouds. She thought she could tell him the whole idea of infinity had terrified her when she was small, but she didn't. "It's so incomprehensible," she said. She felt the slight give of the dock as Luc started back toward her.

"But you can understand the mystery. That there is one. The idea of the mystery is very compelling."

Clare was interested. "In what way?"

"Well, for me . . . father dead . . . mother off doing dangerous things. The mystery beyond that was the constant. The Eucharist actually. It was what I believed in. It's why I'm a priest."

Clare thought she understood. In spite of all the things she didn't believe in, she couldn't quite not believe in the Eucharist. "So you're not one of those men who became a priest to make his mother happy?" she said, well aware that it sounded cheeky.

Luc looked at her. "That, too." He took her hand and pulled it under his arm and covered it with his other hand the way he had in New Orleans, the way she'd loved. "The fact is I went to New Orleans for the drink and the music. If I didn't happen to be a priest, I suppose you'd call it some sort of crisis. A midlife thing. An escape. Maybe even something of a breakdown. But just being in Ann Arbor . . . even that was an aberration."

"Like a time off or something?"

"More or less. Authorized, but yes."

Clare was quiet. She understood there were major gaps here, things she could guess at or that Luc had alluded to earlier like the events that had roiled his years at Catholic University, and the aftershocks still clattering out from Vatican II. They'd made it seem that everything was changing. Though perhaps it was something more deeply about him. "You said 'believed.' Past tense. That you'd believed in the Eucharist. Are you saying you've lost—that you've doubted your faith? You don't have to answer that. But I still don't understand how I fit in. Not that I have to. I meant what I said—that you don't owe me anything. Though I shouldn't say that. Not if it sounds self-pitying. Insensitive . . ."

"Of course I've doubted it. All of it, but it's not that I was ever aligned with the orthodoxy. The fundamental part—the sacramental part—that's the thing that's been my whole life. It's why I accepted celibacy. I see it as the only possible way to be God-centered, which is the whole point, but the one that feels very shaky now."

"Because of me? Luc, I never meant to destroy—"

"I don't mean the sex. The sex was like exhaling after twenty years of holding my breath. Vows included, it's not an inconsiderable thing—I'm French, Clare—but it's not the point. Put it together, Clare: I always recoiled at the idea of a church that made a child wonder about—about *flagellation*, for God's sakes! I should have talked to your parents. And twenty years later, I stare at the abyss with the whole mystery of the Eucharist evaporating—a desperate thing—and you come into my life again. You know what I felt when I saw you in New Orleans? The very first thought that flashed in my mind was that I wouldn't have to face this alone. That was it. You weren't a temptation. Not to put too fine a point on it, Clare, but I saw you more as my salvation."

It was odd, Clare, thought, but she had the strongest sense that she needed to hold her ground. "An illusory thing."

"Yes."

"But you've found I'm actually real."

"Yes. You're very real. It's what I've discovered."

⌣‾

It was the middle of September when her parents came to visit, though it was not a thing for Clare to enter in her diary. In fact, it was something they'd planned that she'd nearly forgotten about. Her father had promised her mother a trip to Mackinac Island with a stop in Ann Arbor on the trip home. They arrived in good spirits, talking about the horse-drawn carriages on the island and carrying a box of maple sugar for her. Her mother had forgotten she didn't like it, and Clare made an effort to forget it as well. She couldn't, though. She couldn't bear the taste of it, and she ended up burying the piece she'd taken deep in the trash when her mother wasn't looking.

"Oh Clare," her mother said, opening the freezer. She was getting out ice for the tea she'd insisted on making, and she'd uncovered the pans of frozen dessert. "You never had your party. I don't have to ask if you invited Father Étienne."

"No, you don't," Clare said. "No party."

"And when is it you defend your dissertation? Is that what they call it?"

"Right. A dissertation."

"I mean the defense, smarty. When is that?"

Clare yawned once. She yawned again, and then shook her head decisively. "No idea," she said. "It hasn't been scheduled yet."

"But you're done with your footnotes?"

Clare went over to her mother and kissed her. "No, Mother, I'm not. But I promise you'll be the first to know," she answered, though the whole time she was thinking dissertation, what dissertation, what defense.

Her mother held on to her. "You seem so happy. Your skin looks so nice," she said, and watching her, Clare thought her mother had walked away from the verge of asking if she'd met someone.

What, though? Hadn't she seemed happy before? Was she different in some profound way so it showed? And as far as her skin was concerned, she'd been expecting her chin to break out, and she'd been covering it all week with Noxzema since she was going to Chicago in two days.

When her parents had left, there was something about her mother's approval that Clare found still weighed on her. What had Madelyn Wheatley McHenry, with her now familiar mix of diffidence and scrutiny, actually seen? Clare was briefly curious, but she put it out of her mind on her drive to Chicago, and Chicago was all Luc, all the time. She was entirely wrapped up in him. She thought they'd entered a new stage of closeness, one she felt might even implicate them in each other's decisions, which excited her but also made her wary. She didn't know at all where any of this was headed. And she didn't really want to think about that any more than she wanted to weigh Luc's sadness or happiness and consider where she fit in. She also didn't want to think about the alcohol question, if that's what it was. She suspected Luc was drinking more than he usually did, but she didn't really think he drank so much, and she assumed the increase, if it was that, was temporary—tied up with the current detour in his life—that it was nothing like what she was used to with her brother, who'd felt stifled in their parents' house but grown expansive when he'd traded home for what Clare sometimes thought, but didn't say, was the bar-centered life of an Irishman. That was Finn. It wasn't Luc. That was her brother. And as far as she was concerned, she barely drank at all now. She'd lost interest; she'd lost the taste for it.

Clare remembered this particularly on the day after she'd come back to Ann Arbor. She'd played tennis early in the morning with her friend Alice, who was her main source of information on current events and current literature. Alice had startled her when she mentioned the Updike book she'd just finished, a hilarious novel, she said, which featured a sex-obsessed priest attempting to reconcile his behavior with the Bible.

"I liked *Pigeon Feathers*. It's the only one of his books I've actually read," Clare told her, and she didn't add that it was the intimacy in it that she particularly liked and that she'd be happy to skip Updike's take on a priest. When she and Alice had finished their match, she started home in the glorious fall, her sweatshirt tied around her waist. She stopped for a moment in the law quadrangle. She wished she could show it to Luc. It was such a brilliant day with the brilliant leaves. She was sweaty, but she was seriously blissed out. Then, suddenly, she felt a wave of nausea.

Clare clamped her hand over her mouth. She was panicked, wondering if she could duck behind a tree or actually make it inside to a bathroom. Then, just as quickly as it had come, the queasiness passed. She was startled. Mystified really. She couldn't remember the last time she'd drunk enough to feel this way, and it was even longer since she'd had an actual stomach bug. And playing tennis had never made her sick. Then the nausea hit again, and she rushed for the door.

It wasn't immediately that Clare came up with a more obvious explanation to consider. She was thoroughly sick in a bathroom stall and, while she was rinsing her mouth and wiping her face with a wet paper towel, she stayed completely stuck on theories of things she'd had experience of—or that in any way seemed plausible. It was only when she'd started a subdued walk back to her apartment that she seriously started figuring out dates.

Impossible! It was true she was running a tad late, though what was late for her? And it was also true she'd felt a sort of unpleasant bloating and her nipples had been sore when she served the tennis ball. But the math was flat-out crazy. She'd actually still had her period in New Orleans and been concerned it would put Luc off. And she'd gotten pills right away. Pills and foam. She couldn't be pregnant. She was sure that she wasn't.

On her next trip to Chicago, Clare was nervous but still hoping she was safe. Luc said she seemed quiet and she supposed that she was. She thought of telling him what she was afraid of and decided nothing would be crazier. Why borrow trouble? Why raise an inflammatory issue when it might amount to nothing more than a scare? She understood that she wanted his comfort and reassurance. She also knew that his likeliest reaction would be something else. It preyed on her a little—that realization as well as her basic worry.

By the time the last saved date in her diary had come and gone, Clare was no longer wondering. She'd walked into the student health service and gotten her verdict. Stunned, she'd written down *September 29th* in the diary, and now there was a new question. What was she going to do with this knowledge? It had shocked her certainly, but what was she going to do?

She paced her apartment like a cat in a cage. On a pass toward the kitchen, she allowed herself a moment of excitement. Her own baby growing inside her. Her baby and Luc's. Stripped away of everything else—the complications and requirements of her life (and of Luc's life!)—the idea had a beautiful and wonderful simplicity. Mother, father, child. How elemental. A lovely thing. A dream.

Then Clare made the turn back toward her table and her view changed to seriously stormy weather. What would Luc say? What would he think? What did she think? What would her *father* think? She'd never heard of anyone even remotely like her who'd raised a child without getting married. Well she'd heard of it, but it was still unheard of. It was hardly the sort of territory she wanted to trailblaze. She understood what her first option was, the one she had to consider right now. She could find another sort of doctor and declare an end to this particular misadventure and keep the whole story from Luc. Protect him in that way. And protect herself from knowing just what he would say.

Nothing doing, she decided, turning back toward the kitchen. Of course she had to tell him. He wasn't a child. And she wasn't ready to be that selfless for him and, anyway, at this point, it wasn't just about them. Or she didn't think that it was, though she wasn't entirely sure.

It was the logistics of telling him that weighed on her now. In college, she'd read "Hills Like White Elephants" and she'd never forgotten how chilling it felt—the pregnant girl, her lover carefully and deceitfully pushing her toward a decision she didn't want to make. Clare could still picture the train station with the strings of bamboo beads on the door of the bar where the girl—her name was Jig, wasn't it?—and the man waited for the express from Barcelona and drank beer and Anís del Toro. Was she headed toward a situation like that?

She didn't know where she should tell Luc. She didn't remember ever fantasizing about a moment when she told a man—her husband certainly—they were having a child. If she had, she thought she would have envisioned it as romantic: candlelight and music, a wonderful dinner. But this, whatever "this" was, had to be different in terms not only of location—she could so relate to the importance of anonymity and transience in a train station setting—but of the actual information. It was quite a different thing telling a man ambush-style you were pregnant than it was giving him the welcome news that he was going to be a father. It was a world of difference, though Clare couldn't imagine a scenario in which Luc would be calculating and manipulative like the man with Jig. It was a sobering thought, though. What if she wasn't Holly but Jig?

In the end, she didn't really decide what to do. Anthony called to ask why he hadn't seen her—was she OK?—and Clare had such a strong impulse to tell him everything that she quickly realized she had to talk to Luc right away. She'd actually started packing things to leave for Chicago when the phone rang again. It was him. She was suddenly so emotional it was hard to talk—she was a mess really—and then, against all her rules, she started to cry. She tried getting control of herself and finally managed to say she had something to tell him, that they needed to talk. He was quiet for a long beat before he answered. He'd be there in a few hours. He was on the way.

———

When she thought of that night, Clare remembered the record she was playing when she heard Luc on the stairs. It was a loaner from Anthony, and she understood what Anthony meant when he said it was traveling music. Listening to the singer languidly following guitar changes while a plaintive fiddle hovered in the background, it was easy for Clare to see herself in a car on a dusty back road, the wind blowing in her face while Luc drove. It was the single daydream she'd allowed herself in the hours she spent waiting for him. When she opened the door, she found herself anchored abruptly in the Ann Arbor night. Standing there, Luc looked so grave his face almost seemed carved.

She let him in. She was afraid that the stillness in his face would extend to his body, that he would feel as rigid as her Grandpa Wheatley had been with his Parkinson's. She moved back from the door without touching him, but Luc reached for her anyway. He put his arms around her, and he felt the same as he always did. Clare wondered if she was the one who was rigid and needed to exhale, needed to relax into him if that was possible. They stood a moment silently. "You OK?" he said in her ear, and she nodded.

She screwed up her courage. "I know you know what I meant. I'm embarrassed about it. I guess horrified is a better word. Luc, I'm so sorry. If I'd thought it could happen . . ."

He didn't say anything at once, and Clare realized she'd feared a quick accusation, an assumption that she would have, should have been prepared—any time, any place—that she was that kind of woman (girl, he might say), though exactly what kind of woman had she been in New Orleans? The most charitable description was harsher than any assumption of sluttishness. She'd been angry. She'd been vengeful and willing to take advantage of another person's vulnerability to satisfy her old anger. Though, to be fair to herself, it was more than that. There was still the fact that she loved him, certainly now if not then.

"It's the sort of thing that takes two people," Luc said. "Do you have any beer? Clare, we can talk about it."

She was glad for the chance to feel guilty about something else: *a poor hostess!* Of course she had beer. She could feed him, too. She had leftover pasta and pans of frozen dessert. She took out one of her placemats and a matching napkin—they were a bright, lovely blue—and worked in a flurry in the kitchen. Then she sat down next to Luc at the table and watched him eat. The record was still on, and Clare let herself drift back for a moment to that imaginary dusty road with the breeze blowing and the crunch of gravel under the car as Luc drove.

The dessert was one of the few things she'd ever fed him that she'd actually made herself, and Luc liked it, which pleased her. When he'd finished, he folded his napkin and put it down next to his plate and then he took out what Clare realized had to be a breviary.

She was startled, though she tried not to show it. She wasn't sure just what she should do, so she excused herself and went into the bathroom. When she came back, Luc was still reading. He had his reading glasses on, newly acquired he'd told her in New Orleans when Clare said she loved them, that they made him look extremely smart. Now, though, she was feeling a little steamed. What was this exactly? Was it a way for him of going to the barricades? Was he pulling something like spiritual rank? She thought of what she'd said to him in New Orleans, that going ahead with what they were doing had to mean she couldn't recognize him as having some sort of superior station.

She was almost ready to say something when he closed the breviary and put it away.

"Sorry to be rude. It's what I'm used to, how I collect myself, though I'm not sure it's worked." He took a pen out. "We need a list."

Clare didn't disagree, but she felt unnerved. Exactly what kind of list? When it came right down to it, did she actually want a priest telling her how to handle this? She got some paper from her desk and her own pen and sat down again. "What goes on your list?" she asked, handing Luc a sheet of paper, and than drawing a line down the middle of her own sheet just so it looked as if she were doing something.

Luc scribbled down a few words and then showed her what he'd written. Clare read the words: *Adoption, Accommodation, Alienation, Alteration, Abortion.*"

"You've given this thought. Very alliterative. It's curious to see that one." She pointed to the end of the list. "I'll need an explanation for some of them," she added. "But scratch off Adoption. I'm not sixteen."

"Keep Abortion, though?"

Clare nodded. "Yes."

Luc drew a line through Adoption and put a box around Abortion. "OK," he said. "Accommodation. You proceed however you can, and I go back to my life and help out financially and get the yearly picture and update. Silent partner sort of thing."

"Very French."

Luc looked at her and then back at the list. "Alienation then. Like Accommodation but without the money or contact. And finally— Alteration. Major changes. I shed one sacrament for another—Holy Orders for Matrimony. Have I missed anything?" Luc lit a cigarette and stood up.

Clare was digging her fingernails hard into her palms. "Very dispassionate," she said. "You can scratch that one off, too. We both know . . . we both know we're nowhere near that. Or the complications."

"But it's all a complication, right?" Luc looked back at her from the window. "Forgive me for sounding businesslike, but the alternative is to sound desperate."

Clare received the blow silently. She knew what she'd wanted him to say, that they could go to France, go to a desert island, that they could keep on exactly as they were together but in something like the witness protection program. She wanted him to make a joke. She wanted him to pass this first real test of the two of them together, and she wanted there not to be a test. She wanted to wake up.

She reached over and drew an X through his list. "Too pithy for my taste. Maybe we ought to feel desperate."

———

As Clare saw it, everything had changed. Things were important now that hadn't been before and things that had earlier seemed of real significance were like so much background noise. She thought of the sappers again and of her own steadily mushrooming self. A clock was ticking. Her jeans felt tighter, and she understood, with a certain alarm, that she was going to be defused sooner or later, though she didn't yet know how.

She changed her mind from hour to hour, and she thought Luc changed his as often. They were essentially in a period of negotiation, of seesawing. At times, they could set it aside. Luc would call her and she would feel excitement again at hearing his voice. Or they could walk together along Lake Michigan as the days slipped deeper into fall and pretend whatever they pretended—that it was just the two of them. Or that there was this unmentioned third party who was really more promise than threat. Clare thought they were being honest with each other, though she bristled when Luc told her rather too brightly one evening that since he'd just found her, he wasn't ready to share.

"You're not going to say that it's like letting the air in, are you?" she asked, and Luc looked at her, puzzled and wary.

"A Hemingway story," she said and she didn't explain, didn't say it was what Jig's lover told her an abortion was. She liked the name Jig. Not actually to name a girl, but she liked it.

She'd given herself a deadline of October 18 for finally deciding. It wasn't a matter she felt she could rush into without finding a certain zone of comfort and she was hopeful she and Luc would be on the same page. Usually they weren't. He didn't answer when she suggested that, given the fact they'd both agreed from the beginning that abortion was an option, it might be the simplest choice. She interpreted his silence as disapproval or washing his hands of any responsibility, and either conclusion upset her. But when he took the initiative and said they were the adults here, and did they really want to saddle a child with the kind of baggage they'd be offering, Clare wondered just what kind of priest he was, recommending an abortion, though of course the readiest answer was that he was a priest who'd gotten his girlfriend pregnant. Not even his girlfriend then. Or now? Was she his girlfriend? Generally, she tried to pull away from thoughts that felt so accusatory and simply told him how uncertain she was. "In theory, I believe in it," she said. "I'm just not sure I could actually go through with it."

They drifted back over the possibilities. What was the problem again with adoption? Clare was unyielding, though she knew Luc thought she was wrong. If she actually gave birth to a child, there was no way she was giving it up. And as far as the gigantic step of Luc leaving the priesthood was concerned, Clare knew he wasn't there and seriously doubted he ever would be. It was her own theory that his crisis of faith was temporary, that he would embrace it again with a particular fierceness. And even if he were to take that leap, the prospect of their making a life together seemed a farther, wide ocean away. It meant that his big-change option wasn't truly an option at all. The remaining choices, along with treading water, which was what they were doing, kept smacking against each other like pool balls that collided hard at the break and then flew away.

Clare was sleepy. Luc was either agitated or vaguely withdrawn, although Clare was aware of the effort he was making to be supportive. The strain showed. She no longer asked herself if he drank too much when they were apart. She was sure that he did. At times, waking up at night alone in her apartment, it felt simply bizarre to her that the two of them even knew each other, let alone that they'd involved themselves in this kind of drama. But they had. Inexorably, they were moving through their scenes. Act 1 . . . Act 2 . . .

As the 18th came closer, Clare thought that both of their positions were hardening. On a night when they were together—Luc had been maddeningly rolling his fingers on the table once more—she realized he had actually started to lobby her, and with a particular intensity. She tried to deflect his argument. "*Add* option? It's more like subtract option," she said.

He looked at her strangely. "This runs in my head," he said. "*For God so loved the world, that he gave his only begotten Son, that whosoever believeth in him should not perish, but have everlasting life.*"

"That's not the Douay version, is it?" Clare asked, skipping the meaner things she'd thought of (are you God in that sentence? so you think it's a boy?), but angry with him that she felt so tough, that she had to be tough. "I get part of it, Luc. Your only begotten child. But I've finally decided, and please don't forget it was the idea you led with. I'm making an appointment. I'm putting an end to this."

He rolled away from her, closing a pillow over his ear. Clare screamed silently into her own pillow. Then, still silently, she began to cry.

Later, she thought it was the closest thing to a true couple's night they'd ever had. The irreconcilable conflict. The thorny, wounding decision. The unhappiness that so thoroughly encompassed them both and which they shared like some blanketing miasma. All night long, they barely touched each other, yet Clare thought of them resolutely holding hands as if waiting to be struck by an angel. She wanted to ask Luc if he was all right, but the question, though it floated in and out of her consciousness, was too absurd. She thought of the night at the lake when he'd stood at the door drinking beer and looking out at the water—of how much it had worried her. Somewhere inside her own misery, she felt that same unnerving sense of unease.

In the morning, they spoke very little. They ate croissants. They had coffee, and Clare dosed hers heavily with milk. When they said good-bye, Luc held her back from him, looking at her with an expression that she couldn't read. She didn't want to, really. Then, carefully, he smoothed her hair from her cheek in a gesture of such tenderness that she had to lower her eyes.

She was methodical back in Ann Arbor. So many phone calls to make, and all with the utmost discretion. Luc had told her to let him know the time, that he'd be there, but she knew she wouldn't, and she was certain he knew, too. Even without the impossible scenario of Father Étienne publicly escorting a woman on such a forbidden mission, it was clearly out of the question. She thought briefly of calling Anthony for moral support or even Lara, her well-informed but not very trustworthy friend. She didn't of course. It was something she knew she had to do by herself. She was in fact so steeled for the whole thing that she was caught completely off guard by the sharp emotion that racked her when she stood up from her desk and felt the unmistakable auguring movement. What was happening? What was this sudden cramping? Had something gone wrong? What? Had she frightened this child into letting go by itself? She wasn't ready for this.

She spent the day huddled in bed, a box of Saltines and a pitcher of water within careful reach. The radio was on low on the classical music station, and Clare tried to concentrate on the music she heard—to identify what key it was in and the shifts, to follow the themes. By evening she was feeling better. Hopeful actually. Hours earlier, she'd detected a pink trace, a hint of blood though not much more. The pain had almost stopped. She sat up a little, listening for something to break, to crash, though it didn't.

Afterward, it was the timeline that tormented her. This was first: she'd stood up from her desk and as soon as she realized what was happening, she immediately sat down again and called Luc. She hadn't thought at all of what she would say when she heard his *hello*. The *hello* again, and then a puzzled, slightly irked *is somebody there? I'm hanging up now if nobody's there.*

She'd put the receiver quietly back in its cradle. It was cowardly. Worse—though it was only later when she knew this—it was the act of a murderer. Why hadn't she said it's me, something's happening, I'm scared, I'm really not sure anymore. Luc, we can talk more about it. We don't have to stop talking. In fact, if another option is still on the table, I accept. Whatever you want.

But she hadn't said anything. That was the horrible thing. She'd heard Luc's voice and she hadn't answered him.

This was second: the phone rang. Someone called at least twice, and she'd stayed in bed. Gingerly, carefully she'd stayed in bed. And she'd had to, hadn't she? That part wasn't wrong, though could she even claim that with any certainty? And by the time she'd tried calling again, the phone had rung and rung. There was never an answer. Never. There were only her fears, her terrors—was she going to miscarry?

where was Luc?—and finally the envelope that arrived two days later in his still precise script. Holding it, Clare wondered if it smelled of whiskey. She already had the news that confirmed what the note told her—the story that had apparently raced through the circles of everyone she knew in Ann Arbor until it came to her. Serious voices saying that Father Luc had shot himself in his room in Chicago. It was in the *Tribune*. People believed that he'd been depressed, Anthony said. It was a terrible shock to Lara and Jake.

Listening, Clare thought she knew what it felt like to be gassed. She couldn't breathe. None of her body parts seemed attached. She wanted to hurl herself against the wall or knock herself out so she would stop feeling or thinking. Hadn't a second man died in the wake of her need—of her terrible sexual need for him? What in God's name had she done? And Luc . . . how could Luc possibly be gone?

As cryptic as the note was, it was so very clear to her: *Out of the picture. Too late? I hope not. I hope that it saved something. Some confusion, though it seems that I loved you. L ~*

A passage from Ezekiel had flashed in Clare's mind: *If he who is wicked turns from wickedness to that which is lawful and right, he shall live.* Something like that, though what a lie. And why hadn't she answered the phone? *Why?*

And this too: even the small things beset her, like the fluctuating memory of just how things stacked up. When was it her mother called? And was it a call, or was it the moment her mother was actually in Ann Arbor and carefully not looking at Clare's swollen waist? "Did you know about him, Clare?" she said. "You never told me about Father Étienne dying." Was it then that Clare was so close to telling her? Or was it all those months later, and the promise of summer, when Clare had put Sylvie in her mother's arms and her mother had clucked softly at Sylvie and then said without looking up, "You don't have to tell me, Clare, but be certain, darling, you keep your secret where it's not lost. Whoever her father is, there'll come a day when your child needs to know."

It may have been then. Probably. Hard to say. Always so hard to say.

———

Rain running through downspouts. Ice jamming up gutters, drifts of snow on the lakefront. Clare has moved to the city. She has told her mother all the ways she means to arrange her life for the child she'll have. The city is anonymous (who needs to mention that it carries the memory of this baby's father in its incessant winds?). Perfect. Clare will make sacrifices, give up all that she has to. All that she has. Where could she teach? Improbable once, impossible now. It won't be just her. She'll have a child. She'll find some kind of work. And when can she play the piano if her child has to sleep? Perhaps she doesn't need to, doesn't want to. Perhaps Clare has moved on.

She's protecting this child in every way she can think of—even from her mother's ability to guess. Is Clare condemned once more by the old ghosts of the church to losing her mother? She thinks so.

It's not that she's prescient. It's never been that. She's not into predicting the future or thinking she can. There simply are things she seems already to know. (In her mind. In her body and heart.) That she will be firm and unyielding when her parents ask that she come home to live. That she will even put up a hand—say no, that she doesn't want her mother to come when the baby is born. That she can do it herself. That she will.

And it's just as certain that her brother will turn up, stick his nose in, that when she's ready to leave the hospital, baby in tow, Finn will be there to see her out through the lobby and she'll be almost grateful: the people who watch might think they're a couple. It's all so inevitable. Her mother. Finn. The lovely summer day when she looks out at the water, baby in arms, and sees the shapes in the distance. They're no longer sailing just in her mind. The beautiful ships.

THE NUNS ON THE ROOF
OF ST. PETER'S

Clare McHenry considered herself skilled at analyzing the nuns of her childhood. In her early twenties, she sorted them by ages. The young ones were fresh-eyed and full of idealism. The middle-aged nuns were sour, confirmed in their barrenness and grinding out the years until eternity, pinching their acts of kindness. The very oldest were holy by default. Their appetites erased, the earth held them by a mere thread.

For Clare, all of them still had faces (Sister John Davida's skin the texture of settled flour; Sister Geraldine's eyes narrowing as chalk dust flew and she covered the blackboard with the circles of hell). Clare could picture every nun that she'd known, including ones who'd not been her teachers. At twenty-four, she thought mostly of what she considered the distressed middle, of lives that were tacky, mean-spirited, and perverse. Smugly perhaps, she ignored the coltish nuns like Sister Arlene and sometimes even the saintly and ethereal nuns like Sister Margret. She thought of the brides of Christ who had given themselves in borrowed wedding dresses and, as symbol of that union, willingly flayed their buttocks with fine chains to mortify flesh (a fact she had recently verified), who from righteousness abused children mentally, and sometimes physically.

In a word, Clare was angry. In two words, she was angry and obsessed. She could not let go of these nuns for she'd not unwound them from the central relationship of her life and everything about it that had grown awkward. Daughter. Mother. She blamed her teachers for her unease, the Sister Mary Andrews and Immaculatas of her life, though she'd not even known them but a milder, Sunday-catechism sort of nun when she first suspected there was something wrong with her mother. *Spiritually* wrong. Fundamentally. A wrongness that Clare breathed in with the incense on a morning in Delaware when her mother dressed early and went with the family to Sunday Mass.

Clare had been nine. There was still grace in church when she prayed, grace that was the part of the church way up at the vaulted ceiling. They were still in church because of God. But Clare sat next to her mother and could not lean against her father's shoulder and ask to use his handkerchief and think grace was love, that it came down from the ceiling and was part of the handkerchief, part of her father's shoulder, and that her brother—that Finn, who always sat on the other side of their father—might not feel it. Her mother, unused to kneeling but stiffly upright, for the very first time was in the way.

"How come you went with us?" Clare asked afterward, lying on her stomach on her parents' bed, her stockinged feet snugged between the mattress and the footboard while her mother changed her chambray suit for a housedress. "You always say you like your church better."

Her mother leaned into the mirror. She unsmudged her lipstick with a finger, and then leaned down and squeezed Clare's heel on her way out the door. "Just an experiment," she said.

By the following March, when they'd moved to Minnesota and Sister Immaculata and Sister Mary Andrew, there was the old trio in church again—Clare, Finn, and their father—and perhaps because she now felt too grown up, Clare did not lean through the space of her mother's absence to rest her head against her father's shoulder. The experiment was over. Clare had heard what her mother told her father. "If it were just a family thing, I'd join in a minute. I know you want me to. But, Bobby, these people expect so much faith."

They'd driven the fourteen hundred miles from Delaware in their Nash. The miles were freezing winter miles. Clare's toes were cold. Her father's shoulders bent tight over the steering wheel, and he peered silently through the space in the windshield that her mother kept scraped clear. Clare felt they'd climbed the map itself, out and up over half the continent to the far north. They had left the sea for this. For bitter cold. For Minnesota. Clare was deeply excited.

But at lunchtime on her first day ever of Catholic school, when Clare saw her father's shirts on the clothesline, shoulder to shoulder, blue and frozen above the arcs of white snow, she felt suddenly strange, certain the colors were upside down. She'd walked home past the rectory where the priest was scraping ice off the steps. The young priest. The assistant. He had a French name, and she'd already learned it. *Father Étienne.* Smoke curled from the cigarette stuck between his fingers on the shovel handle, and Clare watched, fascinated, wondering if he would look up and see her. He didn't, and she'd hurried on up the block to their new yard where her father's shirts made her ache for their real home—the one with the blue waves of sea and eddies of white sails and clouds overhead, and not this ocean of snow. Clare tugged at the line and stuffed clothespins into her pocket and carried the shirts in a stiff armload to her mother, who was waiting at the door.

After lunch, when she'd started back to school, Clare sized up the neighborhood again. There was a house across the street from their house, then two more houses and a lot drifted full of snow, but everything else—school and rectory, the church and the convent—was all St. Francis de Assisi's. Clare looked for Father Étienne, but he wasn't outside any longer and the steps were clear. She crossed the street to the schoolyard and joined the girls from her room in a plot of battered snow angels. The awful cold stung beneath her mittens and her scarf. It was so freezing out it hurt her nose to breathe. Next to her, Jeannie

Carson was balancing one-footed on a wing tip. Clare's boots squished a V shape into an angel head. She glanced quickly at Jeannie and then shifted her eyes. She wondered if they would be friends. Jeannie was eleven already, eleven since January, and she had black hair she said was naturally curly and she had features without anything wrong with them.

"Timmy Porter says he likes you," Jeannie told her, still one-footed. "He's got your missal. He says you'll have to talk to him when he gives it back. All the boys think you're shy. Or else stuck up."

Clare's legs felt blocky from the cold. She didn't know who Timmy Porter was and she hadn't realized her missal was gone. "When does the bell ring?" she asked. She could still see her house. She thought of her mother moving boxes and hanging up pictures, maybe ironing shirts with her hair kept off her forehead with one of Clare's barrettes.

"Exactly one minute before we're too frozen to walk. Sister Josetta spies out the convent window and lets them know in time so we don't drop dead. She is so old. Someday she'll die in the window watching and never tell them and we'll all go with her. Frozen solid dead."

The girls were giggling and Clare was, too, but she wondered if it wasn't maybe a sin or a fault to laugh at a nun, especially an old one. But this was new territory for her, nuns full-time. She didn't really know.

She changed the subject. "I know Sister Immaculata's the principal, but is she smart?" It seemed a pressing question to Clare. All morning recess she had watched Sister patrolling the playground without making up her mind. She had a chalky face shaped like a keyhole, and it made her look a whole lot like a ghost. Her eyes, though, were a bright, Henry Fonda blue. Clare had seen her smile, but she didn't think it was easy for her. Her lips were narrow and stern like George Washington's on the dollar bill.

"You can't tell with nuns. If they're smart they're supposed to offer it up, so you don't really know."

"My brother says if they're smart they wouldn't be here. At least the good-looking ones."

"How do you tell if they're good looking?"

"Did you know when they put their hand under their scapular in front it means they did something wrong?"

Clare was following the conversation, which came from all directions, but the bell rang and everybody lined up double file on the sidewalk. "How come the boys go first?" she whispered, which was the question she'd meant to ask since morning recess.

"Because they can be priests," Jeannie answered, and Susan Taney, Jeannie's best friend, shushed her before Sister Immaculata got to their place in line. Sister walked on past, her lips pursed in a quiet sign and her black cloak trailing on the snow. Jeannie turned around again. "Monsignor was in Japan after the war and he likes ladies last," she whispered. "It's both of those reasons. Uh-oh."

"Jean Anne Carson, one hundred times on the blackboard after school. *I will not talk in line.* Tell Sister Mary Andrew."

"Yes, Sister," Jeannie said, and Clare felt the line moving, and saw Jeannie cross her eyes and sneer at Sister behind her back.

Even with the perspective of young adulthood, Clare viewed Jeannie Carson's old irreverence as both startling and slightly shocking. From her first look at Sister Immaculata, she herself had been wary, and though part of her guardedness came from the awe she might feel at any nun with the apparatus of authority and raiment, of church history and chosenness, Sister Immaculata represented something more. She was commanding. She was full of spiritual certainty. She was bent on sniffing out sin. Grown, Clare was sure of this. But as a child straight from Delaware, she had only sensed it and then brushed it aside for another fear when, fumbling her missal into her desk and mumbling a thank-you to the boy who was Timmy Porter, she watched Sister Mary Andrew turn from the list of pHs she had written on the blackboard and come straight down the aisle toward her.

"There are numbers of spiritual value, of mystical wonder," Sister said. "We must always seek them out." She was rubbing the chalk dust from her hands, and Clare could see her darty-eyed smile, smell a scent that was almost but not quite powder.

"We are studying the ocean in geography, and we may all consider it God's work that Clare McHenry has moved here from the sea-coast to tell us about it in person."

"About the ocean?" Clare asked, surprised.

"Yes. The ocean and the coast."

"Tell us the pU," somebody whispered behind her. Clare wasn't sure if Sister had heard.

"I don't know the numbers," she said and the class, who had all been snickering, laughed out loud.

Sister Mary Andrew thumped her hand on Clare's desk. She was puffy behind her glasses. "I didn't ask you for numbers. I didn't think you were a child to make fun. Is this something to do with your background? With your mother being Protestant?"

"No, Sister." Clare didn't want them to, but her knees had started shaking under her dress so the lines of the plaid jumped. "About the ocean?" she repeated.

"Yes, of course the ocean."

Clare thought her mind was shutting down. She felt scattery. But this was important. Last year in fourth grade, she'd taken a trip with her father and Finn to the ocean station at Woods Hole, and she thought she could remember the report her mother had helped her write. She'd practiced it so many times before she'd given it to her class at Hanbury School. If she could think of the first words, the first sentences . . .

Sister Mary Andrew motioned for her to stand up and Clare did, her hands gripping the wooden lip of her desk, one twitchy knee on the seat. *Shore.* That was the word that she needed. She tried her voice. "The ocean *shore* is different in different places." She sounded all right. She cleared her throat. "Even . . . even on the Eastern Seaboard it's different wherever you go. In the south there are coral reefs. What they're made from is skeletons of sea creatures. Cal*car*eous skeletons."

Clare said the word again in her mind. Cal*car*eous. She could feel all the words coming back now, the pushing rhythm of what she had to say. She went on. "Farther north, the shore is sandy, and the water shapes it into dunes and ridges. And farther north even than that, there are cliffs way above the water. The surf hits the rocks, trying to climb up.

"The sea smells like salt and fish. When you swim, you can taste the salt on your lips. When you float, it holds you up like a big hand. There are seagulls that cry in the air over the boats, and you can count the sea like music. The sea foam always falls back. It can't get loose. It's ivory. It's the color of piano keys."

Clare sat down. She looked at her desk. She crossed her lap with her arms but her legs were still shaking, though not as much. Sister nodded and went back up the aisle. She was talking about echinoderms. She was drawing on the blackboard. "Every inscription is a code from God. Think of the sand dollar. Even its slots. We see the Infinite Wisdom in the very smallest designs of His universe. Consider the governing organization of the five rays in the organs of such creatures. Always five. A celestial plan."

Clare let her breath out. Finally her legs were still. She reached into her desk and took out the book that said geography on it. She opened it to the page written in the corner of the blackboard. She had her own sand dollar. It was in the box on her dresser with her seashells. She'd put the box in last in her suitcase and, when they'd arrived, she unpacked it first and held the shells up to her ear, one by one, and listened to the sea. Her mother had sat on the bed in her new room, in the emptiness, the whiteness, and watched her.

"See, Clare? The sea, Clare," she said. "You've brought it with you."

At afternoon recess, Jeannie Carson practiced backbends on the snow angels.

"I'm sorry I got you in trouble," Clare said.

"What?" Jeannie looked at her, her face upside down between her legs.

"In line. I'm sorry you have to write on the blackboard."

"Like I'd tell Mary Andrew." Jeannie flipped over and scraped the snow off her gloves. "Can you ice-skate? There's a pond behind Schaeffer's. At night the boys that like you try to take you over the banks. But Timmy doesn't like you anymore. All that stuff about the ocean." Jeannie and Susan Taney and the other girls laughed.

Clare was quiet. "What are banks?" she asked then.

"Snowbanks." Susan twisted the end of her ponytail. "From when they clear the ice. They push you over where it's dark and hold you down in the snow and then they kiss you."

"Oh." Clare was surprised, very interested in a cautious sort of way. But she forged ahead with the question that was still on her mind. "Is it always Sister Immaculata for catechism like this afternoon?"

"Ever since Mary Andrew started on her numbers."

Clare nodded. *Numbers. Sister Mary Andrew and her numbers.* And *Mary Andrew.* She tried it to herself without the Sister. "Is Sister—is Mary Andrew a little different?" she said.

"Try a lot," Jeannie answered. "A whole lot. My mother says she was the last one left in the whole convent. Probably she was locked up before we got her. They brought her from the motherhouse when Sister Ellen died."

"I knew a nun who died," Clare said.

The sun was hitting them and Jeannie was knocking icicles off the corner downspout. "Sister Ellen was really old. She was as old as Josetta. She was practically dead for a long time, and she couldn't hear, which meant we could talk all we wanted." Jeannie turned around and looked at Clare. "It was a lot better than Mary Andrew. Mostly we had spelling."

Clare was suddenly eager to tell her own nun story. "Sister Margret wasn't old at all. She's the nun I knew who died. She got so sick you could see right through her. Her face and her hands. She was the music teacher who came to catechism on Sunday." Clare paused, wondering if she should add that Sister Margret was actually the second person she knew who had died. Mr. Macklinaw, the handyman, had had gangrene. *Gangrene.* Finn had told her about it, and she'd looked it up in the dictionary.

"Sunday catechism?" Susan had joined in. "You didn't go to Catholic school?"

"No."

"It's a sin if you live five miles or less from a Catholic school and you don't go." Susan said.

"We lived more," Clare said quickly, and she was sure that was true.

"What do you mean you could see through her?"

"She was so thin. Well not exactly through her. It was like she was blue from the inside. The way you can see through fish sometimes." Clare stopped. Not fish. Not anything to do with the ocean. But she still wasn't done explaining.

"People thought she was holy. They thought she had a halo inside, but William O'Connell said she'd swallowed a flashlight."

"Was that your boyfriend?"

"No."

"So who's William O'Connell?"

"A boy from catechism." Clare opened and closed her fingers, wondering if maybe she was getting frostbite. "His aunt went to Vatican City. To the Sistine Chapel. She bought him a picture with velvet on the back. It was the Sacred Heart. She got it from the nuns on the roof."

"They've got nuns on the roof?"

"His aunt said so. At St. Peter's."

"They're living up there?"

"They make things and they sell them. William didn't really know." Clare was quiet, remembering the picture and the rough and smooth feel of the velvet back. She'd never doubted before that nuns lived on the roof, but it occurred to her now that believing they did wasn't so different from what she'd thought about the priest and the altar boys when she was five—that they never got out of the sanctuary but kept gliding around like the stuffed bears in window displays at Christmastime.

"Immaculata should live on the roof," Jeannie said. "She could stand right up there and watch us all."

———

Unpacking books in her room after supper, Clare thought about Sister Margret again. People had said she had died glowing. She was gentle. She was pretty. Even before she was sick it was as though the hidden part of her body was only air beneath the layers of black cloth. When she sang, her voice was beautiful and clear and she could hit high E. Clare had actually heard her do it though, after she got sick, Sister Mary Corona did the music for catechism and Clare found the notes for everyone since Sister was tone-deaf.

Well she did know some nuns. Or had known. Even if she hadn't gone to Catholic school, she'd met her share of nuns. But Sister Immaculata—Clare stacked the empty book box next to her door—Sister Immaculata was the tough one, the worry in her stomach that wouldn't go away.

Clare took her rosary out of her drawer. She rubbed her finger across the glass faces of the beads. She felt the weight of the beads in her hand, felt their weight as she dropped them back into the drawer. She hadn't gotten over it yet that Sister Immaculata, her own rosary shifting against her habit, had called her out of the room after catechism class. The door had closed. The knob had clicked shut, and they stood in the long, quiet hall. Clare had locked her hands behind her back.

"Your mother's not Catholic," Sister Immaculata said. "Is that correct?"

"Yes, Sister."

Up close, Sister Immaculata was blinkless with her steely eyes. "That's your responsibility," she said. "If you want your mother to be saved, you have to pray for her. It's up to you. You have to do every-thing in your power to bring your mother to the one true Faith."

Clare inched her fingers to the small of her back. She bit at her lip and then asked the question she had to ask. "Sister, isn't it sup-posed to be if you don't believe you have to be Catholic, you can still go to heaven if you're good?"

Sister Immaculata studied her with a look like Finn's when he wanted to hit her. "Is your mother intelligent, Clare?" she asked finally.

"She is," Clare answered.

"An intelligent person, Clare, should know that Our Lord founded His one true Church on Peter—*upon this rock*, Clare—and that the apostolic succession is only through the Papacy. Pray for your mother, Clare. Pray to Our Blessed Lady that your mother will not reject the grace of God and lose her soul."

Sister had turned to go, but then she looked back. "Return to your classroom now."

Clare had been quiet before she made herself answer. "Yes, Sister."

Yes, Sister. Was that all she could say? Clare was mad at herself. She was mad at Sister Immaculata. She wondered if Monsignor Evans and Father Étienne thought the same way that Sister did, though she doubted she'd ever find out. She had the strong impression that priests were off limits, that nuns were like a huddle of protectors surrounding them, or maybe like blockers in the football games she'd watched with her father in the Hanbury den.

Then there was her. Clare McHenry. When Sister Immaculata went on the attack, Clare McHenry hadn't stood up for her mother. She'd asked one question, and that was it.

Clare banged the dresser drawer shut and went back to the shelves. She evened the books along the front edge. Then she plopped backward onto the bed, pulling her pillow into her stomach. She'd wanted new curtains, but she knew she wasn't getting them, though she was getting a new bedspread. Her mother had told her it would be an early birthday present, and Clare thought it was mostly to make up for the paint. She'd asked for yellow walls—not a bright yellow but a cozy, delicate shade. She had had it all pictured in her mind: yellow walls and bookshelves and then a spread and curtains and rugs in the colors of seashells—soft corals and pinks, pale yellow and cream. And blue-green for accent. Definitely not a plain blue but aquamarine like the stone she'd seen once in a museum.

Her father had put his foot down. They weren't painting again when the last owner had just done it and they'd paid for it in the house price.

"And white goes with everything," her mother had added. "I like it."

Clare had wanted to argue, but she'd stopped herself. She knew she couldn't say that it felt like the snow came right inside, that it was as if her room was in a great big icy loop with the whole outdoors.

She got up and plumped her pillow straight and then went to her dresser. She'd already put away her jeans and wool slacks. Her underwear and blouses were in the top drawer and her jumper and blue dress and saddle shoes were in the closet. All she had to do was stick her shorts and summer tops and then her swimsuit in the middle drawer and she'd be done with boxes in her room.

But that would make it official. Moving summer here.

Clare stood with her elbows bent on the dresser, looking in the mirror and tugging at her earlobes and wondering if other people thought her ears were her best feature the way her mother did. She wasn't really sure she needed a swimsuit. She didn't know where it was people swam here. When it came down to it, she wasn't even sure they had summer.

Clare made a face at herself in the mirror and decided she was in a bad mood. She could hear Finn's radio in his room, and every once in a while something banged against the wall and that was like Finn—an occasional sound from his room when he was home, but not much more. At supper, he hadn't said two words. She didn't even know if he liked the high school.

She heard her mother's voice and then a bump at her door. Clare opened it. Her mother was there, holding curtains. The top half of her—the glasses and the gingham housedress part—looked the same as usual, but from the arms down, she was all white organdy and ruffles. "Washed and mended and ironed," she said, putting the curtains over the end of the bed, and Clare went out to the kitchen to get a chair so she could reach the curtain rod hooks.

Her father was at the table with his work papers in front of him. Clare waited next to him and when he finished the sentence he was writing, he leaned back and put his arm around her.

"So it was a pretty good first day?" he asked.

Clare thought of saying that it really hadn't been. Instead, she nodded, aware that looking at her father's eyes was a lot like looking at her own. They were the same blue—medium dark and a little grayish.

"It was fine. Do you still like your job?" she asked, and she hoped she didn't sound as if she wished that he didn't. She knew about moving. It didn't get undone. You said good-bye to your friends and went to the next new place and even if it was in Delaware and you wanted to go back to the last one, you couldn't really do it. You could write letters and hope your friends would write back, but it probably wasn't going to happen.

"I like it," he said, and Clare put her arm around his neck and felt the wool of his sweater and the prick of his whiskers against her cheek when she hugged him. He'd started his job at the college at the beginning of the semester, and eight weeks later he'd taken the train back to Hanbury so the whole family could drive here. Clare had missed him those eight weeks. She'd missed him a lot.

"Clare, are you bringing the chair?" her mother called and Clare let go of her father and slowly started walking the chair back, moving it one leg at a time. She turned around. "Mother says she's not going to church with us Sunday."

"So?"

"I thought maybe she would." Clare waited a second, but her father was looking at his papers again, his pen moving in its sideways stutter before he began to write. She picked the chair up and lifted it over the boxes.

In the bedroom, the curtains, with the rods her mother had ruffled through them, were spread out across the bed. Her mother was cleaning her glasses. Clare put the chair down in front of the window. She knew her mother was tired. In the morning before her father had left for work, he'd been down in the basement moving things, swearing and working on the washer hoses. Now his shirts, with their double-starched collars and cuffs, were not only washed but ironed and put away. The boxes in the kitchen were gone and the café curtains were up on the window over the sink.

"You're a poky," her mother said.

"I was talking to Dad."

"Stand on the chair and I'll hand you the end of the rod."

The curtains were the crisscross ones from the upstairs hall in Hanbury. They were big for the window, but when she and her mother pushed the tacks through the tiebacks into the window frame and pulled each curtain up through the loop so it draped in an arc, Clare thought they looked OK.

"Here's your dresser scarf," her mother said, and Clare smoothed it out, slipping the far corner under her lamp that had the milkglass hurricane shade, and thought she was batting a thousand. Or maybe zero. Everything in the room was absolutely white.

"You can have Aunt Sophie's rug," her mother said getting up from the bed, and Clare looked at her, surprised. It was an all right rug. Her great aunt had made it for the entryway in Hanbury. It wasn't really any color, and she guessed it didn't matter since she wasn't using her seashell shades. But things were getting filled in awfully fast.

When her mother came back with the rug, Clare helped unroll it next to the bed. Her father had come, too. He had a brown Sears package in his hands. "Surprise," her mother said, taking it from him and handing it to Clare.

Clare unwrapped the paper. There was plastic inside and she took that off, too. "A bedspread," she said. She held it up. It was shiny with a ruffle and it had stitching that made diamond shapes all across the top. "It's blue," she said, and it *was* blue. It was nothing like aquamarine. It was the very same blue as the Virgin Mary's dress—the one painted on the statue she'd kept staring at during morning Mass.

"I saw it on sale before we left." Her mother glanced at her father. "We both thought you'd like it. Here. I'll help you."

"It's very pretty," Clare said as her mother shook the spread out across the bed. She made herself take hold of the side and measure it against the floor to get the bottom straight.

"It is. I'll help you with your last box of clothes. Is Finn still in his room?"

"He won't care."

"At least you can show him. Finn?" Her mother opened a drawer and reached down to the box to take out the summer clothes.

A minute went by and Clare, watching her mother, heard her brother's door open and the radio get louder. Then Finn stuck his head in the room.

"Clare's room is finished. See the new bedspread?"

"So it looks like a room," Finn said, and Clare heard his door shut again, and the volume was quieter on the radio.

"It's very nice. Thank you." Clare kissed both her parents. Then she stood by the bed and hoped they would leave so she could get ready for bed and turn out the lights. Her whole room seemed like a shrine. It was like some immaculate shrine to a thing that was cold and distant and scary. She didn't know at all how she'd stand it.

⌣

In April, the snow began to melt. Sunlight streamed into Clare's eyes when she walked to school. Water ran down the snow to the curb. It reminded her of rain when it carved its way through the sand on the way to the ocean.

Clare stopped in front of the rectory and waited for the crossing guard. She knew if she'd been five minutes earlier she would have seen Father Étienne coming out the front door on his way to say Mass, his coat open over his cassock and a cigarette in his hand. She knew he would have smiled at her and said hello, that he even remembered her name since Sister Immaculata had had her help him stuff envelopes in the cafeteria after school one day. It had been dusk, almost night-fall when they finished and Father Étienne had said he would stand outside the rectory until she got home. She'd run the whole block so he didn't have to wait long. She'd gone as fast as she could, hoping he would realize how speedy she was, and how thoughtful. But the next day when she saw him, he laughed and asked if she'd been afraid of the dark. Clare was hot with embarrassment and incapable of saying what she'd really meant. And she was acutely aware that all the girls were right. Father Étienne was very handsome for a priest.

It was Finn's fault she was late this morning. Their mother was hosting her music club, and Finn had left for school without taking the garbage out. It meant Clare had to do it, and the bag had broken, spilling coffee grounds on both her and the snow. She still had a stain on her sock.

The crossing guard was done letting the traffic go. He had his parka on with the hood up and Clare wasn't sure who he was until he walked into the street with his flag. She looked just long enough to see it was Jeff Grauer, the boy Jeannie said was the cutest boy in eighth grade, except that his ears stuck out.

When Clare dipped her finger in the holy water at the church doorway, Jeannie and Susan were already in the fifth-grade pews. Clare crossed herself and went down the side aisle. Quickly, she glanced over her shoulder. Sister Immaculata was across the center aisle, ram-rod straight in the pew behind the eighth graders. She was like a big shadow, and she had the whole, dark, vaulted space of the church behind her. Clare thought maybe she was praying to St. Peter (gatekeeper in the sky, as her father called him). Maybe she was scolding him: *Clare McHenry's mother goes straight to hell unless you intercede with that child, unless you turn her stubborn heart to the will of God.*

Clare genuflected, and Jeannie moved over so there was room for her to kneel down. Clare crossed herself again and folded her hands straight up, which Sister Mary Andrew said was the most reverent way to pray, and the best for people's posture. Sister was full of such admonishments, and Clare didn't really know which ones to take seriously. All the girls thought Sister was crazy, and maybe she was, but Clare had only seen her stymied once. She'd been talking about Mary's example of purity, which was her favorite subject, and Jeannie asked her why Joseph saying he hadn't acted as Mary's husband before the Angel Gabriel appeared was proof either one of them was a virgin afterward. Sister had choked red and stared Jeannie back into her seat and said the question was inappropriate and that every girl should remember never to let a boy touch her between the shoulders and the knees. Then Jeannie had asked if that meant holding hands was a mortal sin and French-kissing was OK, and Sister had sent her to the corner, and Timmy Porter had turned around to Clare and said, "Give me a Frenchy."

The bell rang in the sanctuary, and the altar boys and Father Étienne came out for Mass. Clare stood up with everyone else, and watched Father genuflect at the altar. Once, when Sister Immaculata had asked her to put funeral programs in the pews, she'd caught sight of Father through the door to the sacristy. He was getting ready to say the funeral Mass, and he'd stooped to kiss one of the vestments before putting it around his neck. It surprised her. It also made her feel she was witnessing something private that she shouldn't have seen. Later, she asked Finn what he was doing, and Finn said he didn't know, that they all did it, that priests had a whole rigmarole for getting their vestments on and he was glad he was done being an altar boy. He hated wearing a dress.

For Finn, it had been a lot of commentary, but Clare had hardly been satisfied. On library day, she'd hurried getting a book to check out, and then looked up vestments in the *Catholic Encyclopedia*. She knew what they were now—not just the cassock and chasuble, but the amice and alb, the cincture and the maniple, the stole. She liked thinking of Father Étienne—of any priest—following the exact order of things, which started with putting the linen amice over his cassock to cover his shoulders.

But all that fabric. Did priests sweat? Did they smell like her father when he spaded the garden. Should she even be wondering that?

Father Étienne knelt down and so did Clare. She looked back at the stain on her sock and then at the side altar where the statue of Mary rose blue-robed and eight feet tall over the vigil lights. There was nothing she could do about either the sock or the statue, but they both bothered her. In the night she'd had the same dream she'd had at least twice since her room was done. Mary stood life-sized on the dresser in front of her mirror, her hands stretched out, and Clare smelled flowers and felt tears that were sticky. They were her tears, but they were the statue's, too.

Clare closed her eyes, then blinked them open on the main altar where Father Étienne had started the Ordinary of the Mass. Everybody was giving the responses, and she tried matching her pitch to Jeannie's, making it lower. She knew she wasn't really used to this yet—to Mass every day. She didn't have the practice the others did, and she certainly didn't understand how to take it for granted. Susan Taney could rattle off Latin and file her nails at the same time, and Jeannie sorted her holy cards like a poker player, which seemed basically like sacrilege to Clare. But of course Susan and Jeannie weren't expected to pray about their mothers. Their mothers were OK. In the whole class, only Clare came from a mixed marriage, which was what Sister Immaculata and the church directory both called it. Her father's name had an "M" printed next to it. It stood alone in the white space.

But Clare could feel the holiness of the Mass. She had always felt it, though it had come to her more and more in Lent. And now in the time after Easter, when the bell finally rang for the Consecration she felt the stirring strangeness of it, the solemnness of Father Étienne in his white vestments making God out of the host in his upstretched hands. At Communion, she knelt at the altar railing and let the Communion wafer seal her tongue dry when Father placed it on her tongue, and that was God, too, though she struggled trying to sense it, to think of the presence of God instead of her fear she would bite the host and Father Étienne would see her do it. But when she stood up and the host came unstuck—when it softened and she folded it over with her tongue and then swallowed it—God, the faraway God she had always known, returned. He lived in the airy heights of the church and in the candle flames that burned and shifted on the altar.

Back in her pew, Clare folded her hands tight. Every day now she fasted and went to Communion. She took a sack breakfast to school to eat after Mass, though she knew her classmates had started to whisper, that they watched as she cut the "I" on the side of her cereal box and bent the flaps back to dribble in milk, and then told each other she was too religious, that she was headed for a vocation, for the convent, going to Communion every single morning. Clare didn't know how to say what she really felt, that whatever it was it wasn't holy, that she was searching for God, all right, but not for the Word made flesh that Sister Mary Andrew asked for with her eyes blazing heavenward in prayer. Instead, Clare wanted a word made of sound. She felt desperate for a God who spoke, a God who could tell her firsthand if Sister Immaculata really had things right, if her mother's soul was in mortal danger.

What she needed was a miracle, and not the kind in Delaware when Sister Mary Corona said the name she'd drawn from a hat was the Holy Ghost's pick of the person in catechism class who'd made the best preparation for First Communion. She'd read the name to herself and then put the boy's black missal with the red marker away for a year when a boy would be holiest and handed a white missal with gold leaf pages and a blue page marker to Sandy Thomas—paper-thin Sandy Thomas, Sandy Thomas who was the color of paper. William O'Connell said it was all a hoax, that the whole thing was nothing like the miracles his aunt had heard about in Rome, but even though Clare hadn't been chosen, she had wanted very much to believe the miracle was real. Now, though, she needed a miracle she really could count on. She didn't want some Sister Mary Corona kind of go-between. She needed something absolutely certain.

There was a noise, a scuffle behind her, and Clare looked around. Sister Mary Andrew was leaning over the pew back with her hand on the neck of Timmy Porter's shirt. She was hissing something at him, and Timmy looked bulgy-eyed, but Clare knew he could look that way even without getting strangled.

Jeannie nudged her. "He's got egg on his face," she whispered. "Look. In the corner of his mouth. He went to Communion without fasting. He's in for it."

Clare looked at Jeannie, sensing the scandal, and watched Sister pushing Timmy out of the pew and up the aisle toward the door.

"Where's she taking him?" she whispered, but Jeannie didn't answer. Mass was over and they stood up when Father Étienne left the sanctuary, and then they filed out after the fourth grade.

In the classroom, Clare ate her cereal and put the box in the wastebasket. Timmy and Sister Mary Andrew hadn't come back, and the whole class was quiet. It was eerie how still the room was. Clare took a notebook out of her desk. She wondered what was happening to Timmy—what his punishment was and if it was going on right now and if it was what you'd expect from Sister's face: hell since she'd kill him before he got to Confession, and hell for her, too, because of the murder.

Clare drew a picture of the devil in her notebook and gave him a pitchfork with five prongs. She drew Sister and Timmy next to him, and then she scratched everything out. She'd seen Sister hit Timmy. Blood had come out of his ear. But Timmy was thick and strong. He could get away before she'd really hurt him, and by now Sister Immaculata would be involved. Maybe Father Étienne. Maybe Monsignor Evans. Maybe even the bishop.

"Clare, give me a red so I can finish up," Susan Taney said, poking her in the shoulder.

"Finish what?" Clare turned around.

"You didn't do one?"

Clare looked at the design on Susan's desk. It was every color, and all the shapes in her brother's geometry book. "What's that?" she asked.

"Nobody told you? Geez, Clare, you'd better hurry. She'll probably be here any second."

"Told me what? Do *what*?" Clare had her crayons out, but she held on to the red one, waiting for an answer.

"Give it to me. You're supposed to draw a picture of the Holy Ghost. It's squares and weird triangles and it turns out with wings shaded in the middle. Like this." Susan turned her paper around. "When somebody gets dragged out of Mass, we have to do it for a penance."

"Doesn't she forget?"

"Not in the morning. How do you suppose she'd forget when everybody's got one?"

Clare scanned the classroom. With all the patterned squares on the desks, it looked a whole lot like her idea of a quilting bee. "You can copy mine when I'm done," Susan said, taking the crayon. "But give it back the second she opens the door."

"Hurry," Clare said, trying not to panic. She stared at the top of Susan's head, where her French braid started. She chewed at the corner of her lip. Finally Susan handed the picture over, but the room wasn't quiet anymore. Everybody else had finished working. Everybody was talking. A squishy spitball landed on Clare's desk, and she pushed it off and saw Jeannie plug a spitball right between Rocco Mulleto's eyes. Clare drew her pencil down her ruler edge. She drew more lines while paper airplanes whipped past her head. She felt stupid and worried. More than anything, she was mad.

By the time the door opened, the whole class was wild. The wastebasket had a ring of spitballs around it and one was stuck to the wall. There was a squadron of airplanes under Sister's desk. Rocco had climbed onto Brent Anderson's shoulders trying to stick an airplane on the light fixture, but Bret dumped him off fast and slid into his seat. Clare saw him when she reached down to pass Susan's paper back. She had three more colors to fill in, and she pulled her notebook onto her lap and kept on working.

"What's going on in here?" It was Sister Immaculata, not Sister Mary Andrew, and Clare felt her hand stiffen, but she kept on coloring, kept pressing with the crayons until she felt sweat on her lip. But there. She'd made it. It wasn't as neat maybe as it should be, but her Holy Ghost was done.

Sister Immaculata was silent and erect in front of the blackboard, her hands folded. She was facing the wastebasket, but her gaze was straight ahead and Clare thought she was too tall to see down to the floor. There were the lips again, the outline like thread sewn into the same color fabric so it nearly disappeared.

"Sister Mary Andrew has been detained." Sister Immaculata pushed her beads all the way under her scapular. "Jean Ann Carson, you will lead the class in its reading assignment. There will be silence except for reading. Clare McHenry, come with me." Sister Immaculata turned and then stopped at the door, her back to the class and to Clare, who'd gotten up to follow her. "And Rocco Muletto and Brenton Anderson, clean up that disgusting mess."

Walking toward the door, Clare felt even more irritated and embarrassed than she usually did when Sister Immaculata came to get her. She almost tripped. She caught herself but, for a second, she thought the floor would come right up and smack her in the face. Sister had left the room, and Clare hurried to catch up with her as she strode down the hall and straight past the office and down the stairs. For a second Clare thought Sister's beads would catch on the railing, but she whisked them under her scapular again and kept going. Clare hurried to open the outside door for her. As she pushed on the handle, the sun flashed off the windows into her eyes.

Outside, the sidewalk was mostly dry and the snow had shrunk away from its edge. Clare could see a brown fringe of grass started. She could see the shadows her legs made and the round shadow that was

Sister—the moving shape of her skirts darkening the sidewalk. "Don't we need our coats?" she asked. "I mean your cloak?"

Sister didn't turn around. A car was going by in the street and its tires slapped against the melting snow. The sunshine glinted in stripes over Sister's shoulder. It was warm on Clare's face, but the cold air was like the shower in Hanbury when the hot water ran out. She felt goose-bumpy on her arms.

"We're only going to the convent," Sister answered, and Clare sidestepped a puddle in the alley and looked down the old convent wall toward the new wing where there were cement blocks and pieces of lumber frozen into the snow. She felt a little push, the scary little pulse of excitement in her chest. She'd never been inside a convent.

"Clean your feet," Sister Immaculata said on the convent porch. "A brisk walk on a warm day and you're shivering? Here's Sister to let us in. You'll wait inside."

Clare was hoping for maybe young Sister Arlene hurrying back to the second grade with something she'd forgotten, but it was Sister Josetta who opened the door. She smiled at Clare out of her wrinkles. Clare stood by the door and looked at her shoes to make sure they hadn't left a mark. Sister Josetta smelled ancient. She smelled like musty leather and Clare wondered what it would be like to touch her. She watched as Sister Immaculata went down the dark hall with her long stride. It was almost as if she was gliding—skating really—and Clare looked at Sister Josetta and then blushed, which was about skating, but under a moon that had turned both the snow and Timmy Porter's face blue when he flattened her over the banks and they sprawled in the rough snow beyond the pond. She'd gotten away from him. His kiss had landed on the back of her scarf, but she'd had a bruise from his skate blade for more than a week.

"Goodness, dear." Sister Josetta was so old she was tiny. It was like she came in a different size. "What would your mother say with you outside in that thin dress?" She smiled again and touched Clare's sleeve. "Sit down over there. On the sofa. What's your name? Did Sister tell me? I don't always hear."

Clare spoke up. "Clare McHenry. Clare."

"Oh. The new girl." Sister Josetta looked uncertain and Clare could see how yellow her eyes were behind her glasses. "I suppose even a Protestant mother would worry if a child caught cold," she said, and she sat down in the chair by the door. She picked a book up from the window ledge and Clare thought it looked like a missal, but Sister didn't open it. She held on to it with her old hands and closed her eyes.

Clare looked around. The room was something like an entryway or maybe like a parlor that was open on one side. There were bookshelves and an old spinet and overstuffed furniture with doilies on the backs, and the walls were green and there weren't any pictures, only a crucifix. She was sitting in an alcove. The curtains were drawn and it was almost dark, stuffy, but on the other side of the doorway in front of the stairs, sunlight from the window spun dust specks in the air and turned Sister's habit brown.

Clare pulled at the nail of her index finger. She wanted to ask if she could look at the books or try the piano, but she thought Sister was asleep. She shifted her feet, then pulled at the curtain behind her to look outside. She heard a door open and close. She thought she heard footsteps, and she listened for the sound coming toward her.

"Clare?" Sister Immaculata's face came out of the darkness and, in her hurry to close the curtain, Clare kicked the sofa leg and stumbled upright.

"Come with me. Now."

"Yes, Sister." Clare tiptoed around Sister Josetta and followed Sister Immaculata's back, and even in the dimness, the near dark, it was all angles. Clare counted doors. One on the left. Two on the right. Sister had her hand on a doorknob and was turning it, pushing it open—all the way open.

"Here she is, Mrs. Porter," Sister Immaculata said.

At twenty-four, when she regaled her friends with her nun stories, Clare could always make them laugh. Seated at a table in a bar, her tongue just loosened by whiskey, she sketched out her comedy of stock characters and situations. To Sister Geraldine, her seventh-grade nun, she gave a mustache and a frequent belch. She embroidered the story of Sister John Davida, whom she'd liked well enough, so that Sister not only banished an actual future rock-and-roll groupie and an actual future convicted rapist to the closed wardrobes for an hour together, but ordered them there for whole afternoons of suspicious thumpings. She plumped up Sister Mary Andrew by a hundred pounds and added spurious lectures on gluttony to Sister's actual and frequent lectures on sexual purity, which Clare had found both interesting and worrying and which she was certain had finally led Timmy Porter to his transgression and the first serious four-letter word she'd ever heard.

Clare forgave herself these exaggerations. They let her contain her anger at her general residue of nun-induced guilt. But she had no need to change her picture of Timmy Porter's mother. Marianna Porter had stood next to Timmy in the convent study, and she was young and beautiful. She was also very pregnant. She was, in fact, the most startlingly pregnant woman Clare had ever seen. Older, Clare knew it was the sensuality that had surprised her, a pregnancy somehow redolent of its origins. But as a child she was curious and embarrassed without knowing why. Her mind had become a war zone of puzzled names and images: the Virgin Birth. Mary, virgin and Mother of God, diocesan tributes in the form of corsages for mothers of large families, yet a hint of taint even for them since they'd lost the chance to join the choir of heavenly virgins who sang a song that no one else understood (or so Sister Mary Andrew said), her own mother, with just two children and no church approval of any kind, biting off the thread from a sock she was darning and telling Clare with a little smile that sex made babies, that it gave pleasure, and that some married couples had a schedule for it.

Timmy Porter's mother's swollen stomach and heavy breasts spoke to all this, to Clare's mental turbulence, and Clare couldn't take her eyes away.

"Timothy, tell Clare what you told your mother and me," Sister Immaculata said.

There was a sort of hiccough from Timmy, and Clare realized he'd been crying. In a great effort at politeness, she turned away and studied the room. There was a typewriter on the desk, and there were rows of empty shelves that were dusty on the edges, and boxes stacked along the far wall. The molding was off along the floor and somebody had started to take the carpet up.

Timmy's mother said something to him in a low voice Clare couldn't hear and then turned to Sister Immaculata. "I don't think he needs to repeat it, Sister," she said. "He's told us once."

"Very true, Mrs. Porter," Sister answered. Her fingers rested on the desktop. "Clare, it is correct that you told Timothy your mother gave you permission not to fast before Communion?"

Clare pulled her head up in surprise. "What?" She thought she'd heard wrong. She was sure she'd heard wrong.

"Your mother lets you eat before Communion?"

"No, Sister. Of course she doesn't. Timmy, I never said that."

Sister's face was compressed in a frown. "Clare?"

"I always fast. I bring my breakfast. My mother never told me that. Never."

"So you deny it, Clare? You deny you dared Timothy to break his fast?"

"Dared him?" Clare stared at Sister's tapping fingertips.

"It seems we have a difference in stories," Sister Immaculata said.

"It seems you have a difference, Sister," Mrs. Porter said. "Timothy wouldn't do this without encouragement, although I doubt this child's at fault." She looked at Clare—kindly, Clare thought, and Clare felt emboldened, ready to defend both her mother and herself. She was about to say something when Mrs. Porter gasped. Her face went pale and then scarlet. She reached for a chair, clenching her fists on the back. Clare saw a trickle of blood on her stockings. Then a second one. Then a rivulet.

Clare drew back. She was startled and thoroughly alarmed. What was happening? She thought she should help, but she had no idea what help would be. And it was clear Sister Immaculata didn't know at all what she should do. She was trying to get Mrs. Porter into the chair, but awkwardly, and she looked like she'd just seen a rat. Timmy was useless. Timmy was crying.

"Get Sister. Go, Clare," Sister Immaculata said, her voice still commanding, but also uncertain and shrill. Clare hesitated.

"Sister Josetta?" she said, wondering what in the world Sister Josetta would do.

"*My husb*—" Mrs. Porter managed before a terrible moan cut off her words. Timmy went from blubbering to shrieking. He was squeezing his mother's hands.

"What's his number, Timmy?" Clare asked. "Your dad's. What is it?" she insisted, and when Timmy choked out an answer, she scratched the number invisibly on her hand and walked to the desk and dialed the phone.

Then she was sitting with Sister Josetta back in the entryway where Sister Immaculata had sent her. A hurrying Mr. Porter came for Mrs. Porter and, with all the traffic in and out and Mrs. Porter's cries and screams, Clare nearly forgot to wonder where her own mother was if mothers were supposed to be at Sister's meeting. Timmy's aunt picked him up and, watching him leave, Clare thought if she were actually good, she would forgive him—even about her bruise. But what she really felt like doing was hitting him for lying about her. Just socking him one. And now here was Sister Immaculata ordering her back to the study again.

"Will they be all right?" Clare asked. "Mrs. Porter and her baby?"

"If God wills it. If it's God's will."

Clare thought about this. "May I go?" she asked. "I'm missing geography."

"We have unfinished business, Clare." Sister Immaculata went into the study and closed the door after them. She faced the curtains behind the desk. She waited so long in silence that Clare thought she must be praying.

When she turned around, Clare saw the chilly steel of her eyes, and her chin raised so her wimple stretched. "To sin oneself, Clare," she said, "is serious enough. To encourage another to sin is even worse. But to lie, Clare, in the face of that sin, is to do the work of the devil himself."

Clare felt the words more than she heard them. They were staccato. They were hard like the sound of a hammer on nails. She swallowed. She knew she had to say something. She had to tell Sister how wrong she was, to convince her that Timmy had lied.

But Sister had turned away again. She was reaching for the cord on the curtains and she pulled them open. From her side of the room, Clare saw the brown statue of St. Francis in the corner where the old part of the convent joined the new. St. Francis had his hands raised up. He had sparrows on his robes.

"There, Clare. Watch for the cardinals," Sister said quietly and, as Clare looked up, two red cardinals flew down from nowhere and landed on the statue's hands.

"He works His miracles even in our garden. See how His grace is everywhere?" Sister tapped at the window, but the cardinals stayed put. They were brilliant and red, nestled in the hands of St. Francis.

A miracle? Her miracle?

Clare looked at Sister. She felt very strange. She felt a rush of blood to her face like the beating of the cardinals' wings as they'd landed, and she remembered something. Yesterday morning looking out the picture window, she'd seen Jeannie in her red coat on her way to school. Clare had banged her piano book shut and grabbed her coat and hurried to catch up with her, but her mother had come out on the porch and called her back to get her breakfast. Clare had run while Jeannie waited, and her mother waved at Jeannie and handed Clare the sack. And then she had said it: "Clare, if you'd just give up your dietary laws." Clare had known it was joke. But what if Jeannie had heard and didn't understand? What if she'd told Timmy?

Clare knew she was being terribly quiet. There was something shifting in her, some dark wall going up in her mind like the sea wall against a hurricane. Mrs. Porter was having a baby, and there was something changing inside of Clare.

"You do know, Clare, that His grace is everywhere?"

Clare raised her head. She nodded slowly. "Yes, Sister," she answered.

"Then you admit now, Clare, what you've done?"

Clare stood there. She wanted to say she didn't know, but that was like saying she hadn't seen the miracle, and so she was quiet.

"We'll pray together, Clare," Sister said. We'll pray for God's grace for you and for your mother. This way." Sister Immaculata had knelt down, but now she stretched herself out across the floor, her face down and her arms above her head.

"Pray, Clare," she said, her voice muffled, and though something fierce inside her still held back, Clare did.

———

In the middle of April, two important things happened. Clare, to her surprise, was elected Queen of the May. Then Sister Josetta died. The election was a problem for Clare's mother, who tried to sort out the household budget to find money for a long white dress. For a while, Clare thought she would have to wear her curtains.

"If only I could sew better," her mother said, eyeing the ruffles, and when she frowned but didn't say anything more, Clare told herself the rest of what she knew her mother was thinking. Yes, really she *would* like to sew well. She'd like to sew and to crochet wonderful shawls and afghans like Aunt Sophie did, but she didn't have the right sort of hand-eye coordination, though of course she did play the piano very well and Aunt Sophie said she envied her her music, her education, that for herself she'd give up sewing and crocheting and throw in her hooked rugs if she could just carry a tune in church.

Clare didn't know if Aunt Sophie was right. She loved music but you couldn't touch a sound the way you could trace your finger over wool or find a pattern locked inside the stitches. And besides, she thought as she pulled her slippers on, you certainly couldn't wear a song to climb the ladder to crown the statue of Mary.

She opened the door of her room. She was up early because she wanted to talk to both her parents, to say she was ready to give up her allowance for as long as it took to pay for fabric and somebody to sew a dress. She could hear the sounds in the kitchen, the radio on low and the ting and scrape of silverware on dishes. She went through the hall and into the living room, padding on the rug. She heard the quiet murmur of her parents' voices. They were not having a conversation, not the normal out loud kind. There was something whispery, private in their voices, and it made Clare hesitant. Once in Hanbury, she'd come on her mother crying in the bathroom, scrubbing her nightgown and robe in a tub of bloody water. "It's nothing. I'm OK. I'll explain later," she'd said, but she never had and Clare had grown careful, fearful of secrets that belonged to adults.

Clare waited for a moment longer to see if she could hear any actual words. Then she tiptoed back across the rug to her room and got in bed. She held the blankets under her chin and thought about the dress and whether she should write to her friends in Hanbury and tell them she was May Queen. She didn't think she would. It would seem like bragging and, anyway, her Hanbury friends didn't go to Catholic school and wouldn't even know about crowning the statue of Mary. For that matter, none of them were Catholic except for William O'Connell, and she couldn't write to him because he was a boy. And, anyway, the friends she'd written to hadn't written back.

Clare was still thinking about the dress on the way to school when she learned about Sister Josetta. She'd decided the trim should be eyelet, and then she saw Jeff Grauer and the black ribbon on his patrol flag and had the breathless thought she could ask him what it was for, actually talk to him herself. She was considering dropping her long tablet that didn't fit into her satchel or even dropping the satchel, and wondering if he would pick it up and she could ask him and she'd hear what his voice sounded like up close. But when she started across the street, trying to get her nerve up, her spelling list fell out of her tablet all by itself and she and Jeff cracked heads leaning over to get it. Clare felt all the blood in her body travel straight to her hair roots and then straight to her feet.

He handed her her paper. "Boy you have a hard head," he said. Clare didn't look at him. "You girls are supposed to go to the choir loft. Or are you old enough for choir? There're songs for Sister Josetta before Mass."

"I'm old enough. Is it her birthday?" Clare said. "I mean her name day?"

"She's dead," Jeff answered, and Clare nodded, remembering the black ribbon, and hurried on across the street and into the church instead of walking slowly and waiting for Father Étienne to appear.

Heading up the steps to the choir loft, Clare was thinking about the dress again. Then she had the sudden, queer thought that all this worry about clothes was wrong when there'd been a death in the convent. And Sister Josetta—Sister Josetta was dead. Old perfumed Sister Josetta was asleep forever, and not for a catnap sleep like she took the day Timmy Porter's sister was born and Sister Mary Andrew stopped being the fifth-grade teacher. Sister Josetta was asleep for good.

Clare looked up and held on tight to the railing as she climbed. The stairs were one long spiral, a coil that went clear to the rafters. The first time she'd climbed them, she'd thought she couldn't do it. She'd closed her eyes, feeling gingerly for the steps. Then she'd opened them a slit, and when she leaned into the curve by accident, she realized she could go higher. She kept leaning and she held her eyes level and she was like her father, learning a lesson that she had to learn, though for him it was climbing the ladder on his ship in the navy.

Clare was at the darkest part of the stairs. She could hear voices whispering farther up, and she wondered if the sound was coming down the rail the way William O'Connell had said words carried halfway around the Sistine Chapel when you said them quietly and in the right place. Clare held on to the rail, listening. It was Jeannie's whisper: *Immaculata must have rigged the box. She's her pet.* And Susan's answer: *But how? I counted thirty-one ballots.* Jeannie again:

Some nun way. They work it so it comes out the way they want. Susan, shhh!

Clare caught at the rail with her other hand and held on. The stairs were ringing and vibrating. They were tuned to the G-sharp below middle C with somebody coming up, somebody heavy like a grown-up. Clare took the last steps that curved into the loft and saw Jeannie and Susan with their noses in their missals. *Fakers. Fakers, fakers.* She found an open kneeler next to Rocco Muletto's older sister, and watched the light by the stair dim and go brighter as the footsteps grew louder and came into the loft.

"Clare McHenry."

Clare looked up. *Sister Mary Andrew.* She unbent her knees and slowly pushed herself upright.

"Good morning, Sister." Clare was wary, her mind racing through the weeks of rumors that said Sister, who'd gone completely bonkers—drooling like a rabid dog when she'd dragged Timmy out of church—was locked up in the state hospital in St. Peter—that, given its name, she'd thought she'd found the perfect pH and ascended into heaven, that if she ever showed up here again it would mean she'd escaped.

"Clare," Sister said, bending down, and she was larger than Clare remembered, squarish and with one brown mole under her glasses and another on her hand. "Clare McHenry, Queen of the May. While you're crowning the statue of Mary, Sister Josetta will be holding the crown for Our Lady in heaven."

Clare nodded and was very careful not to look at Jeannie and Susan, though she assumed they were smirking.

There was more noise on the stairs, more girls were arriving, and then Sister Immaculata herself had come into the choir loft. "So here you are, Sister," she said. "If you'd kneel in the back." Sister Immaculata stood by the organ and looked around at the girls. "Sister Josetta was novice master for Sister's class, and she's been allowed to join us this morning. The bishop will cook his own eggs." Sister Immaculata was almost smiling, though her lips still looked salted and left to dry.

But Sister Mary Andrew was a cook and worked for the bishop! She wasn't locked up.

The stairs clanged again and Mrs. Thompkins the organist panted into view. She had little beads of rain on her hair that were like a net on top of the frizz. Clare wondered just when it had started to rain out, if Jeff Grauer was getting wet, if the rain was dribbling down his patrol flag and if the ribbon on it had gone limp. She felt sprinkles herself. Mrs. Thompkins had taken her coat off and water was flying. She was raining on the choir loft.

It was only a low Mass, so when they finished their singing and before Father Étienne entered the sanctuary, they filed downstairs. For a second Clare thought Sister Mary Andrew was going to kneel down next to her, but Sister Immaculata was directing traffic again. She put Sister Mary Andrew across the aisle and, after the Mass started, Clare only looked at her once when the church lit up and a boom of thunder shook the Stations on the wall. The red in the stained glass windows behind Sister went light and then dark.

When Mass was over, Clare waited in the pew behind Jeannie and Susan for the fifth grade to file out. She wanted to pinch them both, but she didn't, and anyway, Sister Immaculata was heading for her. Sister bent her head down so her veil touched Clare's shoulder and told her to wait with Sister Mary Andrew for her car.

"Take the big umbrella in the rack by the side door," Sister Immaculata ordered, and Clare nodded. She walked over to Sister Mary Andrew and let her hold on to her elbow. They stood at the door, peering out through the stripes of rain on the window, at the gray fog that fuzzed the air but turned the church steps and pavement wet.

"There it is," Sister said. She squeezed Clare's elbow and Clare spotted the longest car she'd ever seen, a big black car that rolled up and stopped outside. Clare pulled at the umbrella clasp and pushed on the door.

Sister Mary Andrew was beaming. "You won't find this at your ocean, Clare McHenry," and Clare thought she meant the car, but then realized she meant the weather. "Look at the rain now, the acute angle to the ground. Forty-five degrees. You cook an egg at an angle, Clare, and the line of the yolk stays parallel to the ceiling. It's like water in a glass."

They were blowing down the steps and Clare thought the umbrella would go inside out. She gripped the handle against her side and got the car door open. "Clare McHenry, Queen of the May," Sister said, tucking her skirts in under her. She looked at Clare and a rain drop that had balanced on her glasses ran down her nose. "Pray for your mother, Clare. Pray to the Blessed Mother for your own mother."

Clare looked at the back of the chauffeur's neck where his hair met his cap. "Yes, Sister," she said. She wanted to say that her mother was fine, that she was more than fine. Instead, she closed the door, and watched the car go ahead up the street. A black Cadillac. The bishop's car. And Sister being driven back to his kitchen and his eggs.

Clare smelled the rain and watched it cutting the snow apart. She was dripping, even with the umbrella; she was blowing left and right, her skirt gusting full and then flat. All the houses on the block looked dim—gray and not white. Even her house. Even the rectory. She ducked up the church steps and back inside. When she got the umbrella closed, she put it in the rack, and she was ready to go out the side door and run across to school. Then she remembered she'd left her things.

She couldn't find her tablet, but her satchel and missal were lying in the pew. She genuflected and got them, and genuflected again and headed for the stairs. In the choir loft, she looked down at the main altar, at the tabernacle, and at the side altar where the votive lights were burning to Mary. The church was empty and still, and Clare thought it was holiest this way, all quiet and dark and shadowed. She wondered if Father Étienne was still in the sacristy. She wondered where Sister Josetta's coffin would go, if they'd have it open in the back of the church the way Sister Margret's was in Hanbury.

Clare hunted through the loft until she spotted her tablet kicked under one of the pews. There was a book, too, that somebody hadn't put back in the music racks. Clare picked it up. It wasn't music. It wasn't one of the regular books. She turned to the inside leaf and read *Immaculata, O.S.B.* It was Sister's handwriting all right, all at a slant and with black, black lines at the angle the rain had been. The loft went light for a moment and Clare waited for the thunder and clapped the book shut with the noise. She read the faded letters on the spine: *Spiritual Exercises.* Carefully, she opened the book again, curious, wondering if maybe she'd see pictures of nuns in their habits with their ankles crossed or their heads tilted to the side. But there were only words, and she tucked the book away inside her satchel.

She'd turn it in, of course. She'd give it to Sister. But it seemed an odd weight in her satchel as she went downstairs. She felt anointed. She felt the bearer of some kind of secret life.

With her childhood gone—with the knowledge she had gained and simple deduction, Clare understood that her mother had had a miscarriage in Hanbury. She remembered not only the bathroom scene, but a cryptic comment from her mother about pie-in-the-sky church theories and birth control, and a particular sadness and tenderness in her father that had preceded the move from Delaware. Yet her late-found sureness about the facts of the matter in no way altered her sense of what had happened, her knowledge that particular childhood experiences had been linked in her mind: the bloody water in Hanbury and the blood on Mrs. Porter's stocking. Her mother's talk about sex and Mrs. Porter's voluptuous pregnancy. Timmy Porter's four-letter words and transgressions. The nuns and blue-gowned Mary (more virgin finally than mother), and Mrs. Porter, who had been purified by churching after her baby was born. All of them had slipped under the wire of virtue while Clare's mother, unchurched in every sense that counted, could not.

Clare had hated this idea of her mother, and yet, like a person running out of escalator, she could only back away so long. Her mother was baptized and therefore not pagan, but she was not Catholic in thought or word or deed. She was excluded by her lack of zeal, which was not about goodness—Clare knew her mother was wonderfully good (easy to snuggle with and volunteer of the year in Hanbury)—but about faith. She didn't have it, and she didn't want it. And as that faith, its perimeters stalked by black-robed nuns, more and more encircled Clare, she understood her mother was suspicious of both it and its apparatus.

"So there's a price to being holy," she said when Clare brought home a miniature scapular and medals the week of the May Queen election. "Of course it's their main business to sell. From the get-go they're selling, Clare." She shook the medals in their box and when she picked up the scapular and touched the clingy flannel underside, Clare thought of the nuns on the roof, of the velvety Sacred Heart William O'Connell's aunt had bought in Vatican City.

"I guess I understand," her mother said. "When they've given up so much, they should find it very self-validating to sell other people on their idea of truth." She was still fingering the scapular. "Curious little contraption, though. But all right, Clare. I'll give you the dollar-thirty. The thirty's an advance on your allowance." She leaned over the couch, swooping a kiss onto Clare's cheek that Clare didn't really find comforting.

Dressed in grad school woolens years later, her dresser top strewn with jars and tubes of drugstore cosmetics, and the black-and-white scapular still buried under the scarves in her drawer, Clare had known that the miracle of the cardinals was more about Sister Immaculata's closer view of the sky than about any sort of magical appearance, but its effect had been no less real, a fact she was very aware of as she remembered the guilty prayer she'd made looking up from the couch into her mother's face—her earnest entreaty that her mother might feel the stirrings of faith. As her graduate school self, a person schooled in analysis, she wondered as well just who she would be if, from childhood, she had been less centered on her inner life, on a tendency to play the small moments of her days over and over until they settled in as memories. She imagined two possibilities: an adult born from a carefree child who clambered easily up the May Queen ladder; an adult raised from a child still prone to worry but so beset by large and tangible crises she was forced outside herself. What if her mother had died and left her the de facto keeper of the house? What if her brother, and not the boy they'd known in Hanbury, had tripped on a hunting rifle and given himself an IQ of 50? What if her father had been the neighborhood invalid on the heart machine whose heart ticked louder than a grandfather clock? None of these things had happened, or anything like them. Clare had had a childhood with the luxury of time for introspection, and it had left her, she felt, an easier target for spiritual curiosity, spiritual worry. Spiritual terrorism.

She had experienced them all, but she had felt the curiosity most on the day she found Sister Immaculata's copy of *The Spiritual Exercises*. At lunchtime she carried it home in her satchel, where it stayed on her mind but unopened, its cover so worn that its spine flapped loose. She did not tell her mother that she had it. Instead, she asked if she had heard of Ignatius of Loyola. Her mother chewed at her sandwich and nodded, and said that she had indeed, that he'd founded the Jesuits and written their book of self-help exercises, which was a lot like *Poor Richard*.

Clare considered this. Sister Immaculata wasn't a Jesuit. She wasn't a man or a priest. And from what she'd seen, the book she'd found looked hard and lacking in humor. She wondered if her mother was right. "I need to be back early," she said, finishing her lunch.

Her mother went to the door with her when she got her things on. She pushed the storm door open. "I was thinking of asking your father if we should invite the young priest to dinner. What's his name— Father Étienne?" she said. "It must get lonely—"

"You can't!" Clare surprised herself at how emphatically she cut her mother off. She was holding her satchel latch against her leg so the rain wouldn't leak in and get the book wet.

"Really? Why not?" her mother asked, and then a funny expression came over her face, a little smile. "If you feel so strongly—If you'd rather I didn't . . ."

"I don't want you to," Clare answered quickly. "It's a silly idea. And that's his name, but I don't believe priests eat meals at houses where there're mixed marriages," she added, rushing the words out and then hurrying down the steps without looking to see her mother's reaction.

The rain splashed against her boots as she walked and half ran. Her face and neck felt hot, and it occurred to her she'd added a sin for her next confession. She knew she'd been disrespectful to her mother, though she'd only told the truth. But her errand seemed doubly urgent now. She wanted to hunt in the book to see if there was some kind of spiritual exercise that might make the link for her mother between goodness and faith. She was eager, too, to leave the book in Sister Immaculata's office anonymously (the word had intrigued her since the parish drive when an *anonymous* donor had given a thousand dollars), and she knew she was short on time. Inside the door of Sister's empty office, she held the book flat between her hands and squeezed her eyes shut and pressed her thumbs down hard, spreading the pages back at the center of the book. She opened her eyes and glanced swiftly at the open page. She read one underlined word, *flagellation*, and put the book quickly on Sister's desk. She left the room, vowing to look it up. *Flagellation*. She counted syllables in her head, and told herself to remember the l's and the "flag."

⁓

Then Clare was seriously May Queen-in-waiting. There was no parish funeral for Sister Josetta as there'd been in Hanbury for Sister Margret. Instead, Sister was taken to the motherhouse for burial, and prayers were offered for her throughout the diocese. Clare, as May Queen designate, was given the first of what Sister Immaculata called purity assignments. She was to pray to a saint of her own choosing and ask for aid in keeping her body inviolate. Clare chose Sister Margret because she was certain she was a saint. She could not imagine her not in heaven with her ghostly thinness that seemed pure to Clare, and self-denying, though William O'Connell had called her Her Skinniness.

Clare was required, too, to stay after Mass each day and say a rosary for the repose of the soul of Sister Josetta. She meditated on the Glorious Mysteries. Sister Immaculata had told both her and the new substitute teacher, a heavy, taciturn woman following on the heels of Mrs. Thompkins and a solid week of singing lessons, that her daily time alone in church would make her feel Mary's purity and queenliness and Sister Josetta's great joy in their heavenly meeting. Clare concentrated hard, as hard as she could, though her mind strayed at times to her trips with her mother for dress fittings. (Her mother, after her initial reluctance, had taken out two full months of her budget buffer money and found a seamstress and dotted Swiss, both reasonably priced.) Clare thought, too, of flagellation—a mystification of whipping, flogging, scourging, and punishing (or impelling) as if by whipping—and back again to an identified mystery of Mary at her Assumption: Mother of God carried sinlessly to heaven. Could her own mother, loving but faithless, ever hope for that trip? Clare prayed. She thought of the statues of Holy Week Virgins borne in procession in foreign countries, of the pictures in the diocesan paper that showed their glassy tears, which Finn said were glycerin.

At night in her white room, her dream of Mary returned. First, though, Clare had a vision. She was thinking idly about Jeannie Carson and muddy snow angels and about Sister Immaculata and her blackboard meditation for catechism class—"Whatsoever things are pure, think on these things"—and about the private meditation Sister had given her in a note she slipped out from beneath her scapular—"'Tis not the dying for a faith that's hard, but the living up to it." What she was thinking most was how she'd kept every last word about salvation and her mother to herself forever, and she wasn't sure why. It felt lonely, but it had seemed important and it was maybe something about not just her mother but her mother and father together—about their being together, which was the only way Clare could imagine them. If her mother really knew what was going on with Sister Immaculata, she might say Clare couldn't stay at St. Francis, and Clare didn't want to know at all how her father would react if she did. In the meantime, the words were all still in her head, going round and round like a broken record. *If your mother's to be saved, Clare. If your mother's to be saved . . .*

Clare covered her ears. She tried humming to shut out the words. Finally she got up and, hoping it would make her sleepy, she took her rosary out of the drawer. The crucifix dangled from her hand and she hurried back under the covers. She fingered the beads, saying her Hail Marys.

She was still wide awake. She tried to think about the Annunciation. She was lying on her side and she had her eyes closed, and then she blinked them open and that was when she had the vision. It was Our Lord Himself, hanging on the cross, and Clare was bolt upright in bed before she realized what she'd seen was the crucifix on her rosary. It was glowing in the dark, because that's what it did.

Afterward, after her heart had stopped pounding so fast and she'd curled up on her other side and put her rosary under her pillow, she finally did fall asleep. She dreamed again that her room was a shrine. Mary was life-size on the dresser, beckoning and tearful, but this time she looked like Mrs. Porter, and there was a tracing of blood that curled its way along her thighs. She was being embraced, embraced by blood, the velvety Sacred Heart of Christ pulsing as it gripped her robes. Clare lurched awake. She lay trembling in bed—in the moon-silvered, horrible room. She wanted to scream out, to call for her mother. But she didn't. She willed herself silent and still.

———

The week before May Day, Sister Immaculata sent a note to Clare to come to her office after school. Clare got her sweater from the wardrobe and put her math homework in her satchel and hurried down the hall. Her mother had told her to come straight home from school so they could pick up her dress at the dressmaker's, and she waited anxiously, antsily in Sister's empty office. She scanned the bookshelf for the flappy spine of *The Spiritual Exercises*, but it wasn't there. She could hear the other students jostling on the stairs on the way out of the building, hear the sounds of their voices that started at the door. Shrieks. Bellows. Rocco Mulleto's baseball bat thumping down the railing.

"Monsignor, she's in the office." Clare turned at Sister Immaculata's voice and saw her with Monsignor Evans, who was coming down the hall in his cassock. Monsignor was not fat, but he was tall and he was big. He was so big that he filled the space when he came through the door. Clare squeezed herself against the desk as he moved by her. He had a pouch in his hand and she smelled Latakia, a scent from the dimming past of her grandfather's pipe when she sat on his knee.

"So this is our May Queen," he said.

"Please have a seat, Monsignor," Sister Immaculata said behind her. "She's Clare McHenry. Clare, Monsignor Evans wishes to speak to you. Stand straight," she said, and Clare listened to her footsteps going off down the hall.

Clare waited. She waited and thought about her mother waiting. She watched Monsignor fill his pipe and blow a big, lopsided smoke wreath. He shook his match out and leaned forward in Sister's chair. "Sister tells me you've been saying the rosary after Mass every day to prepare yourself."

"Yes, Monsignor."

"You know why we honor Mary in this way?

"Because she's the mother of God."

"And?"

"She's the Blessed Virgin."

"And?"

"I don't know what else. Because of her goodness?"

"You know about the perfect game? About Don Larson? Clare, are you a baseball fan?"

"My father is. My brother is. He listened to the game at school in Hanbury."

"And how did Don Larson pitch that perfect game?"

Clare was silent. "Very carefully," she said finally.

"I mean *how* could he do it?"

"He's very good."

"Yes, he's talented. He has skill. But what else did he have?"

Clare looked at her satchel and then back up at Monsignor Evans. "Good fielding?"

"The *will*." Monsignor's free hand came down on the desk the way it struck the pulpit during his sermons. "He had the skill and he had the *will*. And how is that like you and not like you? What does Don Larson's perfect game have to do with the May Queen at St. Francis?"

"I *will* do it?" Clare said. "Crown the statue?"

"Yes, but perfection, child. Mary's perfect purity and goodness. That's the ideal you need to represent. You can will yourself to attain it just the way Don Larson willed his perfect game. But you need something more. If Don Larson needed skill for perfection, you need grace. That's what you're praying for. Demand goodness of yourself, but pray to God and the Blessed Mother for the grace to achieve it."

"Yes, Monsignor." The smoke had settled in Clare's hair and she couldn't stop smelling it.

"Any questions?" Monsignor asked. He was clearly ready to let her go, and Clare was curious if he would stay in Sister's office smoking his pipe, if Sister would be back. But mostly she wondered why he had started to seem bored, why his words left her thinking, but not frightened.

"Monsignor," she said. "Monsignor Evans, is flagellation important for faith?"

"What?" He looked at her. He put his pipe down, and she thought she saw a surprised hint of laughter in his eyes before they settled back into grayness. "Jesus was scourged in his Passion. He was whipped with reeds. It was part of His goodness. But that's too big a word for a child. Go on now. Scoot. Pray for grace. That should be enough. Yes? What is it, Father?"

Clare looked behind her. She hadn't heard Father Étienne come up, but he was standing right there in the hallway. He was wearing his street suit and collar instead of his cassock, and she could see the outline of his cigarette package in his pocket.

"Yes, Monsignor. Good afternoon, Father," Clare said quickly. She took a step backward and saw that Father Étienne, with his dark eyes, was looking at her. She dropped her gaze. She grasped her satchel tighter and slipped by him, feeling nervous and odd and wondering how long he'd actually been there. Sister Immaculata was at the end of the hall, and Clare turned around and walked as fast as she could in the other direction and down the stairs by the first grade. She pushed the metal bar to open the door, and listened as the door hitched shut behind her.

Finally. She was finally on her way home. In front of the rectory there were crocuses still blooming and a bed of red tulips. A dog sniffed them and, lifting its leg, sent a hard, yellow stream of pee splashing onto the ground. Clare stared at him. He stared back and, though she was late, she walked instead of running so he wouldn't chase her.

When she opened the door into their living room, her mother was at the piano in her hat and her spring coat. She was playing the fluttery Brahms ballade Clare wished she could play. Clare ate a cookie and waited on the couch until she heard the final chords.

"Sorry I'm late," she said.

"Playing with your friends?"

"I had to talk to Monsignor Evans."

Her mother picked up the car keys and her purse. "And what did Monsignor have to say?"

"Just about being May Queen. Purity and goodness. Mary. He talked about Don Larson's perfect game. There was good fielding in that game, wasn't there?"

"Ask Finn. Ask your father. You ready to go?"

"I am," Clare said, and she gave her mother a quick hug.

When they got to Mrs. Carney's, her mother had a cup of tea and Clare went into the bedroom to put her dress on. It was crinkly. She checked the French seams, rubbing the fabric between her thumb and finger to feel the thickness. She touched the puffed sleeves. After she'd stretched her arms back and pulled the fabric up to button the buttons, she smoothed the skirt and decided plain was good, that her mother was right about no ruffles, or right enough. In the front room, Mrs. Carney was saying Mr. Carney had written to New York to find out if he was Art Carney's cousin and if he could meet Jackie Gleason if he was. When Clare stopped in the doorway, Mrs. Carney got up from her chair, her tape measure dangling from her neck, and said Clare was as sweet as an angel. She tugged at the dress seams to show they would never split.

"Turn around for your mother," she said and Clare pirouetted in front of the long mirror by the stairs.

Her mother laughed. "You like it?" she asked, and when Clare nodded, she put her cup down and wrote out the check.

Clare thought they were going home, but when they drove down the street in the Nash, her dress hooked up in the back seat where she could see it over her shoulder, her mother surprised her. "I'll buy you a cherry Coke," she said.

At Ascher's Drugstore, they stopped at the pharmacy counter first. "We need Mercurochrome," Clare said. She stood still, pressing her toes into the floor. She touched her mother's coat sleeve and twisted her finger in the wool, idly tracing a nubby curl. She could just smell the cleaning fluid her mother had swabbed on a stain when she'd unpacked this coat at Easter.

The pharmacist took her mother's prescription, which Clare knew was for anemia, and she listened to her mother talking to him in her easy, out-in-public voice with its familiar slide of laughter, heard her ask about his wife, who wore fur-collared coats to the Methodist church and was the person who'd recommended Mrs. Carney. Clare watched as the pharmacist scooped out pills and quartered them into piles with a wooden blade that was like a tongue depressor. He counted them swiftly by twos, counted them again and picked up the paper they were on so it made a kind of funnel, and then slid them into a bottle. And while he was doing that and running up the sale on the cash register that binged open and while Clare's mother dug in her purse and put out coins on the counter, they were both talking in that adult way that made them sound interesting and seemed far easier to Clare than her talking to a boy like Jeff Grauer or even Rocco Muletto which, basically, she couldn't do. But she had talked to William O'Connell. She hadn't had any problem at all doing that.

"And you, miss. Any prescriptions for you?" the pharmacist said eyeing Clare, and when she shook her head quickly no and then told him Mercurochrome, he and her mother both laughed. Clare felt her mother's arm go around her shoulder. "We've been to get Clare's May Queen dress. We do need Mercurochrome. Mrs. Carney does very nice work. You can tell your wife we're very pleased."

When they'd bought the Mercurochrome and found a booth on the soda fountain side, her mother put the package from the pharmacy down on the table and took off her coat. Clare waited for her to take her hat off, too, and shake her head so her hair fell a little over her glasses, but she kept it on. "Coffee and a cherry Coke," her mother told the waitress, and then she reached across the table and put her hands on Clare's. "Well little May Queen, what are you thinking about?" she said.

"Can nuns smoke?" Clare said, still smelling the Latakia in her hair. "Monsignor Evans has a pipe. Father Étienne smokes cigarettes. But are nuns allowed to smoke? I don't believe they are."

Her mother drew her hands back across the table. "That's a concept. Let's see. Smoking nuns. With their vow of poverty they probably can't afford to."

Clare nodded. "Then secular priests can smoke but monks can't?"

"A secular priest? What's that?"

"One that's not a religious priest. You know—oh, not not-religious that way. Sister Immaculata told us a priest that's in an order is a religious. Like brothers and sisters are. And the plain parish priests that aren't in an order are called secular because they don't take a vow of poverty."

"Interesting," her mother said, and Clare felt a little tingle that she'd known something her mother didn't.

"You're learning a lot about being Catholic," her mother said, and Clare watched the little creases that pinched above her nose and glasses. Clare sat back while the waitress put her glass with its maraschino cherry in front of her and wondered if drinking the Coke would be a violation of her day's assignment to deny herself a special pleasure. She made a quick decision. She took the bobbing cherry out of her glass and put it on her napkin to take home to Finn. Then she leaned forward and sucked thoughtfully on the papery straw until the Coke was on her tongue. She watched her mother stir the cream into her coffee.

"I do know Christ founded His one true Church with Peter as the head," Clare said quietly.

Her mother looked at her. She put her spoon down. "An administrative detail," she said finally. She took a sip of her coffee, and Clare could tell she wanted to say something more, something that might even be ominous, something that fell into the category of the promise she'd made and kept about raising Catholic children, which, as Clare understood it, had been a requirement of the church and of her father, too. Her mother waited a long time, and then she patted Clare's hand. "You're young to understand this," she said, "but someday, Clare, you'll know that having faith in an idea because you're smart enough to understand the logic it's built on is different from just plain having faith. And it's very different from having respect for the faiths other people hold."

Clare was quiet. She didn't really understand what her mother meant, though she thought it had something to do with what she'd blurted out about Father Étienne and priests not going to houses with mixed marriages. But she didn't ask her to explain. Instead she traced the words in her mind, feeling them like the edge of a puzzle piece, etching them in with the taste of the cherry Coke—that fruity sweet bitterness faintly like medicine, like the sticky Cheracol her mother spooned out for her cough when she had the flu.

In the night, her May Queen dress hanging on the back of the door, Clare awoke with a sense of someone else in the room. She had not had her dream of Mary. There was no moonlight shining on the dresser or the floor. Her room was dark, and she felt certain that Sister Margret had come—that Sister had passed from her wasted body into the motes of the air. Oddly, this did not frighten her. Instead, it gave her the dozy feeling that the exercises from Sister Immaculata were working, that Sister Margret had heard her prayers and given this answer through the hummy air—a murmur from her and all the other dead holy women of the Church, their inviolate bodies a chain from Mary through the lists of all the martyred virgins. Clare thought of St. Peter's and the nuns on the roof. They were so pure. They were rimmed by cloudless skies while they sold their wares.

Carefully, she did not touch herself. If she understood Sister Mary Andrew's clues and Sister Immaculata's convoluted sentences, this denial was the starting point of purity.

Clare carried this sense of her body when she entered church for morning Mass. Her *body*. It was an encumbrance, a thing off limits, a thing sanctified by the absence of touch and the centerpiece of the damning triumvirate Sister Mary Andrew had inscribed on the black-board in her own illuminated letters—*The World, The Flesh, and The Devil*—before she'd gone off the deep end over Timmy. Clare listened to the murmuring Latin. In the shimmer of candlelight, she sensed the echo of night in her room, the humming otherness of light and sound where holiness might take you.

But in a while, her mind drifted off. She remembered her May Queen dress. She watched Father Étienne at the altar and wondered what he'd been thinking outside Sister Immaculata's office and then when she saw him downtown after she'd gotten her dress. She and her mother had come out of the drugstore, and there he was across the street putting money in a parking meter. Clare had looked quickly at her mother, wondering if she'd spotted him, too, and then Father started across the street in their direction. She knew that he'd seen them. He looked purposeful, and Clare wondered if she was going to be caught in the middle of something unpleasant, if Father Étienne would tell her mother something that alarmed her, or if her mother would say something embarrassing.

"I'm cold," she whispered, catching at her mother's coat sleeve. Her mother looked at her a little quizzically, and then she nodded at Father Étienne and headed on to the Nash with Clare. Clare was relieved. Then she felt strange. She had the sudden, very real sense that something that should have happened hadn't.

In class, there was a new substitute. Clare, sitting down, could smell her heavy perfume and hear Timmy Porter tell Brent Anderson that she shaved her eyebrows, which Clare thought was probably true since the ones she had were penciled on. Clare wrote *J.M.J.* at the top of a tablet sheet and then made a list of all the teachers they'd had since Sister Mary Andrew left. There'd been five, including Mrs. Thompkins, and all of them had been lay teachers and none of them eager to stay since the class had grown wild except for the half hour when Sister Immaculata ruled.

The new teacher sat on the edge of the desk and asked what the red "6" on the blackboard meant. Jeannie Carson told her it was six days until May Day when Clare would crown the statue of Mary. Clare looked eagerly at Jeannie when she said her name. She tore a scrap of paper from her page and wrote a careful note asking her home after school to see her dress. She passed it over, and Jeannie read it. Clare waited. She thought Jeannie wasn't going to turn around, but then she did.

"Busy," she mouthed, and Clare nodded and felt a slight flush at the base of her cheek. She also felt quietly miserable. Just as soon as she'd begun to make friends, it seemed she'd started to lose them. Though they'd voted for her for May Queen, now they were jealous and unfriendly. It wasn't just what she'd heard in the choir loft. Two weeks ago Jeannie had been glad to walk home with her and sprawl on the bed reading her autograph book while they listened to records and ate the chocolate graham crackers her mother had made. Now that seemed impossible, ages ago.

"Clare?" The teacher had answered a knock at the door and was looking back at the class, scanning the room. Slowly, Clare raised her hand and waited for the familiar message: "Sister Immaculata wants you in her office."

She got up from her desk. She could hear the usual whisper— *St. Clare, Immaculata's pet*—and she wished it was January and she was back in Hanbury talking to a friend on the phone or lying on the hearth rug, the fire blazing while she ate apples and read. But it wasn't and she wasn't, so she headed for the door and went on out to the hall.

Sister Immaculata was already at the typewriter in her office, typing fast. Clare listened to the click of the keys and the bang of the carriage. She looked at Sister's bleached face. It was all concentration as she rolled the paper she'd typed out of the typewriter and read it through.

"There," she said, pushing it at Clare. "Read it. You're to review your life from the age of reason—seven, six perhaps for you. Remember any impurities. Thoughts. Words. Deeds. Monsignor Evans will hear your confession before Mass on Tuesday. Before you crown Mary. You must be unsullied. That means a complete review."

"Yes, Sister," Clare said. She had the paper and she was ready to go, but Sister pinned her with a hard stare.

"Your slander, Clare, has caused me great pain," she said in a voice that was cold, yet somehow livid.

Clare was warily still.

"Monsignor has my assurance I will not punish you for deceit, but know, Clare, I am aware of it. Flagellation! I've given him a copy of your purity assignments. No flagellation. None. How you could suggest it to him, I have no idea. You've slandered me, Clare, to a vicar of Christ on earth."

"I didn't. Nothing like that." Clare felt a siege of butterflies attacking her insides. She looked at the wall and the cracked plaster, at the light fixture. "I never said your name. I only asked if it was important for faith. I saw it in the book you left in the choir loft."

"You looked in my book?"

"Yes, Sister."

"I can't punish you. Not for that. Not, apparently, for anything. I can only pray for you, Clare. I *will* pray for you. And for your mother. I will pray for you and ask for the prayers of the other sisters that you may overcome your pride."

Clare was still. She wanted to answer, to say she wasn't proud, but simply trying to figure things out. She wanted to ask Sister Immaculata why she'd singled her out to torment, if it was all because of her mother. Instead, she said nothing.

"Go back to your classroom." Sister Immaculata shifted her eyes down and rolled more paper into the typewriter.

Clare waited an instant longer. She looked at the tattered copy of *The Spiritual Exercises* that was back on the shelf. Then she nodded. "Yes, Sister," she said.

When school was out, Clare dawdled starting home. There was a fat, bosomy robin in a bush next to the rectory, and Clare remembered the cardinals. She remembered the statue of St. Francis next to the convent, and she backtracked toward the alley. She walked slowly, kicking at the tufty, new-green grass. She wanted to look at St. Francis again, to see his brown robes and his hands outstretched for birds.

To her surprise, Timmy Porter was blocking her path, solid as a fireplug. Clare stopped walking. "How come you're here?" she said watching him slap his ball into his baseball glove. She could see the leather, the smooth scuffy brown.

"How come *you* are?" he answered, and it occurred to Clare that he'd seen where she was going, and that he'd circled the convent to intercept her.

She hesitated, considered. As far as she knew, the statue wasn't off limits. It was tucked into the back corner of the convent where the new wing adjoined. It was in an open yard that was like a park, though it fronted on the alley that turned south and divided the convent grounds from Dunsinane Woods, a name Clare's mother always made her repeat. "None of your business," she said to Timmy.

He was standing next to the blank wall of the convent where it butted the alley. "You can't get by," he said, and Clare was suddenly back in Hanbury with the sweet, cut wood of the lumberyard and the tacked-up calendar picture of storm-shrouded mountains rising like a sea wall to a raging sea. Her father picked out studs, the smell of Woolite in his Saturday shirt, while Clare stood in front of the calendar, wondering once again if mountains ever did block the ocean in just that way.

"It's not your alley. It's a free country," she said to Timmy, considering whether she was faster than he was and if she could hit him if she had to. She could turn around. She could go home, but that didn't seem an option. "Your fly's open," she said, and when he looked down, fooled like Finn hadn't been in years, she dodged past him and ran. She felt the ridgy alley bricks under her feet, and then the weeds and dirt as the bricks thinned out.

Timmy was chasing her. "You better stop," he yelled. "Hey, Clare, I mean it. Stop."

Her heels flew, kicking dust, the ground bumpy like the seacoast where the sand was crusty and studded with broken shells. For an instant, as she passed the convent, Clare almost smelled the sea air again, almost felt the openness of its horizon instead of this closed-down, land-locked place.

She kept on running. She could hear Timmy behind her. She tried to go faster, but then Timmy had caught up. He was next to her, and she smelled the minty woods, and he was tugging at her sleeve, pulling until she tripped and they both had tumbled to the ground. Clare felt the impact, saw the sky with its popcorn cumulus clouds, and the distant wall of the convent and the statue of St. Francis skinny and upright like a brown stick. She knew that Timmy would try to kiss her and, this time, from curiosity, she would let him.

Her head was next to a root that had broken in their fall, and she saw its white inner flesh, almost liquid, and felt the odd, sponginess of Timmy's lips, which could not be like Jeff Grauer's. "Gross. Oh, gross!" she said, pushing him so he wouldn't know she'd given in, and then she felt his fingers tugging the crotch of her panties to the side, and it was all her fault. She knew it was. It was absolutely her fault because she'd let him kiss her.

"Holy Christopher, your cunt. I saw it. Maybe I touched it." Tommy's face was pink; it was exultant. "You better not tell. If you tell, everybody will know."

Clare's body clenched, pulling away. She tried spelling the word. She tried a "k," and knew something terrible had happened.

―――

As a first sexual experience to recount, Timmy Porter and Dunsinane Woods worked really quite well. Depending on the audience of coffee or margarita drinkers, Clare could count on certain reactions. Men, if they weren't eager to impress her with their sensitivity, were noncommittal. Some women thought it was funny she'd turned to spelling, but mostly they were outraged and said, "God, they're pigs even at eleven." The floundering Catholics wanted to hug her. "How many years of guilt?" they always asked.

But before the experience had become a story, Clare, with a willed presence of mind, had scared Timmy Porter away. She said that somebody was coming, that she'd heard Father Étienne's voice. It was a lie, but Timmy took off running and she got up, brushing herself off. She was worried that her skirt was torn, and she pulled at it, looking at it over both shoulders until she was sure it was OK. Then she started to shake.

By the time she got home, she was desperate for her mother. She went up the porch steps and opened the door to the living room.

It was so quiet and empty that its silence spoke for the whole house. She called out. There was no answer. She waited and called again. Still nothing. No note on the kitchen table. She went through the whole house calling, but she knew she was talking to herself. Her mother had gone somewhere and wasn't home yet.

Clare walked back to the living room. She flopped on the couch and tried resting her head on the back. She kicked her heels against the padded wood below the cushions, which she wasn't supposed to do. So all right. She wouldn't do it. She jumped up and went to the basement door and called again. Silence. She walked down the stairs, peering through the dimness to the far corner where water had seeped in when the snow thawed. She could smell the sealer her father had painted on the cement, and she wondered if things that were living could come through a wall. If spiders could. And snakes.

She ran back upstairs and slammed the door. She leaned against it and thought of the dank basement in Hanbury, of Hanbury and the bloody water. Startled at the image, she hurried toward the bathroom. The door was ajar. "Mother?" she said. She pushed the door open. The room was perfectly clean, the tub polished clear down to the rust spot. Her mother's shower cap was hanging from the faucet. Clare pulled the door toward her and looked behind it. There was a bit of tissue stuck to a hinge, but nothing else. Clare touched her chest. She felt her heart thump, and she sat down on the toilet lid and then got up again, yanking her skirt off and putting it in the hamper. She scrubbed her face. She gargled, feeling the Listerine bite and tickle her throat. She scrubbed her face again until her cheeks stung, and it occurred to her then that pain was a thing you gave yourself for punishment. It made you feel cross and right.

In her bedroom, with her jeans on, she listened for the door and knelt by the bed and tried to say the rosary. Her mind, though, glided past the mysteries without ever touching. She let the beads sway against the floor. She watched them, and part of her wanted to fling herself on her bed and cry and cry until the whole long misery of St. Francis de Assisi School had flooded out. Part of her wanted to cry until her mother put her cheek next to hers and said, "All rained out, love?" But her mother wasn't home, and the part of Clare that was in charge was restless and unsettled.

She got up. She put her rosary in her drawer and went out to the living room. She leaned against the piano. She touched its curving side. Wood. Varnish. She walked her fingers down the keyboard to middle C and stopped. She could practice, but she'd already done it before school. And, too, she knew she would bang the ivories if she played now and might chip one. She headed for the closet. Elbowing back coats, she maneuvered the carpet sweeper out and pushed it over the rug, following the tracks her mother had made. Then she dragged the sweeper backwards until the bottom opened and the batt of dust dropped out. She squatted down to touch it. Cotton. Fuzz. She wondered why dust was gray, why things that got loose made a single color that wasn't a color. And she wondered if this was always true, if it was provable, or if, instead, it was something you took on faith.

Clare felt the grayness slipping up inside her. She snapped the bottom of the sweeper shut and put it away and carried the dust out to the kitchen wastebasket. She was thinking of what Monsignor had said, that Jesus was scourged with reeds, that it was part of his goodness. She was thinking how worn Sister Immaculata's book was, of how fiercely she kept flagellation for herself: that punishment by scourging or whipping, that exercise that seemed the very opposite of denial. That something hidden: a positive act of purity.

Without deciding, Clare knew what she would do. In her bedroom, she took the leather belt out of the loops of her wool slacks. She went into the bathroom and closed the door and slipped her jeans down. Leaning against the wall, she swung the belt at her leg. It flapped loosely without stinging, so she shortened her grip and slapped the belt directly against her thigh. This time she could feel it smart. She adjusted her hand, pointing her index finger like she did for a badminton serve, and she struck her leg once more. And then, because the pain was real but not great, she reversed the belt in her hand and with a quick bend of her wrist, whipped the metal buckle against her skin.

A bead of blood popped up like a tiny ball. Clare looked at it. It broke into a thin streak and she hit her leg again, the buckle and leather both making contact. She kept on hitting. She hit and hit again. She could see tears on her eyelashes like bubbles on a glass, and she thought of the suffering of Jesus and his mother and of the whole enormous and unpure shame of the moment with Timmy Porter.

Tears were running down her cheeks when she heard the front door open. She froze against the wall. She could hear footsteps in the hallway and the thud of books on the floor in Finn's room, and then the sound of his steps coming toward the bathroom door.

"Clare, you in there?"

Clare eased the belt along the wall and dropped it to the floor. "Just a minute," she said. "Wait." She grabbed a washcloth and swabbed it up her thigh. She turned the cold water on. She could hear Finn breathing.

"Hurry up. You fall in?" he said.

"Wait, will you?" She dunked the washcloth under the faucet and saw it puddle red. She squeezed it. She rang it out and pressed it against her leg and reached up on tiptoe for the Band-Aids in the medicine chest. She stretched higher, nudging the box forward. It balanced for an instant on the edge of the shelf, and then it toppled into the sink with a tinny clunk.

"I'm hurrying," she said. She ripped the biggest Band-Aid open and slid the washcloth away, but the Band-Aid didn't stick. It fell off and the blood squiggled down her leg.

"You better hurry," Finn said. "What are you breaking in there?"

"Not anything." Clare dried her thigh with a wad of toilet paper and then grabbed more Band-Aids and strapped them across the bloody punch marks and welts on her leg. She taped the ends with more Band-Aids until she had a kind of poultice. She pulled her jeans back up and stuffed all the scraps of crinkled paper and slick paper into her pockets and flushed the bloody toilet paper. With her hand, she scrubbed the sink, splashing water on all the blood spots. She looked in the mirror and brushed the tears from her face and then remembered to grab the belt and buckle it over her jeans. Her leg burning, she turned the knob and opened the door.

Finn was standing there, a full head taller than she was, but she made herself look straight up at his eyes, which were the same blue as her eyes and their father's and, right now, full of suspicion. But he was still Finn, and Clare was determined to hold her ground. She had nothing to say to him. Nothing. He could threaten her or, that rarer thing, be nice, but he wasn't finding out anything that had happened. There was no way she was going to tell him.

He was standing with his elbow against the door frame so his muscles showed, and he looked very hostile. "What were you doing? Were you in Mother's stuff? You a little May Queen thief?" he said, and Clare wondered if he was going to hit her, though it was years since he had. It didn't matter. She wanted him to get out of her way, but otherwise she really didn't care, and she was certain he knew it. He looked at her for a moment without saying anything, and then he pushed her sideways and went past her into the bathroom. "You're a cretin," he said, closing the door, and Clare went on into her room.

Later, a miserable half an hour later, she heard her mother's voice. Clare opened the door to her room and listened. She heard her father, too. Quietly, she walked out to the living room, moving carefully so she didn't limp. In the kitchen, her father was standing by the sink in his shirtsleeves reading the sports page while her mother unpacked grocery bags. He leaned over and kissed her neck. "Say hey, kid, how do I get used to Willie Mays in his San Francisco uniform?" he asked, and her mother laughed and reached her arms around him.

Clare, all fiery leg and wretchedness, saw them through the doorway. Her father. Her mother, who she really needed to talk to. They were there, but they seemed very far away. More than that, they seemed far from God. Both of them did, but especially her mother.

Still Clare waited, hoping she would look over and see her. When she didn't, Clare tightened her hands into fists so she didn't cry, and went back to her room and closed the door.

———

By the time the May Queen countdown number had shrunk to "2" and another substitute teacher had taken over the class, Clare had lost interest in everything but prayer. Whole chunks of Latin from the Ordinary of the Mass rippled like a stream through her brain. In the classroom, she kept her rosary in her desk and touched the beads, not for the pleasure of her fingers slipping across the cut facets, but because each bead stood for a prayer to reflect on: *Hail Mary, full of grace. Hail holy Queen.* She ate a slice of the orange her mother packed for her breakfast and tasted her bread, but no more. She did not want food. Her body did not want food. Her body did not want. She passed Timmy Porter without seeing him. For whole minutes, she forgot what he knew, and when she remembered, she forgot again in the silent Latin babble. Jeannie Carson shushed anyone who started to tease her, and Clare noticed, but that was all.

At home, her mother watched her and asked if something was wrong. "Maybe growing pains," she said, answering herself more than once, and Clare stayed in her room that was shaded now with new leaves on the trees, but had not once stopped being a shrine. She dusted it, kept it tidy and very clean and, in the patterned twilight the leaves made, stared at her leg, wondering if it would become infected, if she would have gangrene, the terrible greenness, a wound that, if she pierced it, would explode.

But the welts were fading and, though she considered hitting herself with the belt again, she didn't. She was afraid Finn would catch her. Afraid her mother would find out. In every way, just afraid.

The holes had begun growing scabs. Her skin was healing as if it were part of a healthy body with no impurity at its center. To Clare, this seemed incredible. She prayed harder. She waited expectantly for

Sister Immaculata's assignments—to walk last in line, to pray to all the virgin martyrs in *The Lives of the Saints*—and thought, *Is this all? Is this all? Only this?* For the first time she could remember, she was truly angry with her mother, distressed certainly that she didn't sense what was wrong, but more upset that her mother lacked the seriousness of faith.

In the midst of this dismay, an avalanche of notes and holy cards descended on Clare's desk. They were waiting for her when she finished the rosary after Mass. Her classmates nudged and pushed against each other, trying to see. The substitute shooed them back to their seats with the rolled-up diocesan newspaper, and Clare managed to shove everything into her desk, though she had to keep stuffing one stubborn envelope back in until its corners were completely smashed.

At recess, she stayed inside to open envelopes, and Jeannie and Susan were allowed to help her, though Clare hadn't asked.

Jeannie used the teacher's letter opener. "It's like Valentine's Day," she said, "except the hearts are bloody." She handed Clare a holy card that was a picture of Jesus with a satin heart dripping satin blood. Clare wished she felt like telling about the real valentine William O'Connell had given her in Hanbury. It was honeycombed with pink-tissue hearts and flying white birds, and William, though he wasn't her boyfriend, had told her he thought she'd like it since she'd liked his aunt's velvet heart. Clare had. But remembering it now, she simply felt glum.

Clare turned the holy card over and read the inscription. It was from Sister John Davida: "Blessed are the pure of heart, for they shall see God."

"I don't know if I want to," she said.

"Want what?" Jeannie asked.

Clare showed her the back of the card. "To see God."

"Who does? You'd be dead." Jeannie and Susan were opening more envelopes, and Clare realized there was a card from everyone in the convent. There was even a note from Sister Mary Andrew, who told her to pray for her mother when she made her Act of Contrition before she crowned Mary, and to pray for her as she placed the wreath on Mary's head.

"This one's cool," Susan said. "Plastic-coated. You could kill flies that land in your missal."

Jeannie looked at it. "I don't think she's in the mood for jokes," she said. "Clare, is this whole thing maybe creepy? All this praying and stuff. It's like it's making you sick."

Clare carried the empty envelopes up to the wastebasket and then stacked the cards on her desk, putting the one with the bumpy satin heart on top. The *Agnus Dei* was playing through her mind, and she felt the same chill she'd experienced when the class gathered on the church steps to practice the processional for May Day, and Sister Immaculata had herded them into line, the boom of the organ sounding through the open door. Clare placed the stack of holy cards carefully inside her desk. Both Jeannie and Susan were looking at her. "I'm OK," she said.

On the morning of May Day, Clare smelled cinnamon when she woke up. Even before her eyes were open, even before she remembered she was sleeping on hair rollers because it was May Day, she knew her father hadn't left for work yet, that her mother was heating rolls in the oven for his breakfast. To her surprise, she felt hungry. She slipped out of bed and said a quick prayer and then went out to the kitchen in her pajamas. She sat down at the table. Her father, who had the biggest sweet tooth in the family, was at the stove scraping frosting off the cinnamon roll pan. He licked the knife.

"You're up early."

"It smells good." Clare looked at the rolls on his plate. She could see the last bit of egg yolk on the plate rim and hear her mother down in the basement starting the washing machine.

"So today's the day." Her father poured his coffee and sat down next to her. He picked up one of the rolls.

Clare nodded. She watched her father eat and told herself she wasn't that hungry.

"I have to wake Clare up," her mother said, coming up the stairs, and Clare's father laughed when her mother saw her at the table. "Well, that's nice of you, Bobby, eating sweet rolls in front of a faster. I hope you're not hungry, Clare."

"Not really."

"Better get washed. Your dress is on my bed. What time did Sister say?"

Clare scratched her back on the knob of her chair. "Seven. I'm supposed to go to confession."

"This May Queen is part cat," her father said, and Clare smelled his cinnamon mouth and coffee breath when he kissed her good-bye.

"Hurry up, Clare, before Finn needs the bathroom," her mother told her, and Clare remembered May Day in Hanbury when she and her friends filled paper May Day baskets with flowers and left them on porches and then hid in the bushes as soon as they'd rung the door-bells. She pushed her chair against the table and snapped the elastic in her pajama waist on her way to the bathroom.

While she washed and then got her shoes and dress on, Clare rehearsed in her mind what she was supposed to do: count her steps as she walked through the church door; look ahead when she entered the nave and when she walked down the aisle; genuflect when she reached the main altar; walk to the side altar and the statue of Mary and then climb the wooden stepladder. It was a matter of one foot in front of the next even if her shoes pinched, which they did a little.

Her mother came into her room to do up her buttons. Clare unrolled her curlers. The right side of her hair brushed into a smooth curl, but the left side bumped up next to the part. When her mother went back to the kitchen to make Finn's lunch, Clare put water on the bump and held it down with her palm.

"You holding your head on?" Finn said in the hall. "I bet you fall off the ladder."

Clare knew what she wanted to say, that even if he could come to watch, she wouldn't invite him, but she didn't say anything. Instead she offered it up. She got her coat out of the front closet.

"You need that?" her mother called from the kitchen. She was spreading mayonnaise.

Clare looked at her.

"Oh." Her mother nodded. "So you don't have to walk down the street with your dress showing. OK. Don't wrinkle it. You look like a doll. I'll be there watching. Isn't she sweet, Finn?"

"She's lopsided," Finn said, and Clare buttoned her coat and put her hand back over her part.

When she got to the corner, it was way too early for Jeff Grauer or for Father Étienne on the way to the sacristy in his cassock. Clare was glad. Even with her coat on, she felt conspicuous. Inside the church, she knelt with the oldest parishioners in the flickery blue shadows of the vigil lights and prayed to get ready for confession. She had decided what she would tell Monsignor Evans. She would say she had let a boy make her immodest and she had gone to Communion without confessing it. Then she would find out from Monsignor how gravely she'd sinned, how unworthy she really was, and she would say her penance and try as hard as she could to forget.

She had her face in her hands when she heard a movement beside her and felt a thin hand on her shoulder. She looked up into Sister Geraldine's scattery eyes. "Father Étienne is waiting for you in the confessional," Sister said.

Clare looked at her. "Father Étienne?" she whispered, and Sister nodded and genuflected, crossing herself, and went back up the aisle. Clare looked over her shoulder. The light was on over the confessional, and there was no line at all. But Father Étienne. Father Étienne was waiting to hear her confession.

Clare felt her toes growing numb in her shoes. She touched her hair where it was still damp. She couldn't confess to Father Étienne. Not to handsome Father Étienne. Monsignor Evans knew who she was, but he lacked interest or real surprise. She had counted on that. Monsignor could hear without caring. But Father Étienne? Clare looked at the old people praying on their kneelers. She felt the curved wood of the pew under her fingers as she got up. She stared at the floor and at the white hem of her dress that traced it. In the aisle, she turned toward the confessional, and she knew all at once that Sister Immaculata was right. She was proud. She was proud, and she wanted to flee.

———

As often as she had repeated her nun stories, as often as she had said what Timmy Porter had done, the story of her bad confession was something Clare had told only once. She was fourteen and the priest for the high school retreat had been funny but full of fire and brimstone. Clare, listening to him, felt a dark clutch: wings at her throat.

At lunchtime she went to the principal's office and read the sign-up sheet for private conferences. There were choices: Very Important, Important, Relatively Important.

Relatively. Her word. Her word exactly. She had settled on it as the rational choice, for her reasoning mind told her she had done nothing wrong, while the faith part of her—the part of her that was scared—thought she'd lived for years with covered-up sin, compounding it with every additional bad confession that skipped over Timmy Porter and that first bad confession to Father Étienne, every trip she'd made to Communion without ever feeling truly absolved. In the final averaging of faith and reason, she'd been generous to herself, identifying her problem as "relatively important" before she ever saw her choices.

She spoke to the priest. She told him the truth in the euphemisms of her Catholic schooling. He smiled kindly. He said she was good, not a sinner, and that she had a scrupulous conscience she needed to guard against. He sent her on her way, sent her off flying down the cafeteria steps to join her friends with the lightest heart she could ever have imagined, though it darkened later with resentment.

But that was Clare's future. When she entered the classroom on May Day, her heart felt as black as ink. The girls pulled at her coat to see her dress, and she tried to smile, tried to say thank you when they said it was pretty, tried to think of the number of footsteps she must walk, tried to think of Mary's purity and of the women of the church, virgins and martyrs, whose voices had thrummed the air of her nighttime room.

Nothing stuck. She could not get out of the confessional. She heard Father Étienne giving her her Penance—three our Fathers and three Hail Marys—and then absolving her: *In the name of the Father, the Son, and the Holy Ghost.* She heard her own whisper again and again: *I was disrespectful to my parents. I fought with my brother. Once when I was little, I pulled a cat's tail.*

Clare put her coat in the wardrobe, and let Susan turn her around. She didn't say that her dress had French seams and that she and her mother had thought ruffles were babyish. She heard all the girls' careful appraisals and Timmy Porter calling her Snow White, and none of it mattered. The substitute read the roll, and the whole class filed outside to the church steps. The wind whipped Clare's skirt and blew her hair into her eyes. Her place was last in line, this time the place of honor, and her heart felt charred, like cinders and coals, though it was a sunny day and daffodils bloomed in the churchyard. The bell rang in the tower and, when Jeannie asked where the wreath was, Sister Immaculata sent Sister Arlene, who'd been on playground duty, to run to the convent and get it.

Sister Arlene was rosy and breathless when she got back and handed Clare the wreath. "It was in the fridge," she said laughing, and the wreath was damp in Clare's hands, and Sister's fingers were cold, but they didn't really seem that way. Clare had a rush of feeling, a sudden wish that all the nuns were pretty and happy like Sister Arlene. It would be so much better. Maybe it would even make her mother believe.

"Stay in line. Stay in line," Sister Immaculata said. She stared everyone quiet. The eight o'clock bell rang, and the last stragglers for Mass hurried into the side doors. Timmy and Rocco propped the main doors open and, like an inching caterpillar, the class moved forward.

Clare counted her steps. It was not really chilly out, but her arms were goosefleshy. *Fourteen . . . Twenty steps. Twenty-two . . .*

Clare felt her face growing warm as she walked through the doors. She heard the crashing organ processional Mrs. Thompkins had practiced all week, and the bass notes were the sound that crept up her legs. She stared straight ahead. She passed through the inner church doors and felt the clean faces of everyone looking at her, the hard marble under her feet. The church smelled of incense and sweet flowers.

One by one, her classmates entered their pews. A baby cried. The eighth-grade girls rustled their music, ready to start their song to Mary, and Clare shivered inside herself. She was not pure, not fit. And, too, she lacked faith. In her pride, she had seen Father Étienne as a man instead of a priest.

Did she know this yet? Not when she genuflected in front of the altar railing and thought of herself inside the confessional kneeling on her dress so it tugged, and Father sliding the screen, his face silhouetted as she hurried into her confession: *Bless me, Father, for I have sinned. I was disrespectful to my parents, I fought with my brother four times, I pulled a cat's tail . . .* and then the long moment while she thought darkly and Father asked not once, but twice, if there was anything more. Clare took a breath and squeezed her eyes shut tight and then opened them. *I told a lie*, she said, and then they were both waiting as though Father knew there was something else she should say. Clare listened to the blackness and their breathing between them and wondered if she could add it was a lie to a boy. She hesitated, hoping Father would ask again if there was something more, but he didn't. Instead, he asked if she had any questions. Clare could see the outline of his hand as it moved. She heard the back of his fingers rolling lightly against the wood with a sound like a short *glissando*, and she thought of his cigarettes and the smoke that had risen above his hand on the shovel on her very first day at St. Francis. She pictured his face, so close through the screen, and the morning when he'd laughed because she'd run home in the early dark.

No, she hadn't known then when she answered *No, Father*, and she didn't know now as she rose from her genuflection and the girls broke into their song, and Father Étienne and Jeff Grauer and the other acolyte turned to face Mary's altar. Clare's shoe caught on her hem as she started up the ladder. She tipped a little, then righted herself, still clutching the wreath. Mary was porcelain-still. There were no glycerin tears. No streaks of blood. Clare balanced her leg against the ladder side and went farther up to the last step. She reached for the statue. She crowned Mary and, as she backed down the steps, the wreath slipped cock-eyed across Mary's brow.

And even then she still didn't know, for she was only a child. She was Clare McHenry—Clare McHenry who'd made a bad confession, Clare McHenry who believed she'd not prayed enough for her mother's soul and who'd crowned Mary so the wreath sat at a rakish tilt like the hat of a sailor on Wharf Street in Hanbury. In the long unfolding of the Mass, Clare stared at that crooked wreath.

Outside afterward, people gathered as though there'd been a wedding. The first grade had made May baskets and they scattered flowers. Boys ran on the grass, and the nuns were smiling, holding their veils in the wind. Clare tried pushing the heels of her shoes off her new blisters. She spotted her mother. She saw her at the edge of the crowd, the woman in the movies waiting at the station while the train pulls out and the face she loves begins to disappear. Years later, Clare identified that expression and knew how premature and forced their early distancing had been. But in the breezy day, with her heart so desperate, Clare looked for Sister Immaculata, who had all the answers. In the sea of nodding veils, she wanted a nun like the nuns on the roof of St. Peter's.

Someone not yet heaven sent, but not really earthbound.

Somebody selling for God.

ACKNOWLEDGMENTS

My thanks to Paulette Bates Alden and Eva Talmadge for their careful reading and editorial suggestions. Thanks as well to Eva Gallerani, concierge of the Hotel Monteleone, for sharing her knowledge of the hotel's décor in the 1970s, and to the city of New Orleans, perfect muse.